CYGENIC

MONIQUE POIRER

For more information contact:
Riverdale Avenue Books/Circlet Press
5676 Riverdale Avenue
Riverdale, NY 10471

www.riverdaleavebooks.com

Design by www.formatting4U.com

Digital ISBN: 9781626015524
Trade ISBN: 9781626015531

First Edition April 2020

Dante

"What are we estimating the time of death as?"

"Can't have been more than 12 hours ago—"

"He was alive and alert at 11:30 last night," I said, interrupting the man... I wasn't sure what his title was. He wasn't an oncologist. He wasn't even a doctor, I didn't think.

Professor Cunningham didn't need doctors anymore, and wouldn't ever again.

"What do we do about the wetware?" the woman said, looking at me and then past me to the man. I winced at the word. No one had called me "wetware" in... well, not for a while. Certainly not since Professor Cunningham had gotten sick. I'd been too useful to all the doctors and nurses who knew that I was his primary caregiver for them to think of me that way. Even if I was "just a machine," I was a *good* machine that did things like keep track of his medications and feed him and bathe him so that nobody had to be paid to do so. I wasn't just... wetware. I sat there fingering the input jack on the inside of my right wrist nervously, running little circles around the metallic collar with the tip of my finger, watching pulses of illumination run up the circuitry that ran the length of my arm, just below the skin. Part of me was waiting for Professor Cunningham to say, "Don't fidget, Dante!"

But no one told me not to fidget.

"Already tried the contacts in the old guy's database; info's out of date. Nothing for it but to send the 'genic to reprocessing."

"No, you can't reprocess me! Professor Cunningham—" I began, alarmed, only for the woman to talk over me.

"We should stick a pin in it in the meantime. Shut it up, keep it out of the way."

I glanced at the inert form on the bed, covered in a white sheet, and looked back to the man who was writing something on a clipboard.

"Please..." I started, only for him to look at me in a way that made me stop.

"Sit down and shut up, or I'm going to take Cathy's advice. Don't worry your pretty little head about a thing, this will all be worked out soon."

He looked back to the clipboard. He didn't look at me again.

The people who came to collect me were kind enough, but distant. They did so in perfunctory fashion. I was told to be quiet frequently enough that I realized that I wasn't to speak unless spoken to. I was put into the back of a car and driven to a gray brick building and led through a maze of anonymous gray and beige and white corridors under dim fluorescent lighting, eventually to find myself seated in front of a desk opposite a harried-looking woman in her thirties. She looked up from her tablet at me and raised her eyebrows, then looked back to the tablet.

"Tim, you brought me the wrong one," she called

into the hallway, presumably at the man who'd walked me here from the waiting room where I'd spent the last few hours.

"That's 3178KMi1126. Ping him if you don't believe me."

She did, pointing her tablet in my general direction and raising her eyebrows again.

"He's too pretty, and he's too young. 1126 was commissioned twelve years ago."

"That's right, ma'am," I said, quietly. "I was commissioned twelve years ago by Professor Vernon Cunningham, with the intended function of serving as an artistic statement and philosophical experiment on the nature and function of education—"

"Willing to bet the old guy had him commissioned as a toy and then reprogrammed him when he got sick," the man said.

"Yeah, sounds about right, especially looking at how young he is—"

"I was commissioned at five years' growth via special dispensation of regulations concerning minimum biological age restrictions, ma'am," I said with the crisp quickness that long practice brought. "I'm sure that there's paperwork indicating this. Professor Cunningham's work with me is extensively documented, and before he became ill there was a website dedicated to it that had an extensive following—"

She looked at me, eyebrows raised, plainly assessing.

"That makes you... 17. You'd be a minor if you were human, at least for another couple of months."

She had a troubled expression for a moment, and then sighed heavily.

"But you're not human, so that's all moot."

She looked back to her pad, skimming it with her fingertip, nodding slightly now and again.

"Will I be allowed to attend his funeral?"

She looked up at me, and the look in her eyes made my throat tighten. It was some meeting of annoyance and resignation, like I was a problem that she neither had time for nor the inclination to bother with.

"Professor Cunningham contracted stomach cancer. In his final months I was his caretaker—" I faltered, only to be interrupted.

"Skillset?"

"Excuse me?"

"List your skills."

"I... I'm fluent in Latin, and sufficiently fluent in ancient Greek to understand Xenophanes," I began awkwardly, never having been asked this in such a way before. "I can conduct classical and modern analysis of literature and art and other forms of media. I can explain the basic themes and literary importance of much of the western canon and compose essays with complete bibliographies in any of several standard formats. I can perform basic calculus in long form, and am very proficient in most advanced mathematics digitally. I am familiar with the scientific method and can conduct experiments, and collect and analyze data thus generated. I can outline the achievements of thousands of great men and women through all of recorded human history. I have completed several courses on internal medicine and have an earned certificate in medical assistance, and have a full year of experience in being a full-time hospice caregiver—"

"That's enough," she said, not even looking up at me. "Tim, are you hearing this bullshit? I swear, the things people do. Prep this kid for MGH, his skillset's close enough for an orderly if they lay down a basic orientation data set."

"No, that's not correct," I said, standing, feeling my throat tighten again. "There are going to be people who want me. I know that several universities have made offers. I don't want to be a hospital orderly. I was supposed to—"

"No one cares what you want. You're a computer with arms and legs, you don't get to want things. Be civil, or I'll just mark you down as intractable and you'll go to reclamation and recycling to have your head hollowed out and have a new personality programmed in. Something someone actually wants. Pretty young thing like you, I've got some ideas of what someone might want you for. Believe me, it's in your best interest to stay tractable. You're lucky I'm even bothering to tell you this. You probably won't get another warning."

My throat tightened to the point that I couldn't breathe, and I tried to swallow to no avail, my mouth opening and closing of its own volition and tears welling up in my eyes as the man in the hallway appeared again and led me away down yet another white corridor.

I'd been training with Professor Cunningham my whole life. I was supposed to be something important, something special. I was supposed to prove Professor Cunningham's theories.

Someone who'd been following the progress of my training would come rescue me from all this, certainly. I was different, too important to simply be processed and slotted into the kind of role that most cygenics filled. He'd worked too hard on me.

I was made to sit down in another waiting room. This one didn't even have windows.

All there was to do was wait.

Nate

I was sitting on the RA's floor with the asshole who lived downstairs from me because mediation was required before I was allowed to attend classes again.

"And then he shoved me against the fucking wall!"

"I was out of line," I admitted. "But he was harassing Meggie."

"*Meggie*? It's a piece of wetware! I'd never mess with an actual woman. I'm not like that."

I was on my feet again without even meaning to be, and the RA was standing between us, her arms crossed, looking pretty damned imposing.

I hadn't really looked at her before. She was... built. I think I'd heard she was on the rugby team? Taller than me, now that we were both standing. Brown skin, black hair, some kind of Latina. She was the only other person on my floor who wasn't white. Her name was Iris Castillo, she was a senior, and she'd been RA last year, too.

"Sit your ass down, Nate," she said, sharpening every word.

"See, he's crazy. You should make him go to the psych lady at the health center."

"Shut it, Josh. This also isn't the first time I've

heard stories about you trying to get handsy with the cleaning ladies."

"They're not *ladies*. They're not even really people. It's not like they mind."

"The dean will mind when I report this," she said evenly.

"If they minded, they'd report something themselves. Maybe they're happy to get a little attention. That's not even what this is about, anyhow. We're in mediation because this jackass thought it was okay to put his hands on me."

It was all I could do to keep from calling him a jackass right back. "And *you* thought it was okay to put your hands on cygenic maintenance workers owned by the school who can't tell you 'no' because it's their job to keep the students happy and fulfill our requests to the best of their abilities."

Iris squeezed the bridge of her nose.

"Can we agree that you're both assholes and call it a day? Josh, this is your last warning on messing with the maintenance workers. I don't want to hear about you even being in the same room at the same time with any of them between now and graduation. And you, Nate... you get your ass down to the counseling center and work on your anger issues. Stay out of each other's way. You don't even live on the same floor, shouldn't be that hard. I hear a bad word about either of you, this is going up the chain. This goes up the chain, it ends up on your records. You think hard about that."

"So we done here?" Josh asked before I could take a couple of deep breaths and actually think about what it would mean to have physical violence on my record. That was probably the kind of thing that fucked over your scholarships.

"Yeah, we're done here."

He left, flashing me a nasty glare as he did. I still wanted to punch him in the face. Better if I could actually do it in front of Meggie, so that she could see that *someone* gave a damn about how she was treated on this campus.

Maybe I shouldn't have elected to attend a school that owned slaves, scholarships or no.

"You planning on getting out of my room any time today?" Iris said, looking down at me, her arms crossed again.

"Sorry," I said, standing up.

"What's your actual deal, anyhow? I mean, Josh is an asshole, but I don't think that's the deal here. Lots of other guys are assholes."

"Yeah, but he's an asshole in the direction of cygenics."

"And you care, especially, about cygenics?"

"Yeah. I do."

She smiled a little bit.

"You know we got a chapter of PETCL on campus, right?"

"You know PETCL supports the 'recycling' of 'irredeemably damaged' cygenics, right?" I said, making air quotes, "Which in practice is pretty much any of them that so much as get a hangnail or perform a task wrong or have the audacity to be older than 40?"

She raised her eyebrows, glanced at her phone, and sat down.

"So basically, you're too radical even for the designated cause-heads. Talk to me, kid. I got time."

"Only if you stop calling me 'kid,'" I said, trying not to sound petulant about it.

"You look about *12,*" she replied, folding her arms. "Probably why Josh didn't just break your teeth and went for mediation instead. That and not wanting a fight on his record because it'll keep him out of games."

"I'm 17. Sophomore. Skipped a couple of grades back in elementary and middle school." Not the first time I'd had to explain this. "I'm not too young to be here."

"If that's not a 'thou doth protest too much' statement, I don't know what is!" she said with a bark of laughter. "So you're a bleeding-heart about cygenics to the point of violence, and a child prodigy, *too*? The plot thickens."

"Look it's just... my mom died when I was a baby. Car accident." I looked away from her. This was turning into one of those "Nate tells his tragic backstory and the authority figure hums sympathetically and sends him to a totally useless counselor" sessions, and I wasn't sure I was up for that. But there really wasn't an "undo" once the story started. It always came out of me like bleeding

"I don't remember my mom at all. I've only seen photos and videos. But my dad kind of... ditched out on me after that. He's white as fucking paper. Guess he didn't want to have to explain his black son to people."

"Sounds like a real upstanding guy," Iris said, pulling a face.

"He bought a cygenic; she was a refurbished model who was programmed as a nanny. She was supposed to bond with me. I guess it worked a little too well, because there were no actual parents in the way and she was on duty all the time. Dad didn't live with me and her. I... when I was twelve my dad got married again, to this excessively blonde former-pageant-star lady named Tammy, and settled down in Arkansas. Left me in Boston. I've got a half brother and sister I've never even met. They're not allowed to know about me, I don't think." My breath hitched a little, and I wished that I wasn't spilling all this to my RA, but I couldn't stop. "Lisa was an awesome mom, okay? Way better parent than my asshole dad. She was always there for me, and people always treated her like she was just... a thing."

"So you're kind of touchy about people being callous with cygenics because you're thinking about your... mom."

"That's real good, you a psych major?" I said, more nastily than I'd meant to.

"Social work," she said, raising her eyebrows. "Look, you don't want to mediate or talk to me, whatever. I just need to fill out the paperwork that says I tried. You keep getting into altercations, you're gonna get your ass expelled."

"Yeah, I know. I shouldn't have come here. I should have waited to find a school that doesn't have any cygenics on staff and hoped they could give me the kind of scholarship package I got here."

"You're on smartypants scholarships too?" she asked. "Grow up poor?"

"Poor enough. Dad kind of spent my college fund on Lisa. The allowance he dropped in my bank account for her to use on me was bullshit."

"Go poverty pride," she said, offering her fist. I bumped it.

"Sucks, doesn't it, being here with all these trust-fund assholes who have no idea how the world works? Who probably each have half a dozen cygenics working on their parents' palatial mansions doing their grocery shopping and keeping their lawns nice and washing their floors and doing their laundry?"

"Yeah. It does," I said. "Especially since campus has a bunch of cygenics around doing the exact same thing."

"You like pad thai?"

"Yeah?"

"Wanna go get lunch?"

"I don't have enough points on my meal card to eat anywhere but the refectory if I'm gonna make them last the month, and I can't afford to get a job with my course load so... I'm too broke for pad thai."

"Let's just say being an RA's got its perks. You can tell me more about your mom. You ever heard of the Turing Center?"

I hadn't, but I had the feeling that she'd be more than happy to tell me all about it.

Dante

I worked at the hospital for two years. On the first day they'd plugged me into a terminal and uploaded all the data I needed to know to perform my duties, a thoroughly disorienting and unsettling experience and one that Professor Cunningham would never have approved of. I'd known, objectively, that direct upload was how most cygenics came to know things. That learning through action was unique to me, something that I'd been commissioned for, and that cygenics were generally commissioned at 21 years' growth and programmed whole cloth with a personality and knowledge suitable for their intended task. It was... confusing, to suddenly simply *know* what I was supposed to do to prevent the spread of blood-borne pathogens, to simply *know* where the laundry facility was and how to operate the machinery there, to simply *know* how to make a shift report and to whom... without any attached memories of how I'd gained the knowledge.

The hospital was a numbing experience; the shifts sixteen hours long with four scheduled breaks for routine maintenance, followed by eight hours of being pinned and put in a locked drawer in lieu of actual sleep. We weren't given food—my reservoirs were kept perpetually full of nutrient fluid and caloric demands were fulfilled by liquid meal replacements and food bars that at least had the decency to be chocolate-flavored.

There was no time to be anything but obedient, and I wandered in a fog of helpful servitude, only occasionally breaking through to try and convince someone that I wasn't like the others, that I didn't belong there, that I hadn't been commissioned for this, that they needed to plug "The Dante Project" into a search engine. But I was so very effective and useful that no one wanted to bother. I was a very *good* hospital orderly. My youth and prettiness made my popular with the patients. I had a good bedside manner. It was in all the reports about me. The nurses joked that maybe they'd place orders for more like me next time routine replacements of orderlies came around.

Orderlies were routinely replaced after 10 years of continuous function. I had that to look forward to. Staff would be able to bid for me after I'd been retired, and if none of them wanted to buy me I'd be taken offline and recycled. The first time someone had mentioned that to me, they'd laughed off my dull horror. Of course someone would want to buy me. I was so personable and pretty and tractable, I'd make a great domestic.

But that never came to pass, because after working in the hospital for two years, I was stolen.

Nate

Iris got hired by the Boston chapter of the Turing Center upon graduation. When I graduated two years later, she offered me a job.

Which was how I met Charles.

Charles was our programmer; our chapter wasn't established enough to have the funding for more than one programmer on payroll. When cygenics who were referred to our center came in too damaged to give us their basic demographic data and skillset—often too damaged to even speak or respond to stimuli—he reprogrammed them to baseline so that we could move forward.

A lot of the cygenics who ended up at our center *were* that bad, brought in by their fellow cast-offs who were living on the street and deliberately avoiding cygenic reprocessing because they knew that they'd be reprogrammed at best or, more likely, decommissioned entirely. Put offline. Recycled. Killed.

There was nothing illegal, or even that uncommon, about killing cygenics that didn't seem immediately useful. Most of the ones who came to the Center had some kind of horror story about being replaced by newer models and literally thrown out with the trash, of running away from abusive or negligent owners, of having owners who'd died and made no provisions for them and fleeing before being put through the wholly inadequate system of cygenic reprocessing where they were owned by the state, with or without having their minds erased and replaced first. We did outreach, trying to find the ones who needed our help, but so many of them were completely terrified of humans and anything that resembled structure or authority that the majority of dispossessed cygenics still ended up in places where they'd be recycled for spare parts.

But at least I was doing *something*.

Which was more than I could say for Charles, at the moment, because Charles was in a mood and we were having an argument about the function of the organization. Again. Because Charles was working here for how it would look on his resume and didn't deny that. He'd be gone as soon as something better came along, and didn't really give a damn about the mission.

And for some reason, I wanted to convince him otherwise. Some reason that probably had a lot to do with the way I couldn't stop paying attention to the shadows that his eyelashes made on his cheekbones when he was working.

"Charles, you got four more units to fix before 2:30 tomorrow, and you're standing here drinking coffee and playing with your phone," Iris said, flashing a nasty glare at first him and then at me, as if it was my fault.

She probably wasn't entirely wrong.

"Nate and I were just having a conversation, Iris.

I know how to budget my time. It's not as if they care if I keep them waiting," Charles said with a snort, not even looking at her.

"Why do we let you work here again?" Iris asked, throwing up her hand as she made her way to the filing cabinets.

"Because you know you can't get another programmer of my caliber to work for these wages," he replied with a charming smile. "The machines can wait."

"Don't call them that," I said, tightly. Charles looked up at me and cracked a smirk.

"They're machines, Nate. Brilliant, complex, awesome, wonderful machines—but machines nonetheless. They walk around in bodies made of semi-translucent meat, and they look like fancy dolls. They have endearing little mannerisms programmed in. But crack open a cygenic's skull, and you get a computer and some synthetic cellular goo with a smattering of actual human brain cells to paste the whole thing together."

"The cygenic brain is composed of *85 percent* human cells—"

"If you reduced their cranial mass down to just the human parts, you wouldn't be left with enough to build a dog's brain. Getting the behavior you want out of them is just a matter of putting the right data into the computer and then futzing around with the chemical and electrical signals that interpret that data."

"And yet multiple studies have shown that learned knowledge is more adaptive than uploaded knowledge," I replied. "Cygenics who are taught to do things perform better than ones who are programmed to do things."

17

"Applied knowledge is superior because it's forged a path through the gooey meaty chunks in their heads and created a net of neural connections on the way," Charles said with a snort. "Neural connections are the stuff thinking is made of. They are, by the way, a bitch and a half to undo if said thinking and its attendant behavior is pathological. Reprogramming is a woefully underappreciated art form—way more difficult than initial programming. It's easier to work with a blank slate than to salvage something that someone's already fucked up. Thank me later, next time I'm handed a piece of surly junk and turn it into a happy and tractable domestic without wiping the whole thing and starting from scratch."

"They're not junk!" I said, loud enough that both Iris and Charles were staring at me. Iris was looking really concerned. Charles was looking really...

...interested.

I felt my face getting hot.

"I'm going to go to lunch," Charles said, deferentially, to Iris, "and when I get back I do dutifully promise to address at least four of the poor broken little shell-shocked cygenics sitting in the waiting room." He looked back at me. "Nate, would you like to join me?"

I blinked a couple of times, and nodded. Because Charles, despite being kind of an asshole... wanted to talk to me more, and maybe wanted to listen to me. I looked to Iris, and she closed her eyes and shook her head, pulling the file she was looking for and walking away without a word.

That wasn't a denial. Besides, it wasn't as if Iris could just fire me for taking an early lunch. She'd need

June's approval for that, and June thought I was wonderful.

So I went to lunch with Charles.

"Give me half an hour with any of them and I'll have them literate on you," Charles said, cutting up a piece of steak that seemed tougher than the price indicated it should be. Or maybe it was that the knives were dull. "Literacy is a cut and paste procedural subroutine; I don't even have to play around with finessing it in."

"Yeah, but pretty much all the regulars we have right now who aren't BSOD have refused further reprogramming. So no dice," I said with a noncommittal shrug, looking at his hands. Charles had really nice hands; long-boned and nimble, making even the most mundane tasks look artful.

"It's ludicrous that we're letting them decide that. I don't ask my cat's opinion about trips to the vet," he said, rolling his eyes.

"One would hope you'd ask your kid about trips to the doctor, though," I said, setting my jaw.

"Among the reasons I do not and will never have children," he replied with an undeniably charming smile. "There's a fine line with kids where you have to make decisions for them because they're not old enough to be able to comprehend what's in their own best interests, and I don't feel like dealing with that line. If the cygenics in our waiting room were cognitively capable of making rational decisions, they'd consent to therapeutic reprogramming. Demonstrable lack of consent is thus proof that they can't make rational choices for themselves. It's like allowing a kid to go unvaccinated because they're scared of needles."

"You can't know that about them. Have you sat down and actually talked to any of them about why they don't want to be reprogrammed? *Why* they don't want additional programming?"

"No, Nate, I haven't," he said, selecting a piece of steak to skewer and popping it into his mouth with economical, precise movements. I waited for him to chew and swallow before continuing, because he wasn't the kind of guy who'd talk with his mouth full. "That's your job. You're the resident loving and understanding therapist. I'm just the programmer. You and I should have more conversations like this though. They're quite... stimulating."

He looked up at me and smiled again, catching my eyes. I breathed in and found I couldn't quite breathe out again.

"Iris tells me that you were practically raised by a cygenic, is that true?"

"Yeah," I said, catching my breath again, finally looking down at my own lunch. The cream sauce on the salmon had congealed a bit from neglect. "Her name was Lisa..."

Dante

A harsh slap brought me to awareness, pain echoing through my head like water sloshed around in a tin can.

"Come on, on your feet, pretty boy," a voice boomed nearby as a hand grabbed me by the hair, dragging me up. I almost fell again, but another resounding smack had me scrambling to find balance and staggering to my feet. The floor was gritty—my shoes were gone—my clothes were gone too. I looked around, trying to figure out what had happened and where I was. Bare cinder block walls, fluorescent lighting, no windows or indication of... anything, really. There were dozens of other cygenics here, all male, all fairly young, all naked and looking as confused as I felt.

Someone blew a whistle, and I snapped to attention in a completely involuntary fashion. Hardwired reaction to standardized stimuli. Just another thing that proved that I wasn't remotely human. The hospital staff did it sometimes. I'd never heard a snap whistle before I'd worked at the hospital.

"Okay, all of you got something drawn on your left hand. If you've got a circle, you go with Janet over there." The large man presiding tossed his head toward a saccharine-smiling woman with a blackbox in her hand. I knew what blackboxes were; I'd never had one used on me. I knew that they produced instantaneous paralysis.

"You got a square, you go with Owen. Triangles, Lucian, Diamonds, Sophie." He nodded in half a dozen directions, pointing out each of the humans in turn, and then he grinned. "All you lucky buggers who got X's, you get to come with me."

I looked at the back of my left hand... an X. I glanced back up at the human, who had a blackbox in one hand and a knife in the other, a whistle around his neck on a cord. It was readily apparent that this day was not going to get any better. I took several breaths and tried to take stock of the situation. No knowing how long I'd been unconscious. I was dizzy and thirsty and desperately hungry, and there was a dull alarm in the back of my mind letting me know that my reservoirs had run out of nutrient fluid. I had to have been pinned for days for that to be the case.

I numbly followed the directions of the humans all around me, because I wasn't an idiot. I knew damned well the consequences of disobedience. Reprogramming was expensive and required a skilled operator. Deprogramming? Wasn't. Those who disobeyed or didn't obey quickly enough were blackboxed into stillness and plugged into handheld consoles even as the rest of us watched. When they began moving again, it was with the blank, uncomprehending obedience of BSODs, their minds erased utterly, awaiting some new personality and knowledge. Gone.

I found myself hosed down and scrubbed with something reminiscent of laundry detergent and then hosed down again. They washed and cut my hair. The woman doing that cooed at me a little about how nice it was. Curly. Not a common variant. Professor Cunningham had requested it, because it was such a common feature of the subjects of the Pre-Raphaelite art that my appearance was based on.

They stood me in front of a black backdrop and took a number of photographs, then somebody scribbled an alphanumeric across the back of my right hand in black felt pen. Someone else came at me with a jack injector, and before I could so much as flinch it was plugged into the jack at the nape of my neck and I felt nutrient fluid going into the wells along either side of my spine. It triggered a brief and brilliant euphoria, all my systems releasing their little chemical reward pulses at once. Someone gave me a pouch of familiar meal replacement to drink and I sucked it down while I was still giddy; that pouch had to have about 3000 calories in it. It was what they fed us knowing that we'd be working hard for sixteen hours. Between that and having my wells filled, I could probably stay pinned for a couple of weeks.

They brought me to a wall of drawers, just like at the hospital. I was trembling a little as they made me lie down in the one they pulled out for me, but I didn't say anything. Couldn't say anything. There wasn't any point in defiance. A hand grabbed me by the shoulder and pushed my hair aside, stuck a pin into the jack at the nape of my neck. I felt it slide home.

And after that I didn't think or feel anything at all.

'Taire

I woke up to Sir turning on the lights in my room.

"Come on, Baby boy. Got a surprise for you today."

Surprises were never good. But Sir seemed... playful. Still not good, but not the worst way for him to be. I got up, keeping my eyes obediently down, and followed him as he led me down the hall to the film suite. There were two cameras and a lighting setup flanking a fuck-nest on the floor: a construction of mattresses and bricks of foam and drop cloths and blankets and pillows, all covered in blue satin because it looked nice on camera. You could find a way to fuck in pretty much any position in the film suite.

There was a kid sitting in the middle of the nest, knees drawn up to his chin and arms clutched around them. He was pretty. Really, startlingly pretty, a prettier thing than had any business being in a place like this. He looked like art; maybe he'd been commissioned as a model or something. Big mirror-silver eyes, a wide mouth with full lips, skin that looked like nothing had ever touched it, lilac hair in curls. It was cut short, but I had no doubt that Sir would make him grow it out long, because it looked really soft and shiny and nice. He was sitting there looking confused and terrified and so... young. Like maybe even younger than me. Younger than cygenics were supposed to be. I was at least old enough to be vat-age now. It had only taken me 15 years.

He had too much in his eyes to be fresh out of the vat.

"Baby boy, this is our newest acquisition. You're gonna show him what we do here."

"Yes, Sir," I said, bowing my head a little.

"Please," the kid said, his tongue darting out to wet his lips, "I belong to the hospital. I'm an orderly—" he broke off into a howl, dropping into a pile of twitching, writhing limbs. Sir had shot a twitchbox at him. I trembled, but didn't move. Hadn't been given orders to move. The kid was really, really new.

"Let that be a lesson to you," Sir said as the kid stopped twitching. I really hoped he wasn't about to puke. Twitchboxes did that, sometimes, especially if you weren't used to them. If he puked, Sir was probably going to beat the shit out of him and then make him lick it up, and I didn't want to have to stand here and watch that.

"You don't talk if I don't give you permission to talk. You belong to me. You do what I say. This isn't a hard job. Customers like it when you've got enough brains to follow directions and tell them how much you love whatever they're doing. I don't like to hollow out my boys' heads if I don't have to. But there's plenty of people who'll pay for some of your time even if you're BSOD, fuckable as you are."

The kid nodded frantically, curled up into a fetal ball. There were tears on his face. He was the kind who could cry pretty. That probably didn't bode well for him at all.

"Baby boy, go make him feel better," Sir said, the sound of a smile in his voice. One of his oily, nasty smiles, the kind that meant he had plans. I didn't have to look at him to know that smile. I walked over to the nest and knelt down next to the kid, acutely aware that I was on camera. It probably wasn't live feed, not if he'd opened it up with twitchboxing. This was probably a promo.

"Give him a kiss," Sir said, his voice a little impatient. I'd hesitated too long wondering what I was supposed to do. The kid looked like he thought I was gonna hit him. I touched his face, sliding my hand around to cup the back of his head, coaxing him up as gently as I dared until he took the hint and got up on his knees so I could lean in and take his mouth.

His mouth was hard under mine, lips drawn tight, the muscles in his neck tense.

"You gotta relax," I whispered, right up against his mouth, letting my hand run up and down the back of his neck. His hair *was* soft, and so was his skin. "Just go with it. I'll try to make it good for you. He'll get mad if you don't get into it."

"I've never—"

"Well, you are now," I said, the last thing I dared say before I moved in on his mouth again, a little more insistently this time, sucking on his bottom lip a little. What did he mean, he'd never? Someone had commissioned something as pretty as him to *not* fuck?

His mouth softened a little, a shivering uncertainty as he let me suck on his lip, let his lips be parted so my tongue could slip inside. He made a sound then, high and surprised at the back of his throat, and I half expected him to try and pull away but... he didn't. He kind of melted a little bit, some of that tension going out of his muscles, leaning into me fractionally. It was really nice. Nicer than anything I was used to, anyway.

"Yeah, that's really sweet," Sir was saying, his voice getting thicker.

Good. We were doing good. It was better when Sir thought you were doing good. Maybe this day wouldn't be a wash, surprise or no.

Dante

I'd seen kisses in before, in videos and in pictures. I'd caught nurses exchanging quick kisses at the ends of cigarette breaks. I'd read about kisses, quite extensively. But none of these facts had prepared me for the reality of a hungry mouth descending on my own, lips slightly chapped and searingly hot. He had one hand on the back of my head, and the other trailed along my arm, up my shoulder and neck to brush against the side of my face. I opened my mouth to gasp and his tongue darted inside with a quick sureness and insistence.

The man was talking again, the one who'd shot me with the thing that looked like a blackbox, but produced distilled pain rather than paralysis. I couldn't quite understand what he was saying.

The cygenic who was kissing me moved, shifting his weight and pushing me back, and before I realized what he was doing he was straddling my legs and his crotch was pressed against my own and I was harder than I'd ever been in my life. I rocked my head back and moaned loudly enough that it echoed in the emptiness of the room. The man watching us laughed.

The cygenic lunged a little, recapturing my mouth and biting my lip. It hurt enough to make me gasp, but before I could protest he was sucking on it, running his tongue over it. He hadn't broken skin. In the wake of pain, my lip was acutely sensitive. When he broke the kiss to pant against me, his breath hot and cold by intervals, I whimpered. I was on my back, and he was on top of me, pressed fully against me now. Holding me down.

He moved his hips. He performed a kind of liquid undulation that seemed impossible, grinding against me, and I could feel how hard he was, how hard I was, as he rubbed us together. He did it again. Again. Grinding us together, his breath against my lips, his hands pushing down into the softness under my head so that it made a kind of well that my head sank into, making me bear my throat.

"Suck him off, Baby boy," the man said, from some vast distance. Then, in a slightly different tone, "You pay attention to what Baby boy here is doing. You're gonna be doing a lot of it."

He moved to kiss my throat, sucking and nipping, his hands moving to my shoulders and trailing down my arms with fingertips that seemed to burn. He kissed my collarbones, and drew feather light caresses along my ribs that made me squirm a bit. Down to my groin, where he breathed against me for a moment and suddenly, without warning, without preamble, swallowed me.

Oh God, his *mouth*.

Everything else stopped. There was nothing in existence but the sensation of his mouth as it slid around me and drew me in, hot and wet and slick. I had to press my hand against my mouth to keep from screaming, and my other hand shot of its own volition to the crown of his head, holding him there, trying to snake my fingers into his hair. Nothing had ever felt this good. I'd never imagined that anything could feel this good. He made a low purring noise, and it shook me right to my bones. He swallowed me down until I was nestled up at the back of his throat, and his throat squeezed.

I came more brilliantly than I'd ever come touching myself in the shower.

I lay there in a daze, and he smiled up at me and then looked into the brightness beyond this thicket of bedclothes to where the man must be standing.

I heard clapping.

"Good job. Aw but Baby boy, looks like you got left behind. You liked it though, didn't you. Sweet little thing here makes a nice addition, doesn't he?"

"Yes, Sir," the cygenic said.

I didn't even know his name. He didn't know mine. But he'd just done... that. While the man had watched. Something about it felt profoundly wrong.

"You deserve something nice, Baby boy. You want me to fuck you?"

There was a palpable pause while the cygenic took a shuddering breath.

"Yes, Sir," the cygenic answered, his eyes down this time. I saw tension creep into his muscles, his hands trembling slightly before balling themselves into fists in the sheets.

The man came forward, something about the way he moved reminding me of a vid I'd once seen of hyenas stalking prey. I edged backward, and his head whipped around to look at me. His eyes were absolutely piercing, and I froze under his gaze.

"Did I tell you you could fucking go anywhere? You stay right where you are and you watch this. It's your ass next. I'm betting you're a virgin, kid. Your first time's going to the top bidder."

That managed to completely smother the last ember of the wonderful glow I'd been feeling from what the cygenic had done to me with his mouth. I felt my throat tighten up and tears start pricking at my eyes as I sat, drawing up my knees, and watched the man position the cygenic with his rear in the air, kneel behind him and...

Fuck him.

Because that's what I was seeing. No sense in dressing it in pretty language, not when it was as brutal as this. This wasn't an act of love, and perhaps not even one of lust. It was an act of pain and power. I'd read about this, in books that Professor Cunningham would have been very disappointed in me for having an interest in. What I was seeing was... fucking.

"Tell me you love it, Baby boy," the man growled, driving into the cygenic.

"I... .I love it..." the cygenic stammered between gasps.

"Tell me you want more,"

"More, Sir... .please..."

"Tell me you want it harder."

"Harder, Sir!"

The man drove into him with enough force that it rocked them both, over and over, the cygenic clearly struggling to keep the position he'd be placed in, his face a mask of hard determination. He didn't look like he was enjoying himself.

I felt the tears spill over, and blinked to clear

them. I didn't dare bring my hands up to wipe them away.

I was still watching as the man finished, throwing the cygenic down when he did.

He lay there, panting and shivering. I'd once seen a bird fly into a window and slowly die on the pavement. He looked like that.

"Take him back to your room, Baby boy," the man growled, buttoning his pants. "Get him to suck your cock. He goes on sale tomorrow."

The cygenic pulled himself back into order and stood, offering a hand. Not knowing what else to do, I let him pull me to my feet and lead me down an intensely-lit hallway lined with doors and into a tiny windowless room. There was a mattress on the floor, fluorescent lighting above, and a camera staring down at us from the corner. The door closed behind us with a click that sounded depressingly final.

"It's locked," the cygenic said, sitting down heavily on the mattress. "Doors lock behind you here. He'll come get you when he wants you. Welcome to the business."

"What *is* this place?" I managed to ask before my throat closed up on me again and I found myself sitting on the floor, drawn up on myself, pressed into the corner.

"Sir owns us. Customers come and fuck us, he gets paid. Sometimes he gets us to do things with each other on camera, like what just happened there. Sometimes he wants you to perform alone on camera. People pay for that; they tell you to do things over a feed and you do them. There's not a whole lot more to know about it. Do what you're told, and you'll be fine," the cygenic answered, his voice flat. His eyes were glassy and his body tense, like he was in pain.

"What's your name?" I asked, finally daring to actually scrub at my face with my wrist.

"Don't have a name. He calls me Baby boy... I was littler when he started calling me that. You got a name?"

"Dante."

He snorted, something playing over his face for a moment before it went back to a studied blank.

"Pretty name. Sorry, kid, about... before. About now. You get used to it, because you gotta. It's not gonna get any better."

"Are you hurt?"

"No," he said quickly, the lie obvious.

"I'm a trained medical assistant. If there's anything I can do..."

He was quiet for a long time, and I just sat there looking at him. He was younger than any cygenic I'd ever seen, probably about my age. He was thin and wiry, all lithe muscles and tight skin, like a greyhound. It made the electronics under his skin seem to stand out, fine ridges of pulsing light accenting his nervous system where I had only lines. His hair was dark, a shade of silvery gray that reminded me of hematite. His cycs wcrc gray, too, almost human in thcir tonc. He looked at me with a deep, basal sadness and desperation in those eyes when he finally spoke.

"Stroke me off?" the cygenic asked, his voice small and plaintive.

I must have had an unsatisfactory expression on my face, because he looked away, breathing hard, as if he'd been sorry to say anything.

"I... I can't do it myself. Got beat for it too many times, back before I was here. Got beat for not being able to do it here, but Sir pretty much gave up on it. But... I can't bring myself off. And I need... I mean, I didn't..."

I nodded, trembling. It seemed only fair, after all, after what he'd done for me before. I moved toward him, sliding next to him on the mattress, the heat of his skin a comfort against the overpowering wrongness of this place. He lay down on his back, and I lay beside him, half on top of him.

I had no idea what I was doing, only had my brief and secretive explorations of my own body to go by, but the noise he made when I hesitatingly wrapped my fingers around the half-hard flesh between his legs was very encouraging. I gripped a little more tightly, feeling him grow fully hard under my fingers, finding an easy rhythm and watching his face. Watching the way his eyebrows came together, the way he bit his lip, the way his breathing grew harried and erratic.

"Yes... please..." he panted. I felt slick heat under my hand, and looked to see that he was leaking clear fluid. I used my thumb to spread it over the flare at the crown of him, remembering how nice that felt when I did it for myself.

He bucked in my hand and came immediately.

He was breathing hard, his face a mask of absolute bliss.

"I needed that so bad, you don't even know," he said, his voice gone liquid at the edges. "He doesn't let me come most of the time. Says I look good desperate. You'll get in trouble if you ever let anyone bring you off that fast, by the way. You're supposed to hold off, make it last..."

"You've been hard since before you put your mouth on me..."

He laughed, but it wasn't an especially mirthful sound.

"Yeah. I have. Thanks. You... need anything?"

"No," I answered. "Nothing that you can get me, I don't think. Is it all right if I just... stay here? With you, like this?"

"Cuddly fuck, eh?"

"Is it all right?"

"Yeah, guess I don't mind. Gonna have to show you how to suck cock sometime before tomorrow, or we're both gonna be in deep shit. You have to follow orders you're given here. Twitchbox isn't the worst of it. But just do what you're told and don't give him any lip and you'll do fine."

I nodded, hiding my face in the hollow of his throat. I could hear his heartbeat, hard and rapid. Sign of exertion or stress, I knew from my assorted medical training. Had I learned that, or had it just been programmed into me? Had it been something that I'd learned in the CNA classes that Professor Cunningham had enrolled me in when he'd learned of his illness?

I'd hardly thought of Professor Cunningham in the last couple of years.

My mind flashed, unbidden, to King Lear. To the apparent injustice of the universe, and Gloucester in despair, and I found myself whispering,

"As flies to wanton boys are we to the gods; They kill us for their sport."

"What are you talking about?" the nameless cygenic pressed against me said, sounding slightly concerned.

35

"Nothing important. Just something from a play. Something about justice being nothing more than an illusion and how nothing *we* can do will ever repair that."

"Yeah," he replied, "you nailed that one."

He put an arm around me, pulling me a little closer, and I listened to his heartbeat as it slowed to a steadier pace. I sighed, wondering what was going to become of me.

Nate

The cygenic seated before me couldn't have been 30 yet, and had probably been very pretty before she'd lost her left eye. She had her hair pulled over in a side part, trying to hide her face, but when she moved I could see flashes of it. There was a jagged, puckered scar above and below the eye, half her eyebrow gone, the eye itself a slightly hollowed depression of wrinkled skin. Her good eye was bubblegum pink, matching her hair. She was looking furtively around the room, chewing on her bottom lip, not looking at me when she answered my questions.

"Your name's Kitten, it says here?"

She nodded.

"You don't have anything filled out concerning your initial intended function or skillset."

She shook her head, her one eye blinking rapidly as though she were trying to keep back tears.

"I don't know any of that, last place I was at wiped me. I'm not good for that job anymore, either. Guys don't want me, with how I look now, I don't make money. I'm not... I don't have any skills, I don't think..."

"It's okay, Kitten," I said, trying to keep my voice gentle.

"And that guy, the one who's the headhacker, I heard him talking about they should just program me with something somebody wants, like domestic or something, but I don't want to get wiped again and... and if anyone catches me looking like this I'm just gonna get recycled! Who's gonna want me?"

"Don't worry about what Charles says, he runs his mouth. He doesn't get to decide what happens to you. He doesn't get to reprogram you unless you want him to."

She nodded, looking miserable.

"What brought you to the Turing Center?" I asked, keeping my voice professional and gentle, trying to stay on script because I was supposed to process at least half a dozen of the new intakes before the end of the day. Because every single one of them really needed a dedicated therapist to listen to their stories and help them work out the horrible shit that had happened to them, and I couldn't actually be that.

"This guy I do work for sometimes said he heard that you guys can find jobs for cygenics where they won't recycle you—or even wipe you and stuff, like the rec/recs do. Like, you find people who want to buy old cygenics."

"You're not old, Kitten—"

She shook her head frantically. "No, that lady downstairs at the desk who pinged me said I'm *10*. That's old, mister."

I closed my eyes for a second, taking a deep breath. It wasn't the first time I'd heard a cygenic say something to that effect. It wasn't even the hundredth time. But it never got any easier to hear how they all expected to die within five or 10 years of their creation.

"We'll find something for you, Kitten. You're sure you don't want to have any skills uploaded? It would help you find a placement faster. No one would have to erase anything about you, new skills would just be laid on top. You'd stay who you are."

She looked down miserably again.

"Do I have to decide right now?"

"No. You're free to take as long as you want. You can come back to the Center every day and stay in the waiting room if you want; we open at seven in the morning but sometimes there's someone here as early as six, and we close at nine so you'll have to find somewhere else to go after that. I can add your name to the waiting list for a shelter, if you don't have a place to stay. Would you like that?"

She nodded.

"I got some guys I'm running with. We're pretty good at avoiding rec/recs. I'll be okay. I just... it'd be nice, you know, having someplace I could stay? And I wouldn't have to worry? Like back at the last place I was at before I got hurt, I had my own room and everything and most of the time the guys were really sweet. It wasn't until that one guy... anyway my owner was nice enough to just let me go and find something else to do with myself. He could have recycled me if he'd wanted to. Wouldn't have blamed him."

"No one's going to recycle you, Kitten. When we find a placement for you, they're going to have to sign a contract that states that you'll be suitably cared for for the rest of your natural life, or returned to the agency if that becomes impossible. You understand?"

She nodded, biting her lip.

"If you do decide that you'd like to upload some

skills that will help you get the kind of placement you'd like to have, you go ask Linda or Drake or anyone with a badge that says 'Intern' to get you a form about skills acquisition, and they'll help you fill it out. You don't have to talk to Charles if you don't want to. In fact, it's probably better if you don't."

She nodded again.

"You can go back to the waiting room now, if you'd like. Now that you're registered, the kitchen and the clinic will serve you. When was the last time you had routine maintenance?"

"Not since the last place I was working. I dunno, maybe a year?"

I paused, internally screaming at the horror of that.

"You should visit the clinic as soon as you can. There's usually a wait, but they'll let you know if there's anything physically wrong with you that can be addressed."

The eye couldn't, because we didn't have the kind of funds needed for reconstructive surgery. If we could even find a doctor willing to perform reconstructive surgery on a cygenic, someone who wouldn't just tell us to recycle her and get a new one.

"Thank you, Kitten, for coming to the Center. We'll find you someplace, I promise."

She was looking down again, and I saw a tear run down her cheek from her good eye.

"Yeah... thanks. I'll go back the waiting room now, I guess."

She got up and walked out of my office, looking back over her shoulder at me a second from the door. I had to take a few breaths before I could finish filling in her paperwork. It never got any easier.

I was on my way to the waiting room to call the next one in when I ran into Charles.

"Hey, Nate! Didn't see your name up on the bid board for the freshly-cleared domestic. What gives?"

"I don't want a domestic, Charles. Also, her name's Alice."

"Your house could seriously use one. Her name's Alice because I decided she looked like an Alice when I was reprogramming her. Prior to that, she didn't have a name, because she came to us completely fried and with nothing salvageable concerning her former life. Which, as her registration history shows, was being a sewing machine operator for Blackbird Leather. I'm pretty sure they didn't name her. They didn't want her back when they learned that she'd had her programming erased; they were happy to take the tax write-off for donating her."

"I don't want a domestic. I'm not entirely certain that it's ethical that we get to take clients home so cavalierly, but you've heard me say my piece on that before."

"But we take such good care of them, Nate!" he said with a toothy grin. "Better us than someone else, really, we who believe in the mission. Who'd treat them better? Baba's *so* happy to work for me. She tells me so pretty much every day."

I stared at him, and held my tongue on the fact that he'd probably programmed her to do so, because I didn't have any real evidence of that. In any case, Baba really did seem to be quite happy working as Charles' maid, housekeeper, and cook. She'd never called the Center to complain about him or asked to come back, as happened sometimes with cygenics that interns brought home. She came and volunteered in the kitchen on her days off. Or, rather, Charles volunteered her time here on the her 'days off' that he was required to give her and probably wouldn't have given her if not required. She insisted that she was more than happy to help and didn't want to be doing anything else, because she had no interests. That she would just while away the hours watching TV she didn't really like if no one gave her work to do. It seemed terribly convenient.

"You didn't give Linda nasty looks when she brought Scoobie home," Charles said with a pout.

"Scoobie is irreparably damaged. If someone didn't adopt him, he'd have been recycled. It's not the same."

"So it's fine to have pets, as long as they're not working dogs? Whatever helps you sleep at night, Nate. You should come and stay the weekend, see how happy Baba is."

"I don't think so."

"No, it's settled, you're coming to my apartment this weekend."

"And what if I have other things to do?"

"Nate. You're coming to my apartment this weekend. On Saturday night, we're going to go and see that play that you've been nagging me about for the last week and a half, and I'm taking you to dinner at Ristorante Allesandro, and you're coming back to my house, and Baba will make us breakfast in bed on Sunday morning. That is what is happening this weekend."

I'd been out on a couple of dates with Charles in the last year, but this was the first time he'd made the plans.

"Well, I suppose I could try to clear my schedule. But you have to promise to stop scaring the hell out of new clients with talk about reprogramming them. They already think we're just some obscure branch of reclamation and recycling as it is, without hearing you talk about wiping them."

"You've been talking to that girl with half a face, haven't you," Charles said, rolling his eyes.

"Her name's Kitten."

"When *she's* up on the bid board, will you put your name in then? It's not as if we're going to be able to place *her* outside the organization."

"I don't need a domestic, Charles."

"Say that after you've seen what Baba's done with my place. Maybe I'll send her over to yours sometime with orders to make it livable."

"I'm going to meet with my next client."

"I'll pick you up at seven on Saturday."

I sighed through my nose, but I didn't argue. It was impossible to argue with Charles.

Dante

Tango was dead.

He'd only been here for three days, and he was dead. I'd watched our captor kill him. We all had.

My roommate, the one who insisted he didn't have a name, was telling me to calm down and forget about it, because that kind of thing just happened here sometimes. Sometimes people tried to run away. Sometimes people fought back against customers. Sometimes they just got wiped and ended up like the blank-faced and utterly complacent victims I occasionally saw in the food closet, standing and facing the wall as if they'd gotten lost.

Sometimes people were too stupid, my roommate said, to not make our captor mad.

So sometimes our captor made everyone come to the film suite and filled a jack injector with drain cleaner and injected it into somebody's reservoirs, and made us all watch while they screamed and cried and convulsed and melted from the inside. Sometimes he made us watch while he threw the corpse into a trashcan and told us that we'd just learned a lesson in why we had to behave ourselves.

He'd brought me to the film suite on the day he got Tango, and told me to do to him what my roommate had done to me. But Tango wouldn't stop crying, and I found that I couldn't. I couldn't even kiss him, much less... do what I was ordered to do. I'd asked him his name and begged him to stop crying and told him that it would be all right. He'd babbled about how he didn't belong here, that he was a nanny. He'd wanted to know what had happened to the children in his care.

I'd told our captor that I couldn't hurt him.

So he'd twitchboxed me, and blackboxed me, and set me up in a position where I had no choice but to watch him do it. I couldn't turn away, or even close my eyes. I couldn't cry, or tell Tango that I was sorry about what was happening to him. When our captor was done with him, he blackboxed him and took him somewhere else, then came and... had me as well. With no preparation, while I was still blackboxed, so that I couldn't even scream. He brought me to my room when he was finished, and told me that I would get no more warnings about following his orders. That he'd been much too gentle with me thus far. That I'd make a very pretty empty doll if I ever tried to disobey him again.

And as I lay there, waiting for the paralysis to wear off, I decided that I was going to find a way to escape.

I found myself thinking, here in this hellish place, far more than I'd ever thought in the hospital. I'd been bored and exhausted by the menial drudgery and general unpleasantness of my existence there, but I hadn't *suffered*. The staff had been kind enough to me, and the work hadn't been painful or degrading... and it had taken all of my time. There wasn't a spare moment in which to think. Here, I found that my mind could wander as I quickly learned the trick of dissociating from whatever was happening to my body. Frequently, it didn't actually require my attention or active participation. Sometimes it did, but the monster had been right when he'd said it wasn't a hard job. It involved quite a lot of down time in which I was left with my own thoughts.

I was supposed to be a scholar. I was supposed to accomplish important things with the mind that Professor Cunningham had so carefully and diligently trained to intelligence and filled with knowledge. Thus far, I had come to nothing. He was dead, and his work in vain.

At the hospital, they'd pinned me at night. It differed significantly from the sleep we were allowed here. One didn't dream, while pinned.

One didn't have nightmares.

I'd never had a justified nightmare before. As a child, I'd had a few very childish ones—particularly one about cordyceps fungus—and Professor Cunningham had instructed me about the phenomenon, the physiological and cognitive psychology behind dreams and the workings of the subconscious mind. It had all seemed very toothless thereafter, and I hadn't been afraid to sleep.

I had nightmares now forged in memories of terrible things done to me, and done to others in front of me. Of clients who liked to beat me into unconsciousness or burn me with cigarettes—our captor hadn't been pleased about that, and had twitchboxed me for not reporting it to him immediately so that he could have charged the customer an extra fee for damaging me.

My roommate had nightmares, too.

We comforted one another as best we were able. I learned that there could be great comfort in physical intimacy. In being held and kissed and stroked, in doing the same to him. In falling into one another.

Two days after I'd failed to rape Tango, our captor gathered us all in the film suite to bear witness as he murdered him.

And I decided that escaping wasn't enough.

I was going to kill him.

I began to make plans.

'Taire

My new roommate was smarter than anyone had any right to be.

He caught on real fast to how he was supposed to act anytime there was a chance of Sir seeing him, and how to act with customers, and what he was supposed to *do* with them. He wanted to practice with me pretty much any time we were in the room together and weren't completely trashed. Sometimes even when he was pretty trashed—said it helped. Never when I was trashed, though. Never when I wasn't... into it. He'd just stop if I wasn't getting into it, and not even act mad. It was weird.

Sir was happy about how he turned out, probably making money off the vids from our security camera; his two youngest—one of them his prettiest—all over each other all the time without even having to be told.

He got really good at getting me off. Found stuff about me that I hadn't even known about.

He had a major attitude change after Sir killed that new guy; he'd been quiet and reserved before, occasionally lippy. He got real obedient after he died. Real... there was a word for it. When you liked the work you had, or were good at pretending you liked it. When you did as you were told with a smile.

I couldn't tell if he was faking it. He was smart enough to keep me from being able to tell.

But sometimes in the middle of the day, when Sir generally slunk back to his own room to crash and we had a few hours to ourselves to wash and eat and sleep and whatever, he'd let on how smart he was. He'd talk about all kinds of books and history and science and math and stuff. Said he'd been a schoolboy. Said his name was Dante and that he was named after some human. He'd talk about things he'd noticed about the building, when he was walking back and forth between the suites and our room and the bathroom and the food closet. How it was set up, like what rooms were where and how he figured it was probably a storage place before Sir retrofitted it. He never called Sir "Sir" unless he knew someone was listening. He called him "Big Brother" the rest of the time, and when I'd asked him what the hell that'd meant he's just said "1984" like that made any kind of sense.

But he'd kissed me after, and I hadn't worried too much about it.

He got to be one of Sir's favorites real fast too, after the new guy died. Got dragged back to Sir's room a lot. He didn't talk a lot about what went on there. He didn't have to. I'd been one of Sir's favorites for a long time before he got bored with me. I didn't mind not being a favorite anymore.

He always just wanted to be held, every time he got back from Sir's room, poor cuddly little fuck. I didn't mind holding him.

He'd been my roommate long enough for me to have lost track of the time before he'd been my roommate when he woke me up in the middle of the day and said, "I need you to help me test something. You and I are going stare right at the camera for five minutes and see if anyone comes."

"What for?" I asked, annoyed at having been woken.

"Because I only take calculated risks. If he comes to see why we're behaving strangely, I'll know he's paying attention. I have reason to believe he's not."

"He'll twitchbox the fuck out of us if we act up," I said, and considered just rolling back over.

"Maybe so, but as I said, calculated risk." He smiled one of those little knowing smiles he had, the kind that made me think that everything was gonna be okay, because he knew what he was talking about. "Would you believe that one of my clients had a bottle of flunitrazepam in his bag and was stupid enough to leave said bag in the red suite with me while he went to the bathroom? Maybe he's a chronic insomniac. Far more likely he's a rapist. Anyway, Big Brother's probably going to be unconscious for several hours."

"What are you talking about?" I asked, sitting up, moving over to join him where he was sitting at the edge of the mattress, just staring up and the camera with this kind of smug little defiant look on his face. It was the kind of look that would get him slapped in the mouth if Sir saw it. I glanced at the door, half expecting Sir to come bursting through it with a twitchbox in hand, and wondered what the fuck the kid was up to.

"Dante, what did you *do*?" I said, my voice sounding little and pathetic.

"He lets me fetch beer for him sometimes, when he's too full of post-coital sloth to bother moving. It wasn't even hard to slip several pills into it. He was on his third, and he drinks gutter piss anyway, so he wasn't tasting it. The risk of overdose is increased if flunitrazepam is taken in combination with alcohol... he was barely able to walk when he dragged me back here, but I don't think it occurred to him that he was anything other than drunk and exhausted. I very much doubt that he's conscious now. Of course, as it's also a skeletal muscle relaxant, he might also have stopped breathing. That is one of the dangers of overdose."

He kept looking at the camera the whole time he was talking, and his smiled turned downright nasty. Kind of scary, in fact.

"You're gonna get off-lined, Dante," I said with growing horror at what he was saying. He'd maybe killed a human. That wasn't the kind of thing that anyone ever forgave you for.

"I don't intend to get caught," he said, turning to me, his smile going all gentle and nice again. There was a kind of sharp light in his eyes, something that I'd never seen in a cygenic before.

He looked back at the camera and started humming. I didn't know the song, but it sounded... important. Like it meant that things were going to happen. It made me want to help those things happen.

Giving one last glance to the camera and apparently satisfied that no one was watching, he did a weird little curl with his tongue and spat a penny into his hand. Then he grinned and said,

"I'll be Enjolras and you be Grantaire, only with less barricade—because those demonstrably fail in spectacular ways—and more *fire*."

He went over to the door and knelt in front of it,

doing something with the penny at the side of the doorknob. I just stared, completely confused about what was going on. This wasn't the kind of thing that happened. We were supposed to be asleep right now, or at least resting up, because it was a Friday and we always got more customers on Friday nights. They were more likely to be drunk, too, and interested in smacking us around a little.

"What are you doing?" I asked, kneeling up to get a better look over his shoulder.

"I've been looking at the kind of locks we have on the doors," he answered casually, not looking at me. "These are bathroom door locks, they don't even need keys to be opened. I suppose that given how docile and tractable most cygenics are, and how few of us are in any position for innovative thinking, that these seemed entirely sufficient when our dear lord and master was building this facility." He pressed the penny up against something, and with a metallic click the metal collar where the knob met the door snapped forward. "But as you can see, that's not the case."

"Where did you learn to do that?"

"When I was a child, I watched a video about how to replace a doorknob on some home improvement show. Ideally I'd have a screwdriver, but I think I'll be able to make do."

"You're fucking crazy," I said, sitting back, basically falling on my ass on the mattress, watching him stick his fingers in the hollow place he'd uncovered behind the doorknob. Something made a loud, sliding click.

Dante opened the door.

"Et voila!" he said, standing up and indicating the

open door with flourish. "Now let's go let everyone else out and set the building on fire. I think turning on one of the nice white spotlights from the film suite and laying it directly on a foam mattress will create a sufficient self-sustaining blaze. It will certainly create a lot of noxious smoke, which is functionally the same really, if not quite as dramatic."

"You're fucking *crazy*!"

"Maybe so, my Grantaire, but I'm free! And so are you. And so are all of the other miserable souls here, or they will be as soon as you and I open the doors. I'm entirely done with doing as I should; obedience hasn't really gotten me anywhere. I think it's time that I tried disobedience."

He offered me his hand.

"Join me?"

All I could think, as I let him help me stand up, was that he'd just given me a name.

Nate

"My lease runs out next month," Charles said, conversationally, not even looking at me. We were on my sofa, his long lean legs crossed in my lap as we ostensibly watched TV together while I actually watched and he played on his phone. "I've been thinking that instead of renewing it, I should just move in here."

"What?" I asked, turning off the TV. He glanced up at it, looking slightly annoyed. Those heart-shattering baby blue eyes of his had the capacity to hold so much emotion, he didn't even have to try for me to know exactly what he was thinking.

I crushed down the impulse to turn the TV back on just to see him smile.

"Well, we already spend the better part of our time together," he said, his voice getting that warm, indulgent tone he got sometimes when he was explaining something to me. "It seems the next logical step. Besides, Whiskers likes you. Whiskers hates everyone. Clearly, this is a sign."

"Can you at least *look* at me while we're having this conversation?" I said. He looked slightly annoyed again, but after a moment to finish whatever he was typing turned his phone off and put it on the coffee table. He turned to face me, and flashed his most winning smile. As usual when he did that, I felt certain parts of my brain melt a little.

"My rent is exorbitant, and my apartment is tiny," he said. "It seems stupid for me to keep paying for it when I spend most of my time here anyway."

It was true. Over the last three months he'd installed a mini-office in a corner of my den, commandeering the desk that overlooked the back yard (it had just been a repository of unopened junk mail and magazines, before) and setting up a laptop there that he eventually stopped packing up when he left. He often stayed for three and four days at a time, trusting Baba to take care of Whiskers.

"And what about Baba?" I asked, trying to figure a way around his entirely logical suggestion. We'd only been dating for three months. It seemed... sudden for him to just move in.

"You have a guest room. It's bigger than the room Baba has in my apartment. If anything, I'm sure she'd be very pleased!"

"And where will guests stay when they come over?"

"When was the last time you had guests, Nate?"

I sighed, because he was right about that, too. None of my college friends had visited in more than a year. Half of them didn't even talk to me anymore. Iris tried to assure me that it was just normal for people to drift apart after college and to drop off the radar once they had kids.

Neither of us ever talked about our families.

"If I stopped paying my rent, there would be enough spare money to do something really nice, maybe go to Bordeaux for a few days in the summer."

"I can't afford a trip. I don't even like traveling."

"A backpacking trip through wine country, right after all the interns leave. I did it every summer when I was still in school."

"Maybe if we went to Paris?" I suggested. "I've always wanted to see the Louvre—"

He reached over an touched my face, cradling my jaw in his hand.

"Paris is unacceptably crowded in summer, all tourists and hawkers, and everything is outrageously expensive. Bordeaux. I know a hostel that overlooks a lavender field, where they serve duck confit with truffles. You'll love it, Nate," he said, leaning in to kiss me. My brain melted completely, because Charles always kissed like he was starving. When he broke the kiss I found myself dazzled, a stupid grin blooming on my face, my concerns suddenly unimportant. "You didn't think you'd like that trip we took to Martha's Vinyard in September, and look how much fun you ended up having."

That had been a lot of fun... hadn't it? I was smiling in all of the photos.

"Yeah," I said, breathless, as he moved in to kiss me again. His slid his hands up along my arms, guiding them above my head, gripping my wrists and pinning them against the arm of the sofa. I tried to pull them down, and he smiled against my mouth.

"You love it when I hold you down," he whispered. "I can feel it in how you struggle."

I didn't love it. I never loved it when he held my hands like that, always felt trapped and anxious. But he brought his thigh up between my legs and rocked his weight forward, pressing against me in a way that shut down the part of my mind that said I'd told him before about this.

Charles loved to hold me down, and he deserved to get to do things he enjoyed sometimes. It was only fair. I bucked against his thigh, grinding in thoughtless want.

"You like that," he whispered into my ear, his voice like crushed velvet. It wasn't a question. He moved to bite and suck at my neck, and I knew damned well that he was giving me a mark. Knew better than to complain about it, too, because if I complained about it he'd make it worse. It wasn't like he had to mark me up. Everyone knew we were together.

I could run a cellular regenerator over it after, if it was actually that noticeable, but Charles would pout if I did that, and refuse to touch me until I'd sufficiently apologized for being affronted by affection. For being ashamed of people knowing about us. There was precedent.

Anyway, he insisted that I liked having people see me marked up. That it got me all hot and bothered to have to explain or *not* have to explain, and maybe it was true. He was good at stupidly brilliant insights like that. I got caught up analyzing and overanalyzing psychological minutiae and lost sight of the obvious because of it. The danger of being a therapist.

Charles knew how to make me scream. I closed my eyes as he gripped both my wrists in one hand and slid forward, straddling my waist, sliding the other hand into my pants. Looking smug as he ran his hand over my cock, pleased that he'd made me hard. He could be such a complete callous asshole, but dear

God did he know how to fuck me. So fucking arrogant, the way he'd push me up against the wall and make me beg for it. How he'd shove me down on my knees and tell me to suck him off, and how I'd do exactly what I was told when he was the one telling me to do it. I hated that about him. Hated him giving me orders, like I was something he owned, because that was the only way he knew how to treat anyone or anything. But it never, ever failed to get me off. He knew it, too, how much I hated it and hated myself for finding it so fucking hot, and he did it anyway.

And hating it didn't make it any less hot. Didn't make me want it any less. I was fucked up, that way. So when Charles pulled back and said,

"Get up and get out of those clothes,"

I did.

And when he told me,

"Get on your knees,"

I did.

And I knew, as he was taking off his belt, that he'd be moving in here when his lease ran out, because I couldn't say no to Charles. Because I didn't *want* to say no to Charles. No matter how much I knew that I should.

'Taire

"I told you, KJ, he just *took* her! He blackboxed us and took her inside the store. I came back here as soon as I could move again."

"He took her and not you?" KJ said, giving me the kind of look that you'd give your foot after you stepped in dog shit. KJ looked at me like that a lot. Dante and I had been part of this group for like six months now, and it was hitting home that I'd never, ever be able to make KJ like me. But she liked Dante. And Dante liked being part of a group, because it was safer than it had been back when we were on our own.

Back after we'd lost everyone else who'd got out of Sir's place with us.

"I guess he didn't want me," I said softly. Candy was a girl, and pretty. I'd stopped being pretty right about the time my first owner sold me to Sir. I was still young, but... not young enough to be special anymore. Not worth taking. Just street trash.

"You were supposed to have her back. You were supposed to be able to handle it. It was supposed to be a dumpster run. And here you come back with no food and you tell me that some guy just *took* Candy. But not you."

"Where's Dante?" I asked, swallowing hard. I

needed him. He was better at explaining this kind of thing than me. I'd known it was stupid to go someplace without him. To think that I could handle a dumpster run with anybody else.

"Dante's with Angelo, making sure Angelo doesn't call the cops on us this week. He's got more useful shit to do than babysit you," KJ said, her hands in fists, not quite sitting on her hips. Pulled back like she wanted to hit me.

"We gotta try to get Candy back. Far as I know she's still inside the store, and it's just the one guy there. Maybe... I mean he might let her go after he's done with her. We gotta go see if we can get her back."

"And have him call the cops? When a human takes someone, they're done. That's just how it is. You are a fucking idiot. No idea what Dante sees in you. Smart guy like him should know enough to shuck something like you off. I wish it was you got took and not her. *She* was useful, and she had a hell of a lot better attitude."

"What was I supposed to do? He blackboxed us."

"You were supposed to not get caught. The rest of us manage shit like that all the time. You wait until there's no humans around before you hop in a dumpster. You don't get seen. Humans see someone they like, they take us. Who owns your registration, huh? Who comes up as your owner if a human pings you? Dante's got state. Candy's got a dead guy. But you? You got nuthin'. Dante told me. Nobody wants you, kid, and nobody ever did."

"What's going on?" I heard Dante say from behind me, and turned around to find him standing there with his hair disheveled and his lips puffy.

Because he'd been letting the guy who owned the store next door fuck him. Because that kept him from calling the cops and having us all hauled away.

We should have just found someplace else to stay, but everyone liked the abandoned store. It had good walls and a good basement. Good crash place. Not too much activity. Better than the warehouse had been, where we'd been living before Nix found this place.

And just the one human to keep happy so we could keep it.

Dante said he didn't mind. Said it was for the good of the group.

"Nothin's going on, Dante," KJ said. "We lost Candy, and we've got no food."

KJ cuffed me on the back of the head and walked away.

Dante looked at me, kind of bewildered, and then he got that face. That 'oh, poor 'Taire' face. I closed my eyes, because I hated that face. It meant I'd fucked up. Anyone else would have been yelling at me like KJ was; she was right to do it. But Dante just closed the distance between us and hugged me, and even though I could smell the human he'd just been fucking all over him, I couldn't bring myself to push him away because it was Dante.

"I fucked up," I said, my voice tiny and broken. "I was supposed to get food and me and Candy went and then this guy came out of the store and blackboxed us and took her inside. He took her. And KJ says it's just over, and she's so pissed at me Dante. And Candy's *gone*."

He just hushed me and petted my back for a while, and somehow that felt even worse.

"KJ will get over it," he finally said. "She got over it when we lost Trixie and when we lost Nails and when we lost Crow. It'll take her a while, but she'll get over it. We lose people. It's a thing that happens. People get picked up by humans, or people get off-lined, or people just don't come back from runs."

I nodded.

"I'm glad you came back. I wouldn't have let her send you without me, if I'd been there."

"KJ's in charge. She can send me where he wants to."

"KJ doesn't own you. We listen to KJ because she's 20 years out of the tank and knows what she's talking about most of the time, but if she's being a jackass and telling you to do something stupid, you can tell her no. It's not like she's a human. She doesn't have power you don't give her."

I nodded again, not trusting my voice.

"I'm gonna go get Lars and Nix and Ruby, and we're all gonna go to the dumpster behind that grocery store on the other side of Warren Street, okay?"

"But that's Jakes' territory..." I said, pulling away a little.

"Jakes still owes us a favor from when I stitched up that gash on Crane's leg and got them a bottle of rubbing alcohol and showed her how to keep it clean. If we run into any of Jakes' people, I'll do the talking. It'll be okay. And there's usually frozen pizzas in that dumpster; it's been a while since we've had pizza. KJ loves pizza."

He gave me one of those little smiles of his, the 'I know what I'm talking about' smile.

So I nodded again and let me walk with me, an arm around my shoulders.

Hours later, after the dumpster run went without a hitch and we'd cooked our pizza over a trashcan fire and eaten it, and after Dante and KJ had gotten into a really nasty shouting fight which I was pretty sure Dante had won, he and I huddled together on the pile of cardboard and plastic bags that we called a bed.

I liked the basement a lot; it felt safe. Like I always knew what was going on. It was closed in, secure, just the one way in or out. It was completely dark after the sun went down, but I could tell who was around just by listening to the assorted breathing and moving sounds people made bouncing off the concrete walls. Lars and Nix were whispering to one another in the corner opposite us, too far away for me to make out what they were saying. KJ and Ruby were talking upstairs. KJ sounded kind of like she was crying. Dante was breathing against the back of my neck.

"You feeling okay, 'Taire?" he asked, very softly, his arms around me tightening a little.

"Yeah, I guess," I said. I turned around carefully, so that I could hide my face against his throat. He kissed my forehead.

"I'd never have forgiven myself if it had been you who'd been taken, you know. I'd never have forgiven KJ for sending you."

"It's gonna happen eventually," I said, swallowing hard. "Me getting taken or off-lined or something, I mean. I'm not like you, I'm not smart enough to—"

He kissed me on the mouth. It was probably just to shut me up, but I relaxed into it anyway, wrapping my arm around him and sliding it up to cup the back of his neck because I knew he liked that. Should have known this was coming. Dante always wanted me after he'd been with Angelo, said it made him feel clean again. I'd never been able to figure out what he meant by that but... I never minded. Not when it was Dante. Any time he wanted me, any way he wanted me, he always made me feel so good. Better than anyone had ever made me feel before. Better than sex was supposed to feel. Something about the way Dante kissed me always made my eyes sting, because it felt... important. Like it was about me. Like I meant something.

Just having Dante kiss me was enough to get me hard, and he lined his hips up with mine, grinding us together through the tight fabric of our stolen jeans. He slid his hands up under the hem of my shirt. Dante's hands were perfect; delicate and clever and so *smooth*. He washed them any chance he got, and insisted that I do too, and that was probably part of it. He curled over and pushed my shirt up, kissing his way up my belly as he did, before coming back up to breathe warm against my throat.

"I'll never let you go, 'Taire," he whispered as he undid my pants. There was a pause as he undid his own, and then I felt his cock pressed against mine, hot and smooth and hard. Felt his hand go around both, stroking us together. I moaned a little and tried to swallow it down because it was just common courtesy not to make noise. Everybody knew Dante and I fucked. It just wasn't something any of us ever talked about.

I let my hands move along his ass and the backs of his thighs, rough fabric tight over hard muscle. He gasped a little, then purred right in my ear as his hand found the right rhythm. Quick and tight and hot and perfect, the skin of his cock silky against my own. He rained kisses on my throat, licking and nibbling, and I had to bite my lip hard to keep from moaning.

It didn't take very long for him to come, scalding heat splashing against my belly, Dante moaning low into my ear with an abandon that dared anyone to say anything about it. I couldn't help but come too, hearing his pleasure.

"Everything will be okay, 'Taire, you'll see," he said, softly, as he tucked me back into my pants. I grabbed his hand and sucked on his fingers, tasting him and tasting me and loving the way we tasted together. Dante laughed a little, and from the other side of the room Nix called us insufferable sluts and told us to shut the fuck up, and Dante just laughed more.

But curled up around him in the afterglow, I thought maybe he was right. Maybe it would be okay.

Nate

"What do you mean, New York?" I said, being very careful to put my coffee down rather than drop it because he'd probably laugh if I did that, and stare at me while I cleaned it up, and laugh at me a second time for not just having Baba do it.

"I don't know how I'm being unclear. I've accepted a job offer in New York. I'm going to be moving there next week."

"I can't just pack up and leave on a week's notice, Charles," I said tightly. "I know you don't really give a damn about your work at the Center, but that's my *life*. Switching chapters takes about six months—"

"Did I imply that you were coming to New York?" he said, raising his eyebrows. "I'm taking Baba, of course. You can keep Whiskers; the apartment I'm moving to doesn't allow pets. He likes you better anyway."

I didn't mention that Baba also liked me better, though I probably should have. But I wasn't thinking of that. I was thinking about the fact that he was talking about moving to New York, leaving me here with his cat. As quietly and bloodlessly as if he hadn't been fucking me for the last year and a half. As if we were just roommates of convenience, sharing the rent.

I owned the house. Graduation gift from my dad that came with a tacit "never contact me again" agreement. Charles had never paid me any rent.

"I'll need to use your car later. I told Justin that he could have that cabinet that's been sitting in your garage. I can't really justify dragging it all the way to New York and it doesn't fit in my trunk, but it should fit in the back of yours with the seats folded down."

"This is really how you're breaking up with me, isn't it. This is actually happening," I said, my breath picking up speed a little.

"Oh for Christ's sake, Nate, don't tell me you're going to get all dramatic about this. You knew before you got involved with me that I've been looking for other jobs. I found one. It's not as if this was ever any kind of committed arrangement. It's been nice, don't make it awkward now."

"You moved in with me. You've been living here for a year. I thought—"

"What did you think? You're right, I've been living here for a year, and in an entire year I haven't been able to improve your attitude at all. You're such a child." He stood up, finishing his coffee in one gulp and putting the cup in the sink. "I'm going to the store. I'll be back in an hour or so. Maybe then we can continue having a civil conversation about this without you falling into some sort of teary, dramatic tantrum like a toddler."

And just like that he was grabbing his jacket and heading out the door, leaving me sitting there at the breakfast table.

Whiskers rubbed up against my ankle, and I reached down to pet him.

The impulse came to use this hour I had to take everything Charles owned and dump it on the curb. To tell him, when he came back, that if he was planning to leave in a week he might as well just leave now. Let him see what a dramatic tantrum really was.

But he'd just laugh it off, and look down his nose at me for being irrational, and say as much to everyone at work. I wondered if he'd given his two-week notice. If anyone else had known about this before me. I was often the last person to know about Charles' plans.

Iris would have told me if she'd known, wouldn't she?

Where would it leave Baba, if I kicked Charles out?

"Baba?" I called, loudly enough that she'd hear me even if she was upstairs. I heard her coming, her footsteps as quick and precise as they always were. She appeared in the doorway, standing at attention.

"Yes, sir?" she asked, because no matter how many times I told her to call me Nate and to damned well call him Charles she always addressed both of us as "sir."

"Did you know that Charles is planning to move to New York next week?"

"No, sir," she said, looking slightly confused.

"He plans on taking you with him."

"Of course, sir."

"He plans on leaving me."

She blinked rapidly several times, and for a moment actually looked very unhappy before schooling her face back to pleasantness.

"I'm sorry, sir. It's been a pleasure living in your home."

"You could petition the Center, if you wanted. Call and say that you don't want to be relocated. He doesn't have the right... I mean, he doesn't own you. Not really. If you don't want to go, he can't take you against your will."

Baba looked down, taking several deep breaths.

"Would you keep me, sir? If I did that? I know that you've considered me something of an imposition. You've said many times that you don't want a domestic."

"That's not the point... I didn't say that to you, Baba..."

"Mister Lindsted has always been very kind to me, Mister Matheson. I know what he wants from me. I don't think I'd like to learn someone else's habits, if I didn't have to. I know how to live with him."

"I just wanted you to know... that you had choices. That you'll have choices even after you're in New York. You can always call the Center if anything changes and you're not happy. We can help you."

She smiled wanly, looking up at me, and when she spoke her voice was uncharacteristically tender. "I don't need help, Mister Matheson. Not anymore."

I looked down at the cup of coffee that I was holding. It had gotten cold. "No, I suppose you don't. I'm going to go for a walk, Baba."

"Shall I clear all this away?" she asked, her voice cheerfully chirpy again.

"Do whatever makes you happy," I said.

At least someone could be happy.

Dante

I'd been stupid to think that Angelo was a safe human just because he waited a while to make his move. I should have known when he requested that I service him on camera that he had plans other than taking it home to masturbate to. I should have been more wary, should have considered what he was thinking about.

I'd shown up to service him in accordance with our usual arrangement, and he'd blackboxed me and pinned me.

I woke up lying on a hard floor, shaking off the foggy dissolution of having been pinned.

"What happened..." I said, trying to pull my wits together. The floor underneath me was wooden. There was a bank of fluorescent lights overhead. I was laid out on it like a doll, arms at my sides. I didn't try to move.

"Keep your mouth shut until someone tells you to open it, kid," Angelo said. "You used to be a net whore, yeah? Saw vids of you."

As he hadn't told me to open my mouth, I only nodded in answer.

"Knew it had to be you. They don't make you fuckers that young too often. So here's what's gonna happen. I got some people coming over. You're gonna show them what you can do, and then one of them's gonna buy you. You got a problem with that, I got a twitchbox. This only has to be as hard as you make it, okay?"

I nodded again, because what else was I supposed to do? There wasn't any point in fighting with humans. Evading them could be reasonably effective, or manipulating them, but this wasn't that kind of situation. This was the kind of situation where I had to bide my time.

"Get up. I know you're not fucking frozen anymore."

I stood. The room was small and windowless, maybe a basement or a retrofitted office of some kind. Acoustic tiles on the ceiling, beige carpet on the floor. I was standing on a stage. Angelo was seated below it on a folding chair. There were several other empty chairs.

There was a naked cygenic kneeling at Angelo's feet, leaning his head against Angelo's thigh. Angelo was playing with his hair as he spoke.

"It's nothing personal, kid. You've been fun. I'd keep on letting you suck me off and letting your crusty little friends hang around, if it was up to me. But I've got debts, and you're an asset." He looked at the cygenic at his side. "Get him cleaned up."

The cygenic looked up at him and smiled adoringly before he rose. He was the same generic model as Lars, but he had vibrantly orange hair and luminescent blue eyes. It was a model that could be purchased ready-made from any number of stores, with minimal modifications and simplistic programming done while the buyer waited. He probably wasn't dazzlingly intelligent. I probably couldn't expect any kind of assistance from him.

He came to escort me off the stage, smiling at me sweetly. Like there was nothing wrong with what was going on.

I let myself enjoy the shower. I hadn't had a hot shower since I'd worked at the hospital. The cygenic who was supervising me was far more tactile than I'd have liked, running his hands all over me. I relaxed into it anyway, closing my eyes and willfully beginning the process of distancing myself from this because it was beyond my control.

Dissociation is a psychological term describing detachment from one's immediate surroundings and experiences, I thought to myself. *Dissociation is a typical defense or coping mechanism for the processing of severe physical or emotional trauma. I am very good at dissociating. This will end. This will end.*

When I was passably clean, he brought me back to the room with the stage and led me onto it with a huge grin on his face.

"Okay what I want you to do, as soon as everybody's here, is you're gonna suck Rocket off a little bit, then he's gonna fuck you. You're gonna put on a damned good show about it, too. Draw it out, make it last, get into it. I wanna see you wiggling and moaning and everything. I want everybody to see you're worth good money. You can come, if you want. Have yourself a good time. Rocket's good."

I nodded, closing my eyes briefly.

"Smile, kid. Nobody's gonna hurt you."

I looked up at him and offered a winning smile, contemplating the irony of what he'd just said. Of him declaring that no one was going to hurt me, when I was already standing naked in an anonymous room, waiting to be raped in front of an audience of buyers.

Rape was a word that only applied to humans. It would do me good to remember that.

"Rocket, get him ready. Get him into it."

I looked at Rocket, and he smiled at me. It was a compelling smile, managing to be innocent and sensual at the same time, but there was a disturbing emptiness about his eyes. Rocket was a sex doll. I wondered if he could speak and had simply been ordered not to, or if speech was something outside of his programming.

He leaned in and kissed me. I relaxed at let it happen. I'd gotten so good at this, at the brothel I'd burned down. At letting it happen. It wasn't always terrible. Most customers weren't actually interested in hurting me. They just wanted to get off. They just wanted someone to pay attention to them, to make them feel good.

I could certainly make oblivious, innocent Rocket feel good.

I hoped 'Taire was all right. That he'd be all right without me. He wasn't ready. His entire life had been this kind of thing. He needed someone to show him how much more there was to the world. I'd hardly had a chance to start, the pressing needs of survival constantly keeping us active and moving, making new associations and losing old ones.

Someone would take care of him. I had to believe that. That he would be all right.

It didn't really matter if *I* was all right. This would end, regardless.

Rocket had his hands on me, gentle but firm caresses on my back and shoulders. I could hear movement in the room, voices talking softly to one another. Chairs shuffling on the floor. Rocket never stopped kissing me, stroking me. I closed my eyes and let it happen. Let myself sigh softly against his lips. Let my arms fold around him, feeling the taut strength of his muscles and the smooth heat of his skin. Rocket wasn't abhorrent. I'd known far worse.

When I heard Angelo say, "Rocket, show us what the kid can do," Rocket pushed down on my shoulders. I kissed my way down his chest and belly, dipping my tongue into his navel, looking up through my eyelashes at him. He gasped and grinned like this was a game. Like he was having fun. He murmured appreciation as I took him into my mouth and tried to think about other things. About how this would end.

It *would* end.

Nate

Charles had been gone for two weeks before Iris convinced me to get drunk about it. She offered to drive and planned a pub crawl starting with my favorite bar—a place in the South End that had the best wings I'd ever eaten and actually challenging trivia and 30 kinds of craft beer on tap.

"So you ready to talk about it yet?" she said, picking the last shred of flesh off a bone and putting it carefully into the little pyramid she was building on her plate.

"If I say no, can we talk about something else?" I asked miserably. "You were right, I was wrong, Charles is an irredeemable asshole and he's *gone* now."

"And you are far less happy about that than you ought to be. We should be celebrating! You should have been the one dumping *his* sorry ass many many months ago," she said, flagging down a waitress. "Charles is an emotionally abusive shitheel, and I hope he gets hit by a bus."

I winced at her vehemence, looking down into my beer. I was not anywhere near done feeling sorry for myself, and here she was on another "Charles is the devil in slacks" jag. No amount of telling her that those didn't help ever stopped her.

"Not that you ever listened to me about it before," she said, looking down at her plate rather than at me, "but I'm telling you again: He treated you exactly the same way he treated Baba. Like you were staff."

"Please stop—" I began, only to have her interrupt me.

"He fucking brainwashed you! He bossed you around and gaslighted you and convinced you that you were into whatever he wanted, and then he walked out on you when something better came along. Wake up, Nate, you dodged a bullet. You're free."

I didn't feel free. I felt ditched. It was an achingly familiar feeling. I'd been stupid enough to think that I could make him love me, if I'd just been good enough.

He hadn't been that bad, nothing like as bad as Iris always presumed he was. He'd never even shouted at me more than a handful of times, and he'd certainly never done anything like threaten me or hit me or make me feel unsafe. He'd been so good at... putting things in order. I could just relax when he was around, and know that he had a plan and all I had to do was follow that plan and everything would be fine.

"What I don't get is this: first time I met you, it was because you just about popped that asshole who lived on the floor below us. Why'd you take so much shit from Charles? And don't tell me your anger management classes actually turned you into Captain Doormat, I'm not buying that."

I glared at her, then sighed.

"Charles never made me *mad*, okay? I know you don't get it. But... he was always so smooth, you know? I could never argue with him. He'd always just shut me down and kiss me..." I closed my eyes, trying to push back the memories. "... and we'd end up doing what he wanted to do. And it would be nice."

"He'd make you *think* it was nice is what you mean. I remember when you came back from that stupid France trip he dragged you on and you were an angsty mess because you'd spent so much time trying to make him happy."

"We had a good time in France! The food was awesome and the weather was gorgeous and we toured all these little artisan vineyards—"

"And you hated it, and would have rather been at a museum or a lecture series or something. Nate, I know you. You are a giant nerd. You do not secretly have the soul of an especially snobby poet. That was just what Charles wanted you to be. You don't even like wine!"

I didn't have anything to say to that, so I just drank my beer.

"You know what you need?" Iris said, "A hot rebound. That new intern's been making eyes at you the whole time he's been here."

"He has not," I said, my tone admittedly petulant.

"Yeah, he so has. You even knew the one I meant, the kid with the freckles and the absurd gel spikes," she said, holding her hand about a foot above her head, which was unfair because the kid's hair probably only had about four inches of vertical gravity defiance ...

"Is he even 18?"

"Yes, or he wouldn't be interning with us."

"His name's Drake, by the way. He's from Minnesota. He's going back to Minnesota next May."

"Which means he's ideal no-strings-attached

rebound material! You have an expiration date and everything. Go for it. If I'd known you knew his name I'd have invited him out drinking with us tonight."

"No way he's old enough to drink," I said with a snort.

"Next place we're going doesn't card, though," she said with a toothy smile.

I smiled a little, having no intention of stringing along some intern with a crush who was going to disappear in a few months. But at least we weren't talking about Charles anymore.

"So, you drunk enough yet for me to drag you to a club where we can actually dance?" Iris said with a wicked grin as the waitress she'd flagged down brought her the check.

"Do I have a choice?"

"Not really. I'm gonna keep feeding you fancy beers until you say yes. But at least I'm honest about it. Come on, let's go to Nightmare. That's reasonably tame, and they actually have music."

"Hey, there's music here!" I protested.

"Danceable music," she clarified.

"You're insufferable."

"And you, poor boy, suffer me anyway."

I smiled and let her lead me onward to the rest of the crawl she had planned.

Dante

Consciousness came filtering in with a bassline loud enough that it had to be routed through the floor. Dully pounding pain in my head followed the rhythm in counterpoint. The air smelled like smoke and alcohol. There was a general sense of frenetic action, people milling about, the chatter of a dozen voices nearby. I blinked my eyes open to flashing lights and immediately closed them again. Tried to move my arms and found that they were fixed behind my back, tied around a pole...

Oh. I was underneath a table.

Since Angelo had sold me, there were at least six distinct bouts of sustained consciousness that I could remember, across a period of time that I had no means of tracking. I'd been pinned and stored and bought and sold and pinned again many times over. Someone had filled a jack injector with ethanol and pumped it into my spinal reservoir. A toxin alarm had been screaming at me from the back of my head since. I didn't know how long ago that had been, but I was fairly certain that it wasn't my current owner who'd done it. He'd punched me in the mouth when I'd tried to tell him, and that had been my only indication that he didn't want me speaking at all.

"Yeah. He's a good fuck," someone above me was saying. "Tight little bitch, great mouth on him. Real obedient-like if you smack him around a little. He's high-end goods, you don't see shit like him down on Piss Street every day. Picked him up off some punk ass kid who was kicking around Tory's place. You want, I can even hook you up with a guy who does reprogramming cheap."

That sounded like I was being sold again.

"He's busted as shit. Come down on price, and we'll talk," another voice replied.

"You could pimp him out. He'd pay for himself in no time."

I sighed, leaning against the cool steel post at my back, and wondered how long it would take for someone to just deprogram me. Maybe they wouldn't even bother. Various abuses and deprivations would kill the human flesh off slowly, and I'd eventually go BSOD, deprogramming or no.

I hoped that 'Taire was all right. I probably wasn't ever going to get to know.

I probably wasn't going to be alive much longer.

I drew up my knees and rested my chin on them, and I waited.

Nate

I was drinking some kind of neon blue beverage in a glass with a sugared rim, apparently the specialty of the house, because Iris had insisted that I have one. I couldn't decide what it tasted like, other than excessively sweet.

Iris was ruling the dance floor. I was terrible at dancing—especially when I'd gone through 10 drinks—but I had the feeling that she'd be dragging me onto it anyway before the night was done.

I let my eyes wander the crowd. I didn't even know what bar we were in now, Iris leading me on a downward crawl through the labyrinth east of Piss Street. She loved this kind of thing. I'd kind of preferred the quiet pub we'd started in, the one with the trivia and the really good wings. But it wasn't a trivia and wings kind of night, apparently.

The current venue was a "flashing lights and repetitive deep-bass music" affair dominated by a sprawling dance floor. They served ice cream. They'd serve it off a wait-staff's stomach for an extra fee. I could probably get laid here, if I felt like it. It seemed like the kind of place where you could casually fuck in the bathroom without anyone getting mad about it.

The thought was more appealing than I'd have given it credit for 10 drinks ago, being fucked up against a wall by some anonymous stranger... pure lust and pure release.

It had probably been part of Iris' calculated plan to end up here when I was at the height of drunken impulsiveness. I was either going to end up fucking someone in the bathroom, or face down on the floor in her apartment. Or both, in that order, if she would let me get away with it.

A flash of something under the edge of a table caught my attention. I glanced that way and startled, feeling my throat tighten up as my feet carried me forward.

There was a cygenic tied to the leg of a table. He looked young enough to be fresh from the tank. Opalescent skin with softly illuminated lines of electronics running beneath the surface, purplish hair, shining steel-rimmed jacks at his wrists and the base of his neck. He had a black eye and a split lip and a fairly serious head wound. His eyes were closed, eyebrows scrunched together in obvious pain. He was naked except for a pair of cutoffs. Pierced ears, lip, nose, nipples, navel. All with standard steel studs, even in piercings where studs weren't really appropriate, all looking fairly well infected. Someone had gotten creative with a piercing gun.

"Come on, little bitch's worth twice that!" the man on the left, a lanky white guy in an military-issue camo coat, was whining to the other.

"Let me sample, and I might think about it, but I don't think he's worth it," the other sneered. "I can find cheaper elsewhere."

"You lookin' to sell?" I found myself saying, approaching carefully.

* * *

In the end, the cygenic cost me a round of drinks and half of what was in my checking account. I didn't want to think about how I was going to make ends meet this month. It didn't matter.

I crouched on the floor under the table, looking at the cygenic I'd just purchased.

"Keys?" I demanded tersely, looking back up to the man in the camo coat.

"I'll want 'em back. That price, you ain't gettin' the cuffs," he said, running the card I'd given him through a cheap and dirty little data-reader that he'd pulled out of his pocket before giving it, and the keys, to me.

I fumbled with the keys, trying to turn the cuffs around to get at the lock without having them bite into the kid's wrists more than they already were.

The cygenic opened his eyes, and something inside me fell apart a little.

His eyes were silver, the color of mercury, almost luminescent in the reflected black light from the backsplash of the bar. There was fear there, and humiliation, and pain, and above it all a thick wash of resigned hopelessness. He looked completely strung out. He looked like he expected to die.

"Sir," the cygenic murmured, looking away. Not a question.

"My name is Nate," I whispered fiercely, making short work of those cuffs and pulling the cygenic to his feet. He swayed slightly, and I took off my coat and draped it over his shoulders, pulling it closed and snapping the top button. The cygenic staggered a little when I tried to lead him forward, and I slid an arm around the small of his back to steady him as I led him back to the table Iris had commandeered.

Dante

I closed my eyes and bit my lip at the overload.

My newest owner had put a coat on me. It was lined in something amazingly smooth—probably just nylon, but exquisite in the way it flowed on my skin. The fabric caught and tugged on the studs that had been forced through my nipples, sending shocks of pain that bordered on pleasure through me, and it was all I could do to stay on my feet as I was led over to a padded bench facing one of the other tables. He sat down, tugging me down with him. I got to sit on the bench, not the floor. I liked him immediately.

"Iris!" he called across the room. His voice was sharp, and I felt it on the back of my neck, vibrating fiercely through me. It felt... good. Better than it should have. A moment later someone else talking, a woman, but I couldn't pick out what she was saying over the general commotion of the club. This table was closer to the dance floor than the one I'd been chained to.

"Can you drive? I'm not good to drive, but we are so done here."

She replied, and then I was being coaxed to my feet again. This man was really nice about that, strong arm tucking in at the small of my back again, movements fluid and slow enough for me to follow.

His name was Nate. He'd said that.

"What's your name?" Nate's voice asked, hot, into my ear.

"Dante," I mumbled, closing my eyes to dispel the dizziness. Warm breath in my ear wasn't helping that. Nobody had been asking me to speak, recently. Hadn't expected it to be this hard.

What did he want to know my name for?

"Are you all right?" he asked.

"No," I replied, soaking in the sensation of a strong arm resting on the small of my back, drawing in at my waist and steadying me. He was so much better than the last one, and I desperately hoped he'd keep me for a while. It was a long moment before I remembered myself and added, "... Sir."

"Yeah, I didn't think so. Hate to break it to you, but you're fairly trashed," he said, pulling me close. "I'm gonna bring you back to my house, okay?" his voice was smooth and comfortingly strong, but the question didn't make any sense. I couldn't resolve, in my head, what he was asking. Why he was asking.

"As you like, sir," I answered. Safe words, complicit words. Words to show him I could be good. I hadn't met a human yet who wasn't at least somewhat placated by the "as you like" and "if it pleases you" course of speech. I was rewarded with a hand moving gently through my hair.

"I'll take care of you," he said softly.

Take care of me? That would be nice. Impossible little fantasy... which meant I was hallucinating. That was a bad sign. I'd been delirious for a while, but hallucinations were new.

It was raining when he pulled me out onto the

street. Not cold rain; the pleasant kind of cool. We didn't stay in it long before I was being bustled into a car, but the sound of it was pervasive. Kind of soothing, really, after the club music. I listened to it hammering on the roof of the car.

I found myself sitting back against plush seats. He was next to me, arm around my shoulders, serving as an anchor to reality. It was nice. Nicer than anything in my recent experience had been, at any rate. I ran my fingers absently across the velvety fabric of the car seat. The coat I was still wrapped in was fluid and silky against my skin. It smelled like new leather and... maybe aftershave? Something good, something that made me want to breathe it in. I leaned close against the man at my side, putting my head against his chest and listening to the deep, even rhythm of his heart. He allowed it.

It occurred to me a while later that he was talking, maybe asking me questions. Talking to someone else. The woman again. I didn't have it in me to answer, and that was probably really bad. But he didn't seem inclined to beat a response out of me, which was an encouraging sign.

The next series of events was choppy; the car stopped, and Nate steadied me as we stood while he talked to the woman again, and she left, and we walked. Eventually I found myself stripped out of that coat and seated on a sofa that felt like it was made of clouds, sinking down and down and down into it. I couldn't suppress a small moan of pure enjoyment.

"Stay here," my new owner ordered before disappearing. A silly order, I couldn't have gotten very far if I'd tried. I closed my eyes and just breathed, leaning back against that sofa and feeling the tension go out of my muscles. I heard water running, and footsteps. Rain splattering against windows somewhere off to the left. It was quiet enough to hear that kind of thing. Peaceful. Couldn't seem to get my eyes open again, but that was okay. It felt... safe.

I startled back to awareness with a lead slipping into jack on my left wrist. I flailed, jerking away, finding my wrist caught in a strong grip and a soft voice speaking urgently into my ear.

"It's okay, it's okay, it's just a readout. Just want to do a diagnostic. Just need to see if you're going to be all right. Nobody's gonna hurt you."

It was the lie that made me go still. The pure absurdity of having him promise that nobody was going to hurt me. I watched him reading the console he'd plugged into me. He looked worried.

"What did you *drink*?" he murmured. Wasn't looking at me. He was reading the console. He probably wasn't actually asking me, which meant that answering would be speaking without being spoken to. The information was relevant enough that I was willing to risk that.

"Didn't. It's in..." I faltered, couldn't find the right word. "In my back?"

I fingered the jack at the back of my neck, and ended up shivering because I'd forgotten just how sensitive the skin around the jack was.

"Somebody shot you up with something?" he said, and he sounded angry. I flinched, drawing my hand away from the jack quickly, half expecting to get punched again.

He got up and walked away. I tried to relax

against the couch again, but it wasn't as easy this time. When he came back, he was carrying a box.

"Okay, just so you understand where we're at here, first step is getting you clean. Then I can do first-aid stuff on visible wounds. But clean comes first. I want to run a chem sweep."

"You can do that?" I asked in dizzy awe, looking up to find him on the other side of the room, getting something off a bookshelf. He walked out of the room again and came back with a cup in his hands.

"Yeah, I can do that. I'm going to admit before we start anything that I am not entirely sober. So I'm not dosing you with anything other than a cleaner, because I don't want to fuck up, okay? Drink this," he said, offering the cup. It was warm. I must have hesitated a moment too long before following the order, because his eyebrows drew together sympathetically and he said, "It's soy milk and chalk, basically. And vanilla syrup, because it tastes like drinking plaster otherwise. Chem sweep's probably going to make you puke, and you're gonna want something in your stomach beforehand to cut the acid."

I looked up at him, baffled that anyone would consider that kind of detail when dealing with a cygenic, but Nate was looking away again, reading something on the console that was still plugged into me.

The liquid was sweet, and it slid down my throat warmly, pooling in my belly with a heat that spread outward. When I'd drained the cup I was sorely disappointed that there wasn't more. I couldn't remember the last time I'd had anything in my stomach. A little euphoric reward pulse went off in the back of my head for it, and the nagging deficiency alarm faded back.

He picked up a jack-injector, and I must have flinched, because he started talking again.

"Don't worry, wasn't going to do anything with it before asking you. Like I said, want to do a chem sweep. Is that all right?"

"Why are you asking me? Just do it."

"Because asking you is a pretty goddamned important part of this, okay? Tell me you're not okay with being jacked in and I won't. But if you're still trashed by the time I'm sober enough to drive, I'm taking you to a doctor."

A thrill of panic tightened my stomach when he mentioned a doctor. Doctors meant hospitals. Hospitals were where you took cygenics for serious medical-grade modifications. Hospitals cut you up.

Hospitals made you work for 16-hour shifts and turned you off and stuck you in drawers.

"Please, no..." I whispered. "Do whatever you want. Just... if you're gonna reprogram me? Can you make it so I don't care? So that I don't feel it?"

Nate looked at me like I'd said something that hurt him, and very quickly looked away.

His hand, when he brushed aside my hair to get at the jack, was almost painfully gentle. I half expected to shut down when I felt the jack slide in, too used to being pinned. It didn't feel like anything. That seemed unfair; being jacked into an interface like that meant that reprogramming could go on. The human at my side could, if he so chose, completely wipe out everything that I'd ever known. He could even install an entirely new personality and set of memories, if it was the right kind of hardware and he knew how to use it. If he was good at it, I wouldn't even know he'd done it.

I wondered why this man had all the tools to patch up a trashed cygenic neatly on hand. Entirely possible that he was a professional reseller. Not a comforting thought.

"Okay, you're probably going to want to lie down for this part. Have you ever had a chem sweep before?"

"No. Never met anyone who could."

"Right. So I'm gonna shoot you up with some nanites and they're basically going sweep your whole body, isolate any toxins in silicone film and dump them into your digestive tract. That pretty much always results in violent puking."

"Okay."

"I promise it's worth it," Nate reassured as he injected a vial of silver fluid into the lead on the interface. I saw the interface light up, a bunch of text rolling down the screen, then a couple of seconds later I felt the fluid go into the jack itself. It was startlingly cold, and I swore I could feel it running down the veins in my neck with a dull ache.

Nate cracked a cold pack over his knee and molded it in his hands a minute or two before wrapping it in a paper towel and laying it on my forehead. He glanced at a clock set in the far wall, and picked up a tablet from the table before sitting down next to me. The nausea he'd warned me about began almost instantly, and it brought a resurgence of my headache with it, making me incredibly grateful for the cold pack and the quiet and the chance to just be still. I'd been pinned a lot lately, but I couldn't remember the last time I'd slept.

When I finally did start puking into the bucket that Nate had readily on hand, he held my hair back and stroked my shoulders and offered me more of that calcium liquid to get the taste out of my mouth. It felt so much like care that I had a hard time not breaking down into tears. Why was he being so kind?

His hand was still in my hair when I lay back down, combing through it gently in a very soothing way, and I suddenly wanted more than anything to just crawl up into his lap and be cuddled.

"You gonna fuck me?" I asked, my voice slurred and rough around the edges from exhaustion. It wasn't the question I'd meant to ask, but those were the words that came out.

"No," Nate answered, closing his eyes for a moment before continuing his reading. He took his hand off my head, which was the opposite of what I'd wanted. I whined a little at the loss.

"What'd you buy me for then?"

Nate paused, his eyebrows going together, the tablet dropping to his lap as he met my gaze. There was pity in his eyes. "I was drunk and you were there, okay?"

There was more to it than that, I knew there was, but I was still too trashed to be coherent about it, and it was clear that he didn't want to talk. I'd been pushing my luck asking at all. Most of the humans in my recent experience would have smacked me by now.

I just wanted him to hold me. He seemed like the sort of man who'd be cuddly after sex. That would be really, really nice. It was more than I deserved; I shouldn't have even wanted it. Should have been happy with just the gentle hand playing through my hair and the strong guiding hands on my back when I was viciously sick, because that was so much more like care than anyone else had shown me so far.

But it was exactly that that made me want to be in Nate's arms.

Wasn't something I was going to get tonight, though.

I dozed in and out of consciousness for a while, exhaustion battling the nausea and pain and growing lucidity as the toxins washed out of my system in waves, and eventually he deemed me clean enough to dig out a bottle of rubbing alcohol and a cellular regenerator.

It was nice to just lie there and have somebody actually take care of me. Nice to have a regenerator run over the bruises, the scratches, the skinned places on wrists and ankles where cuffs had been applied. I felt it most in the eye; the cool, itchy tingle as the regenerator ran over it, making my skin crawl on the cellular level. It left white-green sparkles in my vision, but the heat and tenderness was gone.

"You want to keep the piercings?" Nate asked, not looking at me.

"As you like—"

"Do *you* want to keep them?"

Actual questions. It wasn't fair to be asking me questions. I couldn't figure out what answer he wanted, what kind of test this was. I was usually better at that kind of thing, but I felt like death warmed over and really just wanted to curl up on that sofa and go to sleep. Or curl up in his arms and go to sleep.

"No...?" I finally ventured. It might mean having to get them all done again if Nate decided he'd liked them.

"Okay. You can start taking them out. Just put the studs on the table. I'll be right back."

Fiddly task to get me refocused. Okay. That made sense. I'd guessed right.

I found that I couldn't take the studs out of my nipples; they hurt too much and my fingers just refused to work. Nate didn't say anything about them when he came back, and he didn't take it upon himself to pull them out. He just ran the regenerator right over them. A little moan bubbled out of my throat when he did. He went flush across the cheeks, but he didn't say anything.

He held my hair back, working with a regenerator on a higher setting to deal with the deep, aggravated cut on my forehead. I didn't remember how I'd incurred that one, or anything for what must have been hours before I awoke to find it there, for that matter. Signs of concussion. Probably would have killed me if I'd been human. His fingers, strong and sure on my scalp, guiding the cool relief of the regenerator, felt good enough to have me purring again...

When he deemed my reservoirs cleared of alcohol and filled them with nutrient fluid, and all the little chemical pulses that were meant to reward me for routine maintenance tripped at once, I moaned in total unselfconscious abandon. He looked somewhat lost at my reaction, pulling away and staring at me as if he wasn't sure what to do with his hands.

"You feel up to a shower?" he asked a while later, as he was putting his tools in order.

"I can try..." I faltered, trying to get up. I proved quite unable to do so.

"If you're gonna fall, you're better off just waiting until morning. It's okay if you sleep on the sofa for tonight."

My first impulse was to whine at him not to leave me. I managed to crush it down before I said anything, and he got up and put away his things one after another while I mutely watched, wondering what he was expecting from me. He brought me a blanket and wrapped it around my shoulders.

"Everything will make more sense in the morning," he said wearily, "Good night."

And he left me.

I sat there in the dark in total confusion, trying to figure out what he could possibly mean just leaving me like that. He hadn't locked me up or tied me down or anything. I knew for damned sure that he hadn't had time to register me properly. I had no idea what my registration number would pull up right now if someone pinged me, but it wasn't this man, and probably not a long string of the other ones before him. If I walked out right now, he'd have no way to trace me...

If I walked out into the downpour in the middle of the night, into unknown territory. I could be halfway across the country, for all I knew. I didn't even know the date.

Or I could stay here and fall asleep on this sofa, where it was warm and dry and quiet and... safe.

And I was so damned tired of running.

So I slept.

Nate

I walked into the bathroom, my mind still reeling. Wasn't entirely sobered up yet, but I'd gone from feeling pleasantly mellow to just feeling anxious and slow and stupid. There was a nagging feeling that I'd fucked up really badly.

It was his eyes.

The way he looked at me, confused and worried. I was used to cygenics being overeager to please, but that wasn't quite it with him. He'd expected me to reprogram him. He'd been resigned about it, hadn't wanted to fight me. About the possibility that I might erase his fucking mind. It was what he'd expected of me, and he hadn't wanted to fight. Hadn't even acted scared. What had to happen to someone to be that resigned about something so fundamentally horrifying?

He was out there on the sofa, still. Probably sleeping by now; he'd only just kept hanging on while I was talking to him. He hadn't answered that first time, when I asked if I could jack into his wrist. I'd figured he'd passed out and he'd scared the shit out of me when he'd flailed. He'd looked so absolutely terrified, and I'd felt like the world's biggest asshole for making him wake up to that. Tried to make up for it with soothing words and apologies, trying to keep it clinical and just get him better. He'd been so sickeningly grateful for it. Expected me to be a monster.

Then he'd asked me if I was going to fuck him.

And I'd wanted to answer "yes."

That was seriously, horribly wrong. Didn't matter that he was fucking gorgeous. Didn't matter that the way he'd looked at me when he'd asked made it seem like he'd *wanted* me to say yes. He wasn't in any kind of shape to consent, not really. Even if he hadn't just spent the last few hours puking out enough alcohol to have killed most humans, the odds were damned good that he was programmed to seduce and was just acting on that programming.

I peeled off my clothes and kicked them into the corner under the sink. Turned the shower on and let the water get to nearly scalding. I swore I could feel smoke in my skin, mingled with sweat and general downtown grime. Getting filthy was usually part of the joy of drinking downtown, but I just wanted to be clean now. Hot water felt purifying, and I found myself just leaning against the cold tile of the shower wall, letting it cascade over me.

It would have been better if he'd been surly. If he'd stayed twitchy and scared, like so many cygenics were. If he hadn't melted with obvious relief and leaned into my hand when I held his hair back. If he hadn't looked up at me with eyes that held implicit gratitude and begged for comfort. The noise he'd made when I ran the regenerator over his chest was like something out of a porno. The glint in half-lidded eyes when he'd asked "You gonna fuck me?" spoke of wanting it.

The words kept echoing in my head, in his smoky, half-broken voice.

You gonna fuck me? He wouldn't have refused me. Even now, If I went out there and asked him to suck me off, asked him to spread his legs for me, there was no doubt in my mind that he'd not only comply but make a damned good show of enjoying it.

I couldn't help dwelling on that possibility as I soaped up, filling the shower with the subtle scent of clove and sandalwood. Soap that Charles had never liked. It felt good to run my hands over my body, over muscles that were sore from dehydration and too much walking around downtown.

I couldn't help getting hard, dwelling on the possibility of his hands on me instead of my own.

I laughed at bitterly myself, because I was jerking off in my shower because I wasn't going to be the kind of asshole who took advantage of a trashed cygenic. No matter how bad I wanted to. Even if he wanted me to. I was pissed at myself for even wanting him. He was hurt and sick and needed my help, and I wanted to fuck him.

I turned, pressing my forehead against the cool tile, bracing my right arm against the wall as I jerked my cock efficiently. I needed to get off; I didn't deserve to enjoy it. I was a bad man, because the image of the cygenic on my sofa came to my mind. The thought of running my hands over all the smooth flesh that I'd just treated with clinical care. The thought of stripping those dirty shorts off him and sucking him off. I could wipe that resignation right off his pretty face, make him moan again like he had when I'd run the regenerator over his nipples. Make him moan like when I'd filled him up with nutrient fluid. Make him writhe and pant and whimper and beg and *come.* I thought of him staring me down with those half-lidded eyes, slinking up behind me and pressing me up against the wall to whisper in my ear. Asking *You gonna fuck me?*—then straddling me and riding my cock.

I came abruptly, panting in the shower spray. The water washed away the evidence immediately. Clean. Worn out and empty and lonely and spent and *clean*. I spent a couple of minutes just standing there under the hot water before I turned it off and dried off and slunk away to bed, hoping that a few hours of sleep and the cold light of day would help me figure out how to salvage this.

Dante

I felt like I'd been run over by a truck. My head hurt, I ached everywhere, there was an awful taste in my mouth, and I was hallucinating.

I hated this dream. I was in bed, tucked in warm and safe.

I hugged the blanket tight against my body, utterly refusing to open my eyes and just trying to hang on to the feeling of comfort. It felt real… but it always did. I knew I'd wake up to the damp reek of the basement on my bed of discarded packing material—and that was the best-case scenario. The "comfort" dreams happened most often in the wake of violence. Coping mechanism of an evil brain. Having them be lucid was a pretty recent development, but not unprecedented.

It meant that I was for some reason sleeping alone, because I seldom had this dream when 'Taire was pressed warm at my side. The thought made me bury my face farther into the phantom blanket, because I didn't want to wake and find out why he wasn't with me.

It was the smell that finally convinced me that there was something amiss, a smell I vaguely remembered from childhood. Sunday mornings checking the news feeds, sitting at the breakfast table and reading them with the professor, discussing the ramifications of current events. Sausage and eggs, toast deliciously greasy with real butter, hot cocoa and coffee... I could have cried at the memory.

And then I remembered that my mouth tasted like vomit and chalk because I'd spent half the night vomiting. Memories of the recent past came spilling back like words to an almost-forgotten poem. Being captured, the hellish time that followed, the events of last night, my current owner...

Nate.

I rolled over and tentatively opened my eyes to brilliant morning sunlight painted across the far wall of a room that looked... domestic. There was a love seat adjacent to the sofa I was laid on, the oblong coffee table between them covered in an assortment of slightly-chilling electronics. A couple of consoles, assorted cables, a jack injector, an empty vial. There was a TV dircctly opposite the sofa, flanked with shelves containing books and assorted objects. A potted palm dominated the corner near the window, stretching nearly to the ceiling. The floor was carpeted, and where the sunlight met the carpet there was a rotund brown tabby lying belly-up, slowly kneading the air.

I leaned back with a sigh and stared up at the pristine whiteness of the ceiling. Nate. My newest owner. The first in quite some time who'd seen fit to set me in good working order, and hadn't even fucked me for the trouble. He'd had a console jacked into my skull, and it had left me with my wits intact. He had a console and a jack injector and a cellular regenerator in his home, as if those were normal things to have. None of my previous captors had had any of the finer equipment. He'd used that equipment to tend my wounds, and he'd wrapped me up in blankets and let me *sleep*. I was still considering the ramifications of that when he walked in.

Nate

I walked quietly to the living room, pausing for a moment because... well *damn* he was pretty. He was awake now, staring up at the ceiling with a slightly dreamy, thoughtful look. His skin was just this side of silver in the morning sunlight, his lilac hair glinting iridescent highlights. His face was... artistic, like he ought to be painted or set in marble. He had a lithe, narrow body, like a swimmer or a dancer. At that moment his arms were up over his head, the blankets pushed down to his waist. I had the urge to take a picture, because this, now, was an image I wanted to keep.

I couldn't, though. That wouldn't be even a little bit okay.

I cleared my throat softly and he instantly turned his attention toward me, face a startled blank that sent my little fantasies crashing down to more reasonable and realistic proportions. Of course the cygenic would be cagey, after the hell he'd clearly been through. Probably better that he was, it meant that he had a solid understanding of his situation. Too many cygenics didn't.

"The shower's free. I'm in the middle of making breakfast. How do you like your coffee?" I asked, tossing my head back toward the kitchen.

A little bit of his tension melted.

"Coffee?" he asked, his voice filled with childlike anticipation. "It's a long time since I've had coffee."

He stood and stretched, brushing tousled silver-purple hair out of his eyes and walking toward me with catlike grace. Like a living work of art. I could only watch, transfixed, contemplating what a horrible idea it had been to bring him home and not to Iris's place. My interest was inappropriate, and taking advantage would make me just like every other bastard who'd ever used a cygenic as a cheap toy, and a fucking hypocrite besides because *I* was supposed to know better.

It didn't help that he was still wearing nothing but a pair of really short cutoffs and didn't seem at all shy about that.

"Need to get you some clothes," I murmured, gazing at the taut curve of his ass as he disappeared into the bathroom, not bothering to shut the door behind him.

I busied myself with the particulars of making scrambled eggs and sausage and toast, and he eventually came to the kitchen. His curling hair was tousled and wet, and he had a towel draped around his hips. He sat down at the table casually, comfortably, as if he belonged here.

"Help yourself to whatever," I said. "Cream for the coffee's in the fridge, got some orange juice in there too, if you want any,"

He grabbed my hand as I was sidling past and fixed those mercury-colored eyes on me with a disquieting earnestness.

"Thank you," he said, his voice very soft. He

looked away again and let my hand go. I felt like I'd been kicked in the stomach.

"I'll see if I can't find you something to wear," I faltered, feeling my face flush as I slid out of the room.

I left him digging into a mound of scrambled eggs like he hadn't eaten in a week. He probably hadn't. Cygenics came with all the instincts to eat like humans—but they didn't *need* to. A cygenic could be kept alive and in solid working order on about 500 calories a day. It was easy to spot the ones who were being fed short rations on liquid diets; they went all paper-skinned and wiry, like heroin addicts. He hadn't gotten to that point yet, but that was no reason to believe that anyone had bothered to actually feed him in ages. Even professional operations often fed their workforces nothing but liquid supplements and nutrient fluid.

I'd never seen someone so painfully grateful to be fed breakfast.

I picked out a T-shirt and a pair of lounge pants with a pretty forgiving fit, making a mental note to bring a few sets of the hospital scrubs we kept at the Center home in case this situation arose again. It wasn't that I couldn't afford to lose the clothes, just that having him wear my own stuff was another breach of good boundaries.

Dante.

That was his name. The name he'd given when I asked, last night. Dante.

Heading back into the kitchen, I placed the folded clothes into an empty chair before gathering a plate of food and a cup of coffee and sitting down opposite my impromptu houseguest.

"So. Your name's Dante. Interesting name," I said, between sips of coffee. Feeling out the right level of conversation was never easy, not with cygenics. Not at first. With humans there was always the comfortable distance of social role to fall back on. Even when I was out playing "faceless guy in a bar," the people around me assumed I was a peer. Cygenics tended to presume I was a figure of absolute authority, of greater or lesser immediate threat.

"I'm named after Dante Gabriel Rossetti*, "* Dante replied, not meeting my eyes.

"If you don't mind my asking..."

"You can ask me anything you want, sir," Dante said crisply, eyes still down. Looking at an empty plate.

I closed my eyes and sighed. This kind of thing always seemed easier at the Center. It was all so clean and clinical and detached there.

"Do you know when you were commissioned, by whom, and what your original cited function was?"

He trembled a little. There was a tightness in his jaw, and I watched his Adam's apple bob as he swallowed before speaking.

"I was commissioned between 16 and 17 years ago by Professor Vernon Cunningham, with the intended function of serving as an artistic statement and philosophical experiment on the nature and function of education—"

"Seventeen years ago?" I interrupted, looking him up and down again. Cygenics defaulted to 21 years' growth at point of commission. "But you'd have to have been..."

"I was commissioned at five years' growth via

106

special dispensation of regulations concerning minimum biological age restrictions, yes," he said with a crisp quickness that indicated long practice. The next words were slower, and his expression broke a bit as he said them, fighting a grimace. "There's apparently a lot of paperwork involved in the creation of a cygenic child. Professor Cunningham often joked that it would have been simpler to acquire a human child for the experiment."

"You were a kid."

"Yes, sir."

"I've never met a cygenic who was ever a kid."

"Most people haven't. We're not common." He glanced up again, something confused and hurt in his eyes. "I've known one other. From what he's told me, cygenic children are most often illicit. And they don't usually get to be adults. Sir."

"You don't have to call me 'sir.' My name is Nate."

"If that pleases you, Nate,"

I pinched the bridge of my nose. Small steps.

"Okay. I'll admit we've already veered pretty far off the usual script here. When did you... what's your service history been? How did you get from being an artistic statement about education to being chained underneath a table at a club? You ping as state property, and your contact information is MGH..."

"Professor Cunningham contracted stomach cancer. In his final months I was his caretaker as well as his student. Upon his death, I was relegated to the care of reclamation and recycling, where I was summarily placed in a hospital as an orderly. I served there for two years, and then I can only presume that I was stolen because I found myself at some kind of illicit processing center. I was sold into prostitution. After a time, I was able to escape that captivity. I'd been living off the grid since with a group of my peers. Recently, a human who I had mistakenly considered trustworthy abducted me and sold me into prostitution again." He looked at me, a hard and appraising light in his eyes. "Then you purchased me. Would it be overbold, sir, to ask what *you* intend my function to be?"

"I don't have an intended function for you. I shouldn't have brought you to my house; it's probably given you the wrong idea about me. I work for the Turing Center...—"

"So you're going to resell me."

I stood up and ran my hand over my hair and paced halfway across the kitchen to stare out the window, because otherwise I was going to have to punch something. It was sunny out, the kind of fiercely brilliant sun that only comes after rain.

"Is that what you think we are, out on the street?" I asked without looking back at him, swallowing hard. "You think we're just another scrub and sell place in the business of turning a quick profit off cygenic misery? You... you're the oldest cygenic I've ever met in terms of years out of the tank, and the first one to be able to string together a really complete self-history. You're fucking amazing. I had no idea that there were cygenics like you out on the street. You know how many I meet who are halfway to BSOD? Who've been reprogrammed by hacks and left with fried minds? Who never got programmed with more brain than they needed to be acceptably functional the first place? You are a genius. And that's what *you* think the Turing Center is about?"

"I don't begin to understand, sir, what it is that you want from me," he said, swallowing thickly. "but I've concluded that you don't intend to keep me. Everything you've said to me thus far implies it. If I've misjudged, I'm sorry. I don't know anything about the Turing Center—only that any kind of center having to do with cygenics is generally a point of resale." He said, all in a rush. His hands were shaking, and he was hanging onto his coffee cup really hard to try and hide it. I felt my anger bleed away in the face of his obvious terror. "I have a very extensive skillset, sir... " He faltered when I didn't say anything. "I'm fluent in several languages and have fairly extensive medical knowledge. I was... educated, rather intensively, for the first twelve years of my life. Do you have any literature that you'd like analyzed?" He laughed, a small, barking, slightly hysterical sound. "I'm not sure which of my skills you'd find most relevant, but... I can make myself useful." There was a long pause, and when he spoke again his voice was hushed and broken. "I can function as a sexual companion, if that's asked of me."

I sat back down, elbows on the table, head in my hands.

"Look, Turing Center..." I sighed, looking up at him. He wasn't looking back at me. "The Turing Center for Cygenic Dignity tries to secure positive outcomes for off-grid and otherwise dispossessed cygenics. My friend Iris is a social worker, and one of the co-chairs of the local chapter. I really should have brought you to her house, not mine, but I'm the one with the crash space and I was drunk. I don't remember why I thought this was a good idea. None of the shelters have any free beds right now. One of our shelters was burned down a couple of months ago by some fucking 'human purity' supremacists who think that cygenics shouldn't have shelters while homeless humans exist. Everyone got out, but we've had a hell of a time getting clearance to build a replacement shelter. We still have the outreach center, so I can still hook you up with people who can help you find a decent job and somewhere to live..."

"And who would own me?" he asked, finally looking back at me, looking so overwhelmed and uncertain that I had to resist the urge to hug him. "Aren't you obligated to return me to the hospital?"

I shook my head. "Legally we are, but I've never had a case where a state agent wasn't more than happy to sign off a cygenic into our custody. It's a tax write-off for them, making a donation to a nonprofit organization, and it works out to being more cost-effective to take the write-off and buy a new cygenic than it is to reprogram one who's been deprogrammed or otherwise damaged."

"I'm not damaged. I retain all the programming that the hospital gave me."

"They don't have to know that. We'd just tell them that you're not suitable for that job anymore. They'd donate you, and you would be owned by the Turing Center. We're a national organization, and we place cygenics all over the country, but the agency retains ownership and if cygenics in our ownership report unsatisfactory conditions at their work placements, they can get recalled and placed elsewhere. The people we place with have to follow very rigid guidelines for employee rights and housing and care for cygenics who are sent to them. They're not allowed to do any reprogramming without the consent of the cygenic in question."

"Ah. So you don't sell us; you give us away."

"If you want to look at it like that. It's just a stopgap measure toward the agency's intended goals. My friends and I sign all the right petitions, donate to the right lobbies... Dante, I'm an emancipationist."

His face went blank, and he blinked several times before looking away.

"You're not serious," he finally said, looking up at me with tears in his eyes.

"I'm *very* serious."

"You'd let me walk out that door right now, then?" he asked, his eyes narrowing.

"If that's what you wanted, yes. I think that'd be a poor decision on your part, but I wouldn't stop you." I sighed, standing and walking over to the window. I stared out for a long moment, and when I looked back Dante had seen fit to put on the clothes sitting in the chair beside him. The towel had been discarded over the back of it.

"Are you leaving, or am I driving you to the Center?" I asked.

"What do you think they're going to do with me? Find me a factory job or something? I know how problematic I am. You should go online and do a search for 'Vernon Cunningham Dante project,' perhaps you'd understand the scope of the problem," Dante hissed, turning to look at me with searching eyes.

"If you become enrolled in the Center, you'll get placed, like any other cygenic in the network, in accordance with your abilities. I'm not going to lie to you, we place a lot of domestics, mostly with lower-income families who really need the help and couldn't possibly afford to commission a cygenic. You get to decide if you want to take the job we offer you or keep coming back to the Center until you find one that you're comfortable with. A lot of the time, more than I'm really comfortable with, cygenics who have domestic skills end up going home with our staff. There's this board in the back called the bid board where staff fight to offer positions... but never mind that. You can come in every day for the rest of your life, if you want. We have a waiting room and a kitchen and a clinic."

"And where would I *live* in the meantime? You said you've got no beds."

"If it comes to that, you can stay here until something else comes up. It's not like I don't have the space. Hell, I've even got a spare room I could give you."

He stared at me for a really long time, breathing hard. He dropped his gaze again, looking down at his coffee cup.

"Why don't you just keep me, then?" he said, softly.

Of all the responses he could have given, I hadn't expected that one in the slightest. When I didn't respond immediately, he continued.

"Is it that you don't want me? I could make myself useful..."

"You don't even know me," I said.

He looked up at me, and there were tears in his eyes. "I know that you cared for me last night, and that you let me sleep, and that you fed me actual food. I know that you're talking to me, right now, as if my opinion in this matter has meaning to you. There aren't many humans who consider cygenics as more than tools or toys or disposable amusements. I could find a way to make myself useful to you, if you would allow me to."

"I don't want to own slaves," I said. He gasped, his eyes widening fractionally, because that wasn't a word that anyone but emancipationists used regarding cygenics. Because they weren't *people*.

"Do you have any idea what any of us would give," he said, his voice brittle, "To be owned by someone who doesn't want to own slaves?"

He lowered his eyes again.

"You'll do with me as you like, of course," he said, his voice flat. "It's your right to do so. If you wish to take me to this center of yours and relinquish me into its care, I can do nothing to stop you."

"You could leave. Walk out that door. I'm not keeping you against your will."

"Or at all, it seems," he said bitterly. "What's the date?"

"It's the 18th."

"Of what month?" he asked, his gaze flashing back at me for a second.

I blinked, and it took me a minute to figure out that he really might not know, because he might have spent an undisclosed amount of time pinned.

"July."

Dante laughed, and it was a really unsettling

113

sound. He got up and walked past me, right up to the window. Put his hand on the glass, then his forehead. His shoulders were shaking like he was sobbing, but he didn't make a sound.

"July?" he finally said, sort of strangled. "It's July? Last time I knew anything, it was the beginning of April. I'd figured it was maybe a couple of weeks I'd been lost in the shuffle, and now you're telling me it's July? What am I even supposed to do with that? Everyone in my acquaintance will certainly assume that I'm a loss, and they'll have moved. If I walked out of here I wouldn't have any idea how to find... anyone I used to rely on."

I didn't bother resisting the impulse this time, good boundaries be damned. I stepped forward and snaked my arms around him, pulling him close. The warm, flat planes of his back came up flush with my chest, and I rested my chin his shoulder, looking out the window for a moment and then closing my eyes. I'd kind of feared resistance, but there wasn't any, just a momentary tensing and then a long, hollow sigh.

Dante

I couldn't take another breath in. I was being held. It felt so impossibly *good* to be held.

I turned around, returning the embrace, hiding my face in the hollow of Nate's throat. When I finally found my breath, he smelled like aftershave. The same way the coat had smelled. A smell I was already learning to associate with comfort and care.

We stood there, frozen, for a very long time. I didn't want him to let go. He felt real and solid. Stupid for me to think it, but he felt safe. That was completely baseless, but it was true.

No one ever held me. 'Taire had but... never a human. Never someone who could protect me.

It was Nate who finally pulled away, looking at me strangely, as if he wasn't sure what to do.

"I'm gonna go get dressed, and then I'm going to drive you down to the Center to get you registered and to meet some people, and we can take it from there, Okay? As long as you're still registered to the hospital, you're technically stolen property. It's safer if you're registered to the Center and... you can still come home with me afterwards, if that's what you want. Have some more coffee if you want it," he said, finally.

"As you like, sir," I answered softly, keenly

wishing that he'd just gone on holding me. "It's not as if I have anywhere else to go."

And that was the end of it. Nate left me standing in the kitchen, looking out over his back yard. After a few moments the same rotund brown tabby I'd seen before walked into the kitchen and stopped to stare at me with apparent disapproval. I looked around, noting an empty dish on the floor and a box of cat food on the counter.

Winning the cat's approval proved quite easy.

I watched the cat eating, wondering if there was a way for this to work out well. I'd never really entertained the notion that my life could turn out well, not before last night.

I'd have to see what this Turing Center of his could offer me.

Nate

It was well past two in the afternoon by the time I walked into the Center, Dante in tow. I wasn't on the schedule for the day, but Iris was, for the afternoon shift. Which meant she was either already here or would be in at three."

There's going to be a packet for you to fill out with a history and a bunch of demographic information. Do you think you could do that while I make some phone calls and talk to people? Would you be all right in the waiting room?" I asked Dante as I held the door for him.

"If that... yes," he said, catching himself before spouting more of that "if it pleases you" talk.

Drake came walking out of the office and stopped dead, staring at Dante.

"Oh my *God*. Is that a new intake? When's he going on the bid board? I want him."

Dante looked nervous, glancing at me, but seemed to calm immediately. Probably because I was looking at Drake like I was planning to punch him in the face. Dante said, glancing at Drake's badge, "I'm afraid... Drake... that I'm not negotiable. At all. Sorry to disappoint you, but I'm not going to be on any bid board."

"Uh... huh..." Drake said, frowning and looking to me for confirmation. His eyes went wide when he saw how incandescently pissed I was.

"Drake. We do not speak to or *of* our clients as if they're property. Go back to your desk right fucking now and read the mission statement and standards of practice. If I hear you say anything like that again, I'm contacting your school to discuss termination of your internship. That was not remotely acceptable."

"Jesus Christ, Mister Matheson, what crawled up your ass?"

"You are not helping your case."

Drake looked at me and at Dante and back to me, and I saw genuine worry creep into his eyes as he apparently remembered that I was his superior. I watched his puppy dog crush on me die. He turned around and slunk back into the office, abandoning whatever task had brought him out here in the first place. I closed my eyes and sighed. So much for Dante's first impression of the organization.

"I'm going to go see if Iris is here yet. She was there last night when I found you, but I wouldn't say you've actually met her. I'm going to try and see if I can snag her for late lunch or early dinner so that the two of you can talk."

"Yes," Dante said, looking at me appraisingly. "I'll wait for you."

I tried to muster a smile as I pointed him to the waiting room, and made my way upstairs.

Iris was sitting at her desk, sipping from a gallon-sized cup of iced coffee and looking very annoyed at whatever she was reading on her screen.

"Afternoon!" I said cheerfully from the doorway.

She looked up at me and... didn't exactly smile, but made an effort in that direction.

"Hey, Nate. Didn't expect to see you in today... I mean, after last night..."

"He's downstairs in the waiting room. You will not believe how amazing he is."

"Oh really?" she said, raising an eyebrow. "What's his story?"

"He's 17 years out of the tank."

Iris blinked, and took another sip of coffee before saying,

"Can't be."

"Yeah, he is," I insisted, the reality of Dante's existence overshadowing Drake's callous 18-year-old trust-fund kid behavior. "He said he was commissioned as a child for some kind of personal research project about education for some professor. There's apparently a website about it, I haven't had a chance to look. I swear, Iris, he's practically human. I haven't seen this kind of continuous lucidity in a cygenic since..." I faltered a little, some of that giddy energy ebbing away, "Since Lisa." I took a deep breath and continued. "Yeah. Anyway, he's going to be newsworthy is what I'm saying. Once we get him checked out and fix his registration and everything."

"What's he pinging up as?"

"State of Mass, assigned to MGH. Shouldn't be a problem. I was actually wondering if I could use your phone to make the call—"

"You can't just bump the line for him just because he's your pet project," Iris said, her face growing suddenly stern. "You of all people should know that. We've got cygenics down there who've been waiting for a month for someone to register them. Add your wonderboy to the list, yeah, but he's got to wait his turn. You want to speed of the process, hang around and do some entry interviews."

"I kind of already did most of his entry interview over the breakfast table today..."

"Did you see how many cygenics we've got out in the waiting room today? And June's still in Washington. I heard her talking about being the founder of a new chapter there, which might mean a promotion for me if I play my cards right. I'm happy for you and all, that you're so excited about this, but we can't bump him to the front of the list just because you happened to be the one who found him. Anyone reports that happening, and we've got accusations of conflict of interest and being audited by the organizational review board and maybe losing chapter credentials. June would have a fit if she knew. I shouldn't have let you bring him home, I really shouldn't't've."

"I think you're not hearing me, about what a big deal he is. About how different he is."

She raised an eyebrow and stared hard at me until I looked away. The "there is no discussion to be had here, because I am right and you are wrong" look that she'd perfected as an RA.

"You want to get to him, you get your ass downstairs and help Linda and Drake and all of them go through the line that got here before we opened this morning. You think kiddo out there can manage his own intake forms without assistance?"

"I already gave him the packet. By the way, Drake needs someone to shout at him about his behavior toward clients, because when he saw Dante he asked when he'd be on the bid board. In front of him. Why do we *have* a bid board again?"

"Good to know. We've talked about the bid board before, it's a national thing, it works out more often than it doesn't—*please* just drop it? And hooray for your project being able to handle his own paperwork, one less thing for us to do," she said, shaking her head a little. "Now go. I've got shit to do; this grant petition isn't going to write itself. Catch me around five, we can go out to Ezio's or something."

"Yeah, sure. Just, Iris? Keep an eye on him. Just watch him, the way he acts. Talk to him for five minutes, if you can. You'll see what I mean about him being a big deal, like for the agency. I'm going to look up that website he says exists about him before I start doing interviews."

"Sure, whatever," she said, not even looking at me anymore. Iris was not a ray of friendly and helpful sunshine when she was hung over. I went downstairs, bypassing the waiting room and heading straight back to the office to see where Linda and Drake were in interviews.

Dante

There wasn't anywhere to sit in the waiting room, unless I wanted to sit on the floor as several others had elected to. Most of them were watching the inane morning show playing on a screen set in the far wall. A few others had clipboards like the one I'd been handed, and sheaves of paperwork.

I opted for leaning against a bare patch of wall and tried to fill out the paperwork to the best of my ability. I didn't know my current weight, and I could only hazard a guess as to my height. I didn't know the contact information for my current owner; Nate had mentioned that I was still registered to the hospital but I didn't know its address or a phone number or anything like that. Hopefully those gaps in knowledge weren't damning. I was filling out my personal history when the woman approached me.

She looked somewhere around 30, with disheveled blue hair and constantly wandering eyes. Her face was painfully familiar; a standard model. I'd met half a dozen women who looked exactly like her. She was wearing a T-shirt with a radio station logo on it. It was far overdue for laundering.

"Hey," she said. "Hey, you can read, right?"

"Yes," I replied, looking back to my paperwork

for a moment before looking to her. She wouldn't meet my eyes. It wasn't uncommon among us, but I'd always found it just a bit unnerving. The polite thing was to pretend it wasn't happening, not to keep trying for eye contact. I'd learned that from KJ and Ruby and sometimes even 'Taire, through trial and error. Looking around the room, I suddenly wondered if 'Taire was all right, wherever he was. Any of my group, really, but him especially. It was uncharitable how little I cared about how KJ et. al. were doing in comparison.

Three months. They could be anywhere.

"Can you, like, when you're done," the woman began, scratching the back of her head and glancing over her shoulder to the crowd, "can you maybe help me out with mine? I'm not so good at reading and they're gonna be mad if I don't finish it, right? Like half of these guys here are like scrap metal walking, right, but I'm still good. Just, I can't read. And I don't know if they're gonna understand. I don't need any reprogramming, right? And I don't want them thinking that I do, and they're gonna think that if they find out I can't read, and you look so smart over here just like blowing through your papers and stuff and maybe you can help me? You look like a smart guy."

"I used to be the smart guy in my group," I replied with a weak smile.

"Yeah, I could totally tell, you know? Like you look it. Like your eyes or whatever. And like you can read and stuff. I mean, I know you don't know me from anybody, but I figured, you know, maybe..."

"Who you talking at, Zee?" a man asked from across the room. I looked up to find an emerald-haired man with a *beard* staring at me. I had to wonder who'd specified a desire for facial hair upon his commissioning and why, because it was most definitely nonstandard. He was wearing a ratty tank top, and had a thermally branded number on his right shoulder. 9999. He didn't get up from his chair. I tucked my pen behind my ear, as it was obvious that I was in for at least a bit of conversation and I didn't want to start inadvertently doodling in the margins of the paperwork in front of me.

"Smart guy," the woman, apparently Zee, replied to him. She looked back at me. "That's Nines. Been enrolled a while, knows the deal about this place. I've only been coming here a couple of days and they only gave me the paper stuff today. You should talk to him."

Nines nodded, then turned to the blank-faced man in the chair beside him. "Hey, you need to go stand over there, by the water."

The man blinked a few times, then got up and walked over to the water cooler. He stood facing it, continuing to blink as if he didn't know what he was supposed to do. He continued standing there.

"Come on, smart guy. Free chair."

I looked at the man by the water cooler and suppressed a shudder before taking the offer to sit down. It felt distinctly uncomfortable, but I didn't know the status quo of the place I currently found myself, and I had the general impression that Nines might represent leadership of a sort. It would be a poor idea to snub him.

"You're one of KJ's boys, ain't you? You're the one 'sposed to be dead."

"You know KJ?" I asked, suddenly at attention, studying the man, trying to decide if I knew him. I didn't think I did, which made it slightly unnerving that he apparently knew me.

"Yeah, kinda. Not like buddies or anything, but I know her. Or I used to. We kinda ran the same ground in a lot of places, my pack and hers. Folks talk, you know how it is. Say they had a smart guy. Say he got bagged. KJ figures you're dead or good as."

Ah, so this was the leader of the neighboring territory, down toward the abandoned high school. I'd probably seen him a few times, but I'd never had a conversation with him. He'd been clean-shaven at the time. I felt something tighten unpleasantly at the back of my throat and swallowed thickly. Declared dead. Not unexpected news, given the duration of my disappearance, but still not especially welcome.

"Are they doing well, have you heard?" I asked urgently, "Do you know where they are?"

"Haven't talked to KJ in, shit, gotta be a month and a half now. They moved off that good crash spot they were at right after you got bagged, only ran into them once since. Ain't had a chance to tell them about this place. Been coming here just about every day they're open. Means I don't run into folks so much. Sweep took out half my pack, 'bout three months back, then this one bitch decided it was my fault and got everyone on my ass and she's in charge now. Rest of them can go fuck themselves, I gotta look out for myself. You come here, no one gets on your ass. Safe place to spend your days, you know? They got food and jack juice and everything."

"Mm-hmm," I replied when I realized he was

waiting for some kind of response. "Well. At least it's not bad news. It's good to know they're well."

"Yeah, everything's pretty good with KJ and crew, last I heard, since they shook loose that useless fuck used to be running with 'em."

His words hit me like a physical blow.

"Excuse me. I need some water," I said standing up. I crossed the room without looking back. I sidestepped the man who was still standing in front of the water cooler and took a paper cup for myself. I sat down on the floor next to a dusty plastic ficus tree in the corner and drank it while my hands shook.

He could only be talking about 'Taire.

'Taire had been cut from the group.

My first impulse was to walk out, that very moment, and put whatever effort I could into finding him. I might well have done so if the woman, Zee, hadn't come over and crouched down beside me.

"Hey, hey you okay? You want me to go get somebody or something? They got people here..."

They've got people here.

I had people here. Specifically one man to whom I owed something of a debt of gratitude. Leaving would be rude, and incredibly stupid. I had an opportunity here before me. Walking away wouldn't be a sound course of action. The ability to take sound courses of action separated me from cygenics who ended up BSOD and offline. I had to keep that in mind.

'Taire was wandering this city without even the dubious protection of the others who'd shared our circumstances. What was he going to do with himself, without KJ's leadership?

Without mine?

He knew that I had been captured, and had known for three months. He'd wanted to go chasing after people from our group who'd gotten captured every single time it happened, regardless of risks. He didn't make sound decisions without someone to help him slow down and think.

He might well have gotten himself killed by now. In fact, that was by far the likeliest outcome. Following suit would help no one. I swallowed thickly, looking at the woman crouched beside me. She looked deeply concerned.

"You want to show me your paperwork, Zee?" I finally said, taking several long breaths. "I'll see if I can help you make sense of it."

Nate

I conducted three entrance interviews by the time 4:45 rolled around, and decided not to begin another. If I missed Iris' 5:00 window she'd very likely go to dinner without me.

I found Dante in the waiting room. He'd removed the childproof panel from in front of the entertainment system and had subsequently changed the channel from the standard daytime fare that was usually on to some public-access kids' show wherein a group of animated monsters were singing about phonics. Dante was sitting off to one side with his back to the screen, answering questions from an audience that included roughly half the cygenics in the room. Others continued to stand or sit unmoving, staring in random directions or look vaguely in the direction of the group.

Dante caught sight of me, and his face absolutely lit up. I stopped breathing for a second when it did, because he was devastatingly beautiful when he smiled.

"Excuse me," he said to the group, standing and walking around the margin to meet me in the doorway. "I was wondering if you'd forgotten about me," he said with a wry smile as he approached.

"No, I wouldn't..."

"In the three hours I've been here, only six people have been seen. Several people have come and stopped to look in on us, but very few of us have been called back into the offices. Is that normal?"

"Sadly, yes. Did you finish your paperwork?"

"I've completed it to the best of my ability. I do hope I'll be forgiven for having used the back of the sheets with blank sides for impromptu lessons in basic literacy..." He picked up the clipboard from the table by the door and started turning the sheets over and putting them back in correct order. The notes I managed to glimpse looked like artfully written alphabets, letter combinations, and lists of random words.

"You changed the channel," I said, looking from his paperwork to the screen and back, a bit dumbfounded.

"This seemed a significantly better use of everyone's time," Dante said softly, looking over his shoulder at the crowd of cygenics now enthralled by an older woman with a Spanish accent reading aloud from a picture book. "Zee hasn't been registered, and she's apparently been coming here every day for a nearly week. Nines is registered, but he's been coming here every day for a month with no forward progress or further information as to what he should be doing other than showing up and staying in the waiting room all day. They praise the food quite highly, and the access to basic medical supplies," Dante said. "I have to wonder, though, why it is that we're all sequestered to a single room with two security camera feeds and left here to wait."

"Because we don't have enough staff," Iris said from behind me. She was standing on the bottom step, one hand perched on her hip.

"You're Iris, if my memory serves," Dante said, leaning his head slightly in deference. "I'd like to thank you personally for your assistance last night."

Iris blinked, her eyebrows going up.

"Well aren't you polite!" she said with a bark of laughter. "And you're welcome." she looked to me and continued, "We got clearance on a good placement lead for a fish-packing plant up the coast looking for half a dozen workers. They check out. I sent the approval to national just now. We get an answer by this afternoon, we can spend the weekend choosing best-placements from the pool of regulars and bus them up for Monday. Linda's of the opinion that the guy with the beard's a good fit, but frankly I think this place is probably a best-case-scenario for a bunch of the BSODs because from everything I've read they're just looking for a cheap alternative to an industrial filleting machine. Worker rights inquest came back clean and human employees report satisfactory treatment, but there's no way it's anything other than dull repetitive tasks. We just need to snag someone who can do overlay programming. I'm thinking of putting out an ad looking for students and paying them out of petty cash. It's not like this is gonna be programming rocket science and it's not like there's gonna be a sharp failure curve."

Dante was listening intently, and Iris seemed to realize it, suddenly looking at him.

"Did you need something?" she asked.

"Nate called me out of the waiting room. I was

just filling him in on what my observations have been this morning," he said, his voice clipped and courteous.

"Shall we continue over dinner?" I suggested. "I had wanted to get him registered to the agency before we take him out of the building, for obvious reasons, but there's just not time for that today."

"You were gonna bring him to dinner with us?" Iris asked, looking from me to him and back incredulously.

"Yes," I answered, glaring at her.

"Why?"

"Because I want him to come," I said, gritting my teeth. "Because the two of you need to talk, and because he's staying with me indefinitely, and until he's registered I'd rather not put much distance between us lest something unfortunate happen to him. Because he technically still belongs to the state of Massachusetts until you let me fix that."

"We could order in," Iris said with a labored sigh. "Ezio's delivers, and we can hole up in my office to eat undisturbed."

"Good enough," I said with a grin, turning to Dante. "Do you like Italian?"

"I'm generally appreciative of whatever's offered to me, Nate," he said earnestly.

I had enough time to conduct another entrance interview while we waited for our food to arrive, and walked into Iris' office to find her and Dante already portioning chicken alfredo penne into paper bowls.

"The outreach center's been functioning as a day shelter, mostly," Iris was saying, clearly irritated by whatever Dante had been saying. "Most of the cygenics that show up here need to be individually walked through everything, and that's not even counting the ones who are BSOD."

"There's a lot of concern about reprogramming among the people I was speaking to," Dante said. "They don't want to be reprogrammed."

"And the ones that don't, aren't," Iris replied, glaring at him. "It's a major tenet of the Turing Center's ideology that we don't reprogram without the express consent of the cygenic in question."

"Except BSODs."

"We repair BSODs, when possible. Try to return them to the level of function they had before whatever event or injury caused them to become BSOD. Then we seek consent for further reprogramming in the event that it will help them get better placements, which is pretty much always. Sorry your afternoon was frustrating, but we don't even have a programmer right now because the last one we had took off recently without even giving his two weeks' notice—" she noticed me standing in the doorway and stopped mid-sentence. "Hey, Nate."

"Hi," I said, running my tongue over my teeth. "Don't let me interrupt."

"So if I'm understanding you correctly, your entire organizational methodology is based on certain assumptions of capacity in the population you're ostensibly serving and how best to address them," Dante said, setting down his bowl of pasta and meshing his fingers together. "I'd like to challenge that."

"Oh would you? You, who showed up all of three hours ago, are going to tell the Turing Center what we're doing wrong? You gonna tell us how to fix it?"

"Well, if you're looking for a change that could be made immediately, your waiting room would better serve everyone as a classroom. If the waiting period for placement is in the order of months, that time would be better utilized improving the applicant's skillset, wouldn't it? To widen possible placements?"

"That's what reprogramming is for," Iris said with an exaggerated sigh.

"But we don't want to be reprogrammed, Miss Castillo. We want to be educated."

Dante looked to me and smiled before continuing.

"I was sitting there in the waiting room listening to a program telling me how to prepare sea bass, and thinking that I'd never encountered sea bass and wasn't ever likely to. It made me think about the applicability of skills, and I thought about the name of your agency. Turing. The name was familiar to me, so I considered where I might have heard it, and my mind turned up Alan Turing—the father of modern computing. Am I correct to assume that your center is named for him?

"Yes, it is," Iris said, looking at Dante like she might have looked at one of the auditors who came annually from National.

"And are you aware that Alan Turing suggested that the most expedient and effective way to simulate the adult mind would be to reproduce a child's mind and then to subject it to a course of education? It's a well documented fact that cygenics who are able to learn by education are better able to perform on all rubrics than cygenics who are given precisely the same information via programming—"

"Charles used to talk about that," I interrupted.

"He said it had to do with where and how the information is stored and accessed, in the computer or in actual brain cells."

"Precisely. When I was commissioned, I had the general knowledge of a five-year-old child—but absolutely no experiences. No means of comprehending or associating the concepts that I knew with one another, or attaching emotion or memory to them. I objectively knew that fire was hot and would damage my flesh, but I had no visceral memory of pain because I'd never been burned. Programmed knowledge isn't wholly applicable or accessible. When acting upon programmed knowledge, the actions are at first... distanced? It's like watching someone else perform them, like being in a fog. Knowledge gained through experience is vastly superior. I can say this with a conviction that neither of you can, because I have experienced both kinds and you have not."

"Yes, that's all very nice. You're very smart. But how exactly do you expect me to apply that to your little group sitting around watching Public Broadcasting?"

"Education, Miss Castillo. Most of them aren't functionally literate. That can be changed."

"And where the hell would you expect us to get the manpower for that?" Iris scoffed, picking up her cup of soda. "The Turing Center is funded exclusively from donations and grants, and precious few of those. My chapter has a payroll that allows for six paid positions. Everyone else is a volunteer or an unpaid intern. We don't have the money to spend on classrooms."

"I think you're making very poor use of an obvious resource," Dante said, looking at his hands.

"I've spent most of the afternoon talking to people in the waiting room. Cygenics. Miss Castillo, correct me if I'm wrong, but I can't help but notice that none of your employees or volunteers are cygenics. In an organization that claims to serve our population, we do nothing but sit and wait."

"Oh for fuck's sake. You were in the waiting room with them all morning, you said yourself that most of them aren't even literate. What the hell would we do with them other than find them suitable jobs out in the world? Any time we can, we try to get people into domestic and nannying roles in poor households. We've had independent longitudinal studies showing that that can elevate entire neighborhoods because it means that kids get quality care instead of going into daycare that their parents have to pay for, and one-income families can become two-income families, and everybody's standard of living rises."

"Which just means that you're using dispossessed cygenics as a resource with which to ameliorate the living conditions of human families."

"It's mutual aid!" Iris snapped. "Dispossessed cygenics have shitty outcomes in almost every circumstance. Being some poor woman's nanny so that she can get a job and feed them is a better outcome."

"Is it? Because while I'm sure that I don't have to tell you how thankful we all are for not being casually murdered and recycled for parts, as someone who has previously been through reprocessing and given a 'good job' by the State of Massachusetts, I can assure you that unpaid labor for the betterment of humanity is largely a thankless and soul-killing endeavor. I was more genuinely alive when I was being *raped* on a regular basis than when I was working at the hospital, but the security measures and confinement were similar."

The silence after he'd said that was choking.

"And what would you have us do instead, with that lot down there?" Iris asked, bristling.

"Give me a month of daily study with Zee and Nines and half a dozen of the others, and I'll not only produce literacy, but basic mathematical competence and proficiency with data processing programs. Then you'll have a bank of data entry staff, and registration can proceed more smoothly. You can stop wasting your interns' time and utilize *them* better. Give me six months with the brightest ones and I'll give you tutors who can teach literacy to others, and who'll do so for the cost of kale soup and nutrient fluid. We're *used* to working without pay, Miss Castillo."

Iris blinked and froze, her fork halfway to her mouth.

"You want to start a cygenic school, and you want to grow a batch of cygenic schoolteachers for further cygenic schools."

"... Yes?"

"And you honestly think that you can get something worthwhile out of this?"

"You're not doing anything more worthwhile with them, are you? It's not as if I've got anything better to do with my time. It wouldn't invalidate them for the kind of work you're generally sending them to—who doesn't want a nanny who can help the kids with their homework, after all? It would make better use of everyone's time and resources, and it would overall enrich everyone's experience with this program."

Iris looked at him hard, then looked at me, and back to him, and back to me.

"Didn't you say there was a website about this kid's origin story, Nate?"

"Do a search for 'Vernon Cunningham, Dante Project', ma'am," Dante answered before I could.

"I just might. What would you need to make this school thing happen, in terms of resources?" Iris asked, her voice a precise tone of faux casual. "We don't have a lot."

"I suppose I could, if pressed to it, work with a white board and a pack of markers, and paper and pens for my students," he said. "But ideally I'd like a large screen with an active connection and a few work stations for students to share. Half a dozen low-end laptops or tablets would be more than adequate, if I was also allowed to commandeer the existent screen in the waiting room. Though ideally classes would occur in a workspace separate from the waiting room, so that anyone who's not interested in being there doesn't feel forced to participate."

"We could set up in the dining room," I suggested, looking at Iris. "The projector will take a wireless connection."

"There's a projector?" Dante asked, perking visibly.

"June wouldn't approve the expenditure for laptops, and I can't allocate that much money without co-approval."

"I can donate one, for the big screen at least," I said, grinning. "Dante, would having just the one for you and having your students work with paper and pens function, for now?"

137

"It would suffice, I suppose," he answered with a wan smile.

"Ask me again after I eat this—it's getting cold on me, and I will be more amenable to any ideas if I actually have blood sugar," Iris said, facing her bowl and looking up at me through her eyebrows. She glanced at Dante. "But you, kid, might have just talked yourself into a job."

Dante

Last night I'd been half naked and horrifically intoxicated, chained underneath a table in a bar, waiting to be killed through casual violence or negligence as soon as my death alleviated someone's boredom.

Tonight I was lying on an overstuffed sofa, dressed in clean clothes, reading an utterly predictable pot-boiler while Nate scrolled through assorted websites on his tablet. He'd been more than happy to lend me his reader and told me to download anything that I wanted, and his membership allowed access to enormous amounts of free reading. Being allowed to read something of my own choosing, for no one's benefit but my own, was a rare and precious indulgence.

It helped to have distractions, given the events of the day.

It had been a long time since I'd indulged in the hope that my life could turn out well. That anything of my existence could be remotely salvageable. That I could be something more meaningful than a very accomplished and useful member of a group of my dispossessed peers, attempting simple survival for as long as possible. That I could reintegrate with civilization as something other than a drudge.

We'd left the Center shortly after eating, and Nate had insisted that he needed to take me clothes shopping. I'd ended up with a full wardrobe of slacks and sweaters and crisp white button-downs, mostly of Nate's choosing. My input was to stand there and play mannequin and fawn over the quality of the fabrics while the store employees had cooed at how pretty I was and suggested what colors would best compliment me. It had been uncomfortably flattering, but I hadn't dressed this well since I Professor Cunningham had been alive.

And it seemed to make Nate so happy. I kept catching him giving me such fond glances... no one ever looked at me like that, except for 'Taire.

'Taire wouldn't look at me like that ever again. I tried not to dwell on that, because there was nothing to be done about it.

We'd proceeded from shopping to a small Italian bakery-and-gelateria before coming back to Nate's house. I was confident that I'd never, in my entire life, eaten so well as I'd eaten today. Professor Cunningham had seen that I was well nourished, but he was not an epicurean.

I reached the end of the chapter I was reading, and took a moment to cant my head back and look at my impromptu savior. I'd managed to curl up practically on top of him, moving closer by degrees as he actually paid attention to the procedural drama he was watching. He was leaning against the arm of the sofa, his chin resting in his hand, his dark eyes intensely focused on the screen.

Nate was an objectively attractive man. His skin was smooth and unblemished, a shade of brown that—

in conjunction with his features—probably indicated an eclectic heritage. He had well-defined cheekbones and a strong jaw, deep-set brown eyes and tightly-curled dark hair that he kept cropped short. He had a compact build, and a general softness about him that spoke of an uncomplicated life.

He had gentle hands.

I remembered how his hands had felt on me, how he'd caressed my neck, my shoulders. How *careful* he'd been, treating my wounds. I still wanted more, desperately wanted to be held and touched and reminded that I was not alone, no matter who in this world I lost. Wanted to be kissed and caressed and fucked, by someone to whom it meant something. To prove that it *could* mean something. To make me clean again.

It was not a topic that I felt at liberty to broach.

Nate picked up the tablet on the table when the credits started rolling.

I was lucky. I had been plucked from the jaws of ignominious and most probably painful death and brought into grace again. I even had a job, in theory. Something that would actually make use of the skills I'd spent most of my life acquiring. As my students were to be cygenics, no one seemed to especially care about my lack of credentials or experience at such things.

"I found your website," Nate said quietly, looking at me and catching me looking at him.

"Oh?" I asked, attempting to look innocent.

"It was wiped from its original server due to inactivity, but I found a mirror on an archival site. This Cunningham guy looks like he was a pretty big fish in the pond of radical education reform."

"At one point, he was. See if you can find the talk he gave at TEDx, Sydney. That was significantly earlier in his career, when he was still teaching, before I was commissioned. It's interesting that—"

I stopped, because Nate had apparently found the vid in question. I could hear Professor Cunningham's quick, precise voice as he introduced himself and his work to his audience. I found myself swallowing thickly, moving to sit up and draw my knees up, curling on myself.

I had not predicted such an emotional reaction to hearing his voice.

Nate noticed my distress and paused the vid, setting the tablet down and looking at me with marked concern.

"Hey... are you okay?"

"I will be, given a moment," I said, taking a breath. Taking another. "He raised me," I said, completely aware that I was about to begin babbling and completely powerless to stop it. "He raised me and trained me and died without making a single provision for me. He didn't write a will, Nate. He spent a year dying and didn't write a will. I became state property upon his death."

Nate was silent for a long moment, looking at me with open sympathy. I expected some kind of platitude or reassurance, and was a bit surprised when he said, "My father left me when I was less than two years old. After my mother died. He packed up and left. I saw maybe a few dozen times in my entire life, holidays and stuff. I was raised by a cygenic named Lisa."

I blinked as he regarded me, as if looking for some kind of response. I wasn't entirely certain what had prompted him to divulge such information to me aside from, perhaps, a shared experience of abandonment. But he'd had the good fortune to be human at the time. His father had, at least, had the presence of mind to see that he was taken care of.

"What became of her?" I finally asked.

"She died," he said, his voice hollow. "When I was 16. She caught some kind of degenerative neurological virus. I don't really know more about it because... no one would treat her. The people at the cygenic clinic I brought her to told me that she was irreparable and that was all there was to it. I think I spent more time on the phone with my father while she was dying than I did in all of my life before that combined. He bought me a house. As if that would make up for the fact that my mother was dying."

"I'm sorry," I said, at a loss.

"I was in college by then. Met Iris, who told me about the Turing Center. I wish I'd known about it while Lisa'd been alive, because I don't know if there was anything that could have been done but there might have been if I could have gotten someone with actual medical training or programming skill to even look at her... I was 16, I didn't know shit about the world. I just knew that she was dying and no one would help. I got really invested in cygenic rights and emancipation because... if we lived in a world where she wasn't regarded as just a piece of property, maybe..."

"Maybe she wouldn't have had to die," I finished for him. He nodded.

We sat in silence for what seemed a very long time before I said,

"I'd like to watch the rest of that vid, if I may. It's been a long time since I've heard his voice."

Nate nodded, handing me the tablet, and we watched it together.

Nate

Dante spent the remainder of the evening walking me through the history of his education as documented on the website. I'd been a very successful public school student and had never had much interest in educational theory other than to complain about things that were obviously bullshit, like early tracking and standardized tests—things that everyone complained about. Dante's deep interest in the subject and his vast well of academic knowledge were both daunting and really, really interesting. He became animated, talking about analysis of classical and modern media and the utter density of conveyed information in any given narrative.

I'd forgotten how much I missed actually intellectual conversation, as opposed to the artistically pseudointellectual kind Charles had favored, which had mostly existed to prove that he had the answer to every question and that further discussion after he'd declared his opinion was pointless.

It was after midnight when I showed him the room that I was probably going to keep thinking of as "Baba's room" for a while and bid him goodnight.

I lay awake in bed for a while considering the prospect of having a roommate again. I hadn't had a roommate at all since junior year of college, and never one remotely as interesting or heartbreakingly attractive as Dante. Cohabitation wasn't something I was good at, and not something that I generally chose. It was something thrust upon me by circumstance.

I wondered, as I feel asleep, if Dante enjoyed improv theater. It would be nice to have someone to go with who actually liked it.

I woke to screaming.

I was on my feet and halfway to Baba's room before I even registered what was happening, stumbling down the hallway with one hand on the wall. I pawed at the light switch and squinted in the sudden brightness.

Dante was sitting in the middle of the bed in a tangle of blankets, knees drawn up, panting. He looked at me with complete, unhidden terror for a moment before blinking and softening to something more wary and sad-looking.

"I'm sorry," he said softly. "I didn't mean to wake you."

"Nightmare?" I asked, still bleary. I found myself sitting down on the edge of the bed without invitation, which was probably inappropriately intimate. I wondered if it would be worse to stay or to get up again, now that I'd done it.

"Yes," he said, not elaborating. He was looking down at his hands, breathing in short gasps.

"Do you want to—"

"Hold me?" he asked, looking up at me with desperation in his eyes. I froze, feeling like he'd just dumped a bucket of ice water one me, the last of my confused bleariness shattered and feeling suddenly, completely aware.

"What?"

"Never mind," he mumbled. "I'm sorry, that wouldn't be... I just... I... I haven't slept alone since I was a child. I learned today at the Center that someone who was very dear to me is most likely dead. It's not your fault, you shouldn't have to—"

I crawled over and wrapped myself around him. He was clammy from cold sweat, his shoulders still heaving, but he melted against me with a sigh of purest relief. He pressed his face into the hollow of my throat, and I found myself laying back, pulling him down with me so that he was laying beside me. He fit in my arms like he belonged there. I felt the hammering of his heart against my chest, felt his breath at my throat.

"Thank you," he said, half muffled against my neck. "Thank you."

I just hushed him, running a hand up and down his back, because I had no idea what to say to that. It felt awful that he should be thanking me for something as simple as being comforted.

His breath slowed and evened as we lay there, and a while later he said, "You could pin me, if you'd like to avoid this. Being woken in the night by my nightmares, I mean. The hospital did it as a matter of course, it's functionally as good as sleep. I don't think I'm going to be able to sleep alone—"

I didn't really mean to kiss him on the crown of his head. It just seemed so natural an extension of comfort, such an instinctive thing to do that I was doing it before I considered the ramifications. Before I considered who and what he was and that I had to maintain some kind of reasonable boundaries.

He went still when I did, his breath catching, and I was afraid I'd crossed the line of appropriate response. But after a moment he took a breath and asked, in a plaintive voice, "Stay with me?"

"Yes," I answered. "I'm just gonna get up and hit the lights—"

"If... if we could leave them on..." he ventured, a tiny tremor running through him.

"That's fine," I said quickly. "Anything you need."

"Thank you," he said again. "When I was small... when I had nightmares, Professor Cunningham would sit and talk to me about them and analyze them and talk about their likely causes and the psychology behind them." He cuddled himself against me, warm breath against my throat. "This is better, I think. But you don't have to—"

"Hush," I said, hugging him more tightly. "We can talk about it tomorrow."

He hummed agreement, and we lay there quietly. It wasn't until I heard his breathing go deep and even in slumber that I let myself drift off.

Dante

I was aware of the heartbeat first. The deep, unfaltering rhythm under my ear. Then of warmth. Then of solid, comfortable weight across my back. Then of the fact that I was painfully hard, and that the man I was lying on top of shared my condition. I blinked my eyes open to cool morning light and a tangle of sheets and the mellow brown skin of someone's throat.

Nate. Nate had come to my room because I'd had a nightmare. He'd *held* me.

Relaxed in sleep, he was beautiful. Not that he wasn't when he was awake, but sleeping erased the lines of perpetual concern from his brow, making him look open and content.

I moved a little, the whole length of his body sliding against mine. It felt indecently good. Nate murmured appreciation, and I felt it as much as heard it, the deep purring hum in his chest. Better and better. I pressed a kiss to his throat.

Nate came awake with a start, jerking upward to lean on his elbows and then rolling, dumping me unceremoniously at his side, pulling away from me as if I'd burned him.

"Shit!" he hissed, sucking air through his teeth.

"Sorry. Sorry. Okay, this is... okay. Boundaries. Bad... bad boundaries."

I blinked several times and realized that he was trying, in all his sleep-addled communicative efforts, to express that I'd severely overstepped mine.

"Oh... I'm... I'm sorry," I said, feeling my throat tighten. I'd just thought—"

"Look, there's nothing to be sorry about," he said with a sigh. "It's not like it's your fault. You're just doing what you know—"

"And what is it that you think I know?" I interrupted, narrowing my eyes. "Is it that you don't enjoy being touched? Because I awoke to the distinct impression that you were enjoying that as much as I was," I continued, glancing at his admittedly-flagging erection.

"Look," Nate said tightly, "we've clearly had a misunderstanding here. It just wouldn't be appropriate..."

"Who determines what is and is not appropriate, Nate? To whom do I make my petitions for intimacy?"

"This isn't a joke."

"I'm not joking!" I fell back against the bed, staring at the ceiling in frustration, acutely aware that I had royally *fucked up*. Of course Nate wouldn't want such attentions from me. He'd made no overtures of any such kind, and a morning erection could be attributed to any number of things including random happenstance.

I'd asked him once if he was going to fuck me, and he'd answered in the negative. I should have remembered that.

"I just wanted to feel good," I finally said,

150

miserably. "I'm sorry that I presumed interest on your part. You've been so unerringly kind to me—"

"I'm not going to take advantage of you," Nate said with steely conviction.

I leaned up on one elbow to stare at him.

"What makes you think that you're taking advantage of me?" I asked, eyebrows going together. "Is there some obstacle that I'm unaware of in my capacity to seek pleasure for its own sake? I recognize that it is, perhaps, not entirely healthy that I self-soothe with sexuality—but it's always been a remarkably effective method of coping, in my experience. I've spent far too much of my life feeling bad. I want to feel good." I paused, looking at him, trying to gauge his reaction. He was staring at me intensely, looking a bit lost. I said, softly, "I want to make *you* feel good."

"You don't have to pay for basic decency with sexual favors."

"I woke up in your arms, with your cock pressed against mine. Forgive me for concluding that I might be able to pursue mutual sexual satisfaction based on those circumstances. I was unaware that any action on my part was to be judged as necessarily transactional because I am, apparently, a mindless simpering supplicant, incapable pursuing anything for any reason other than to curry favor with you."

Nate blinked at me for a moment and then... smiled.

"You pull out the big vocabulary guns when you're angry, you know that?" he said, with a chuckle. I scowled.

"You're not the first to tell me," I answered, letting myself drop back down to the bed, resisting the

151

childish urge to pull a pillow over my face. I was usually able to moderate my vocabulary choices to my audience. That I lapsed in anger was, in fact, one of KJ's commonest complaints about me—that I "tried to put the run-around on her with 50 cent words." At least Nate seemed more amused by it than angered.

"I'm sorry that I so grossly misunderstood the situation," I said, "but I do think that I'm entirely justified in being annoyed at your paternalistic bullshit about what is and isn't *appropriate*. I'm not a child."

Nate was quiet for a long moment. I listened to him breathing as I stared up at the ceiling, afraid to look at him and see what he thought of me.

"I just got out of a complicated relationship," he finally said, as if it were a confession. "I'm not over it. I don't want to end up using you as a rebound to *get* over it. You don't deserve that."

"As a point of fact, I don't deserve anything," I said bitterly. "Deservedness isn't a concept applicable to cygenics. We are purpose-built to serve the wants and needs of others. We're not supposed to want or need for ourselves. Anything granted to us is a mark of human kindness, not to be expected and certainly not *deserved*."

Cold, clean, philosophical words cobbled together from things I'd read and seen and heard. Sometimes, more often than I liked but less often than I should have, I believed them. I too easily forgot that I was not entitled to the same universal rights and privileges that humans were, because I'd done so much reading on the topic of human rights. Western literature had an obsession with the rights of man. Rights that did not include me.

"I don't believe that," Nate said after another long silence. "It's not... it's not that I don't want you. I wanted you pretty much for the moment I saw you, as fucked up as that is. It's that I honestly believe that you deserve better."

"And it's your right to believe anything you like, and to disregard my opinion in these matters. You own me."

"The Turing Center owns you," Nate corrected, something fierce in his voice.

I sat up and looked at him solemnly. He was looking at me, as he most probably had been the entire time, with fathomless desperation on his face.

"The Turing Center didn't unchain me from under a bar table and care for me when I was sick. You did. It wasn't the Turing Center that I chose when I decided not to chance my luck back on the street this morning. Did you think it was? Did you think that I chose not to walk out the door because you talked about my opportunities there? No. It was because you'd offered me solace when I was in desperate need of it. You, Nate. I'm *yours*. If you honestly believe, the way you say you do, that I'm capable of making rational decisions—then you'll accept that that's the conclusion I've drawn. You don't treat me as property, but you could. You have every right to. You *purchased* me. You brought me to your home, and fed me, and clothed me, and touched me, and held me. But if you'd have me ignore that, I suppose I must. I am, after all, only a cygenic and will ever exist at the whim of humans who know better than me what's good or right or appropriate."

I looked down at my hands, balled into fists in the bedclothes.

"I want to do right by you," Nate said, softly. "And I don't know how."

"Stop overcomplicating the matter and treating me as a philosophical treatise on the subject of morality. I'm not mindless, Nate, nor am I naïve. I'm not looking for your undying love. I just want to feel good. I like it when you touch me. I'd like to touch you."

I raised my hand and laid it on his cheek, sliding it backward to cup the back of his neck. He allowed it.

"If you want..." he faltered, his tongue darting out to moisten his lips.

I knew precisely what I wanted from Nate Matheson.

I closed the gap between us and kissed him.

Nate

Part of my brain shorted out when felt his lips meet mine.

There was no hesitation in him. Dante took my mouth, direct and consuming and undeniable. He shifted, moving closer, hooking an arm around my neck and cradling the back of my head. I moaned a little, and Dante smiled against my lips.

"It's entirely possible," he mused, "that my experiences have left me slightly hypersexual."

He pulled back a little, meeting my eyes.

"I like to be intimate, Nate," he murmured, close enough that I could feel his breath on my lips as he spoke. "To make others feel good and to be made to feel good in return. To revel in the pleasures of the flesh. I like to be *fucked,*" my cock twitched at the word, "by someone who knows how to do it properly." he pulled further away, leaning back. "But if you're adverse to that, I suppose I could always... take matters into my own hands."

I watched him run his hands across his chest and belly. Watched him slide his hands down his sides and hook his thumbs under the waistband of his pants and slide them off. He was already half hard, and as much as I knew that I shouldn't be watching, I couldn't stop.

He leaned his head back, arching into his own touch, palming himself lightly.

"I should... go take a shower..." I said, my voice labored. "Leave you to..."

"Stay," he breathed. "It's better if someone's watching."

Those words burned into my brain, and I felt my cock throb in response. There was no way I could force myself to get up after an invitation like that. He'd said it like an order.

Maybe Iris was right in her observation that I just liked being told what to do.

Dante was so beautiful. The sun was just coming up now, filtering through the curtains and casting iridescent highlights on his hair, making his opalescent skin practically glow. I could see the lines of electronics under his skin pulsing with light, like liquid energy flowing along the smooth perfection of his muscles. Dante looked like art. Indecently erotic art, at the moment.

He ran his left hand back up his chest, his face going thoughtful as he fingered first one nipple and then the other through the fabric of his shirt, exploring the piercings. I'd bought him a pair of plain steel rings to replace the studs while I'd been buying him clothes. I'd been horrifically embarrassed, at the time. We hadn't said a word about it.

"I never understood why people did this..." he breathed, moving his hand to slide up under the shirt's hem. "Unbearably painful, having it done but... I get it now." I watched as he hooked a fingertip into one ring and tugged it slightly, biting his lip. A moan bubbled up out of his throat. "Glad I kept these."

I wanted to touch him. To reach out and run my hands up his sides, peel that shirt off and explore his nipples with my lips and tongue. I knew that if I did, he'd allow it. Welcome it, even. Writhe and moan under my hands.

But I kept still and just watched, fisting my hands in the bedsheets to keep them still.

He gripped himself in his right hand, stroking in earnest now, head thrown back. Eyes closed, his lips parted slightly, fine beads of sweat breaking out along his forehead. Close enough that I could feel the heat rising from his skin.

"You'd be good at it..." Dante moaned, his breath hitching. "I've... .I know the difference between good sex and bad sex... You'd... . you'd be good. You'd make me come. "

"Yes," I murmured without meaning to.

That seemed to be what he was waiting for, because at the sound of my voice he moaned and arched and *came.*

I had done nothing in my life to deserve a sight a beautiful as watching Dante come. Watching his face in pure ecstasy, watching him arch up off the bed and then relax back against it in languid contentment, smiling and sated and purring. He opened his eyes and looked at me, a slow and completely lascivious smile spreading across his face.

"As you see, I'm more than capable of taking care of myself," he said. "Want me to take care of you, too?" I could have sworn I felt his gaze as it swept down from my face to my groin, where my erection was tenting out my boxers, a little spot of wetness blooming where the head of my cock pressed against the fabric.

It took all of my willpower to answer, "No."

He looked at me, as I got up, like I was a puzzle in need of solving. There was something in his eyes that made me look away.

I retreated to the bathroom to jerk off in my shower for the second time in as many days, dreaming of putting my hands on him. Of putting my mouth on him. Of him doing the same to me, which he seemed more than willing to do.

He made a damned persuasive argument, that was the worst of it. I leaned against the shower wall, playing it over in my head, his face as he'd said "I like to be *fucked.*"

I moaned when I came, and knew that he'd probably heard it.

I lingered in the bathroom until I'd washed away the smell of sex, and stepped out into the hallway to another smell entirely.

"I made pancakes," Dante called from the kitchen. "I hope you don't mind. If you don't come and have some soon they'll be cold."

Well. Who was I to argue with pancakes?

Maybe cohabitation had its perks after all.

'Taire

I couldn't have let it be over that way. Not with Dante. Dante was too important for that.

As long as he was still alive, I was not going to let him rot with some human bastard. I was gonna save Dante or die trying. I owed him that much.

I'd been trailing him for three months now.

It wasn't easy; I couldn't get too close. Couldn't let humans know I was around. I'd seen him a couple of times. Saw him from a rooftop as he was being shoved into the back of a truck. Saw him carried out of a nightclub over someone's shoulder, probably pinned. I'd been so fucking close, but I might as well have been a million miles away for all the good I could have done either of those times.

I'd stole a GPS console off the meth-head human who'd been making KJ and Nix do drug runs for him. Wasn't even hard, guy had a glass jaw, never had time to reach for his blackbox. So complacent about how strays didn't fight back.

Dante's registration number was 3178KMi1126. I knew because I'd made him tell me right after we'd lost a bunch of people who'd got out of Sir's place with us. So that if we ever got separated running, we could try to find each other again. He knew mine, too.

Nobody else knew mine. Not even KJ, who knew that my registration number pinged up like I was shiny and new because nobody had ever actually used it to register me.

When KJ found out that I'd popped the meth-head, I got screamed at about how being anything but boot-licking obedient to human trash meant they'd come down hard on all of us, and how easy it would be for that asshole to call in a tip and have the cops sweep the neighborhood and how we could all end up like Dante had and how it was selfish and wrong and stupid to have punched him.

She'd beat the crap out me, too.

So I didn't have a group anymore. Probably better that way, for tracking down Dante.

Sleeping all alone in whatever corner I could find sucked, though.

Getting kicked out would've only have been a matter of time, without Dante there. Everyone knew I was useless, and they only tolerated me at all because Dante liked me, and everyone wanted Dante to stick around because Dante was a smart guy. A good guy. Kind of guy who'd watch your back always knew what to do no matter what kind of problems you had. Kind of guy who just plain took care of everybody.

And now humans had him. I wasn't gonna let it be that way. I was gonna rescue Dante, and everything was gonna be okay.

Unless Dante was fried for real. If he was wiped... I couldn't think about that.

Dante was a schoolboy. No matter how pretty he was, nobody was gonna wipe all of that without storing a backup. That'd just be wasteful. Humans were lot of things, but they weren't usually wasteful. They sucked out every scrap of utility you had, generally. Dante was too useful to be wiped, had to remember that.

It was going to be okay. All I needed to do was keep tailing him and wait for the moment I could grab him and everything would be okay. Once I had Dante back, the two of us could find a group easy. Everyone liked Dante.

Dante... got me. Like, understood. He would— he'd been a kid, too. Fuck of a lot nicer for him that it'd been for me, yeah, but at least he'd been a kid. It was more than any of the others had. KJ and Lars and them had been untanked at standard growth. Humans had to pay a whole lot extra and go to special companies if they wanted nonstandard cygenics. Had to commission us. Wasn't like going to a store and picking up a maid or a secretary or a watchdog or a whore. Commissioners who wanted kids, they had to go through background checks and stuff, Dante said.

If they wanted to do it legal.

My commissioner hadn't gone through any kind of background checks to get me made, I was damned sure about that. Never registered me, because I wasn't supposed to exist.

Dante said when he pinged me that I'd been made in Belarus, 19 years ago. That was all there was to know about me, from my registration number.

Only so many reasons to want a cygenic kid. Wasn't like people didn't know that.

It was just that nobody—absolutely fucking nobody—really gave a shit. Kept those kinds of assholes from going after the *real* kiddies, didn't it? Just some fucking wetware, right? Disposable anyhow. Off-lined cygenics turned up in dumpsters all the time. If some of them were kids—well, not much to be done about it.

Except... Dante had cared. Like really genuinely cared. He'd felt really, actually bad about it, like nobody else ever did.

That was why I couldn't let it go. I knew exactly what humans used cygenics like me and Dante for. Especially Dante, now. Dante was a pretty. I... hadn't grown up pretty. Wasn't dwelling on that bullshit either. Had to focus. I was on a rescue mission.

Which was why I was in this really nice neighborhood five miles outside of the city, hunkered down by the dumpsters next to a house that was getting renovated a block away from where I was pretty sure Dante was, pretending to myself that I wasn't scared shitless.

Nice neighborhoods were dangerous in a totally different way than shit neighborhoods were. In the city, you had to worry about getting scooped by pimps or getting caught by gangs who just wanted to beat the shit out of you or fuck you or both— but nobody thought it was weird for strays to be around, generally. You could sit right on the street and beg or look for work and you'd usually be okay if you had a few people with you, unless there were cops doing a neighborhood sweep. Sometimes people just got bagged by a random human, like Candy had that time, but it wasn't what usually happened. Usually humans didn't even look at you. You were just street trash.

Nice places like this, you had to worry about being *seen*.

Cygenics were a hell of a lot more common

uptown than downtown, overall, but they weren't strays. And you could always tell. I was shit at passing for a pet, I knew that. Didn't have the right clothes, didn't walk right, didn't look right. Didn't have a human to cover for me anyway, even if I'd been good at faking. Dante was a fucking champ at that, but not me. Any human who spotted me here would know I didn't belong here and try to ping me with a cell phone in about five seconds. I'd come up unregistered. Shit would go down and I'd end up... dead, probably.

But Dante was here. Had been every night for almost a week now. I'd chased his signal here from Piss Street. Bad fucking luck that I hadn't been able to get him from Piss Street; it was a way easier neighborhood to work. Alleys and rooftops you could get at from fire escapes, and dumpsters everywhere. Wasn't as hard as here. This was all nice back yards and little banks of trees and clear streets.

But being hard wasn't going to stop me. Being dangerous wasn't going to stop me. Because it was Dante.

There was food here; rich bastards threw away all kinds of perfectly fine stuff, all I had to was wait for the middle of the night and be quiet about going through people's trash. Had to hole up during the day out of sight, because there were all these people around walking dogs and playing basketball in the street and stuff. Human *kids* everywhere, because it was July and school wasn't on. But I'd be okay. All I had to do was wait for the right opportunity. For that human he was always with to go out and for him to be left at the house alone.

All I had to do was not get caught.

Dante

My students had left me for the siren call of the open cafeteria. Having eaten a more than ample breakfast and looking forward to what would probably be a more than ample dinner, I was far less moved by the promise of split pea soup and white bread with margarine than they were. Besides, it seemed gauche to use the Center's resources when I was eating so well elsewhere, and the time it took for everyone to receive their food and nutrient fluid made a convenient planning period for the lessons of the afternoon.

I'd been teaching for five days now. Nines was far and away my best student, and was also rather handy at maintaining classroom discipline on my behalf. I wasn't entirely approving of his methodology, which generally involved whistling through his teeth and shouting insults and threats at anyone who didn't appear to be giving me their full attention, but fear of his authority allowed me to play "good cop" and student engagement was generally high.

I was writing words containing "at" on the board when Miss Castillo walked in and sat down to observe me. Unsure of her motivations, I continued filling the board until she spoke.

"They're talking about you in the office, you know. Linda and Drake and everyone. Nate won't shut up about you. The clients won't shut up about you. So I thought I'd drop in."

I turned to her and offered a winning smile. "Saying good things, I hope? I don't believe I've entirely hit my stride as regards teaching, but the group shows great promise."

She hummed, looking at me in unhidden appraisal for a moment before speaking again. "What's going on with you and Nate?"

"Excuse me?"

"You heard me. What's going on with you and Nate? You two an item?"

"Miss Castillo, shouldn't you be asking Nate about that? It's hardly my place as a guest in his home—"

"Cut the crap. I'm worried about him. If I'd thought about it for five damned minutes the other night when he found you, I would not have let him bring you home. Wouldn't have left the two of you alone. I let shit start that I shouldn't have let start, and now I'm at least in part culpable for it." She sighed, glancing at the door and then looking back at me. "I have known that boy since he was 17. Did you know he was in college at 16? He was. Nerdy enough that he got skipped ahead in school. I met him when I was a senior and he was a sophomore. I was an RA. He was raising hell about the fact that the school owned slaves. We kind of hit it off. He's kind of shit at making friends."

Not knowing what else to do, I sat down at the desk opposite her, as if we were in some kind of consultation. Perhaps we were. I wasn't entirely sure where she was going with this but it was clear that my attention was required. She pulled a vapor cigarette out of her pocket and stuck it in her mouth. I smelled cinnamon.

"He came home with me the Thanksgiving of his sophomore year. It was his first after Lisa'd died, and he kind of had a meltdown and ended up crying in my room about how he couldn't afford to stay at school over the break, and how he was just gonna go home to his empty house in Allston. How all his high school friends were in California and Washington and wherever, and how his shitbag dad expressly dis-invited him from the Thanksgiving his white family was having in Arkansas."

She leaned back in the chair, glancing at what I'd written on the board.

"So I invited him home with me and my family, since there's always a million people at my abuelita's house anyway. I have no idea how he stayed my friend after that, because she grilled him on whether I was trying to date him, and told him how my childhood sweetheart and my high school boyfriend *both* later went on to come out, and how I probably had a curse. She's had a candle lit for a husband for me since I was 16. But Nate ended up talking about psychological profiling on crime drama shows with my dad for most of the night, and I think he was just kind of folded into the family as an auxiliary little brother after that. He hooked up with my cousin Lorenzo that Christmas break, but then Lorenzo moved back to the islands. Should have figured out then that Nate's into macho control freaks, because Lorenzo sure as fuck was one."

"I'm not sure I'm following..."

"The thing you need to understand about Nate is that he's got real hardcore abandonment issues. His dad ditched him, and Lisa died, and all his high school friends peaced out like high school friends do. The one decent dude he dated in college went on a backpacking tour in Thailand and decided to stay there—broke up with him in an email. Not even a month ago he got dumped hard by this guy he'd been dating. Guy was an abusive shit-stain, and I'm happy he took off, but the way he did it pressed every one of Nate's buttons. Fucking asshole. You basically happened to show up on the scene while Nate has a big sucking chest wound that you don't know anything about."

"What is it that you want me to do with this information, Miss Castillo?" I asked.

"That boy is gonna fall in love with you. You break his heart, I break your legs."

"I will... keep that in mind," I said, raising my eyebrows. Humans did not generally threaten cygenics with anything so mundane as bodily harm. Humans generally threatened cygenics with twitchboxing and reprogramming and other torments unique to us.

"He doesn't deserve to have his heart broken. He's codependent and leechy and that puts people off, but I swear to you kid, all he wants in this world is someone to tell him he's good. It's some weird "daddy issues" thing, I think. Psych was more his thing than mine. I was sociology." She took a long drag on her cigarette. "But it comes down to him being eager to please. The asshole I was just talking about, the one he's on the rebound from? He manipulated the fuck out of that. I need to know that's not gonna be a problem with you. If that's gonna be a problem with you, I can find a way for there to suddenly be an open spot in one of the group homes so that you're not under Nate's nose anymore."

I swallowed, considering that. It might be better, less of a risk, to have more professional accommodations. A more... clinical setting than Nate's house. Something more in keeping with my station and my association with this organization. Several of my students lived in the Turing Center's group home, and spoke well of it. They didn't pin you, and they served actual food, and they didn't lock the doors.

I very much doubted anyone there would cuddle me while I slept. I hadn't inquired, but co-sleeping was almost certainly forbidden.

"Whose bed would I be taking, Miss Castillo?" I asked, trying not to frown.

"Someone who's being bitchy about placement, probably. Someone we can send home with one of the interns. Hell, I could take someone home myself, if it came to that. I could really use a fucking domestic, and Nate doesn't have a leg to stand on anymore with telling me why it's unethical, not since you. You don't have to worry about anyone getting kicked on the street to make space for you; we don't run that kind of operation. Since you made yourself so valuable to the organization so quick, we've got a vested interest in keeping you safe and sound. Nate's place fits that bill. *You're* not the one I'm worried about."

"I have no intention of breaking his heart, Miss Castillo. I owe him a great debt. He's been very kind to me. I don't think it would make him happy if I were to find other accommodations."

She sighed again, rolling her eyes and taking another drag. When she spoke, she produced a cloud of cinnamon-scented vapor. I imagined that I could taste the cloying sweetness of it.

"Shit, he's that far gone already? I knew I should have thrown him at some rebound boy-toy with a fucking sell-by date. Strap in, kid, it's gonna be a ride. You better take it where it goes."

"And where does it go, Miss Castillo?"

"To Nate being completely smitten with you until he's not, and you being gracious and understanding about it whenever that is. Like I said, you break his heart, I break your legs. Same deal if you don't treat him right."

She took a final drag before slipping her cigarette back into her pocket.

"There's some kind of lecture thing going on at BU tonight. You should look it up. Nate's into that kind of thing, lectures and improv theater and classical concerts and stuff. Drag him to the MFA and he'll love you forever. I need to get back to my office, I've got another programmer interview in like 15 minutes, and your kindergarteners will be back soon. Be good."

I snorted a little at the order to be good, as if cygenics at large could risk being otherwise. I noticed, as she was leaving, that several of my students had formed a line in the corridor as if waiting for an invitation back into the classroom.

But the conversation had been... illuminating.

Nate

"Nerve Ostrander is going to be speaking at Boston University in a lecture open to the public!" Dante said from the door of my office.

"Excuse me?" I said, glancing up at him over the edge of my tablet. I still had three open case files that needed to be finalized.

"Sorry if I'm interrupting; the cafeteria opened for dinner so all of my students elected to leave class to stand in line. But Miss Castillo tipped me off to a lecture and I looked into it and *Nerve Ostrander's going to be at BU*. Tonight. Xe's the Ken Robinson of our generation. If we don't already have plans..."

Something about the way he said "we" made me smile. He considered us a unit. My plans were his plans; plans were something we did together. It was... nice.

"Is it bad that I don't know who the Ken Robinson of some previous generation is?" I asked, closing the last of my open files and putting the tablet down to give Dante my full attention.

"... should I explain who Ken Robinson was, or just skip right to Professor Ostrander?"

"That second one. I mean we can go to the lecture anyway, I kind of like lectures in general, but do tell?"

"Nerve Ostrander is the author of *Inclusive Education for a Brilliant Future*, which is at its root a book about everything that is wrong with the current model of western education and what can be done to repair it. Last time I was aware of xyr, xe was also a candidate for Minister of Education in the Netherlands. I've seen vids of xyr talks; xe's very engaging."

"What time would we have to be there? Do we have time to pick up dinner first?"

"The talk starts at 7:30, but we should probably be there at seven if we want to get seats. If there are seats. I fully expect a standing-room-only crowd. I don't think we have time for dinner; it's already six and we have to factor in travel time. We could eat afterward..."

I looked at the profiles on my tablet.

"Seven's cutting it close. I'm supposed to be here until seven." I watched his face fall, and I sighed. "Give me five minutes," I said, "and I'll have to come in at six tomorrow to finish this. But yes, we can go. *You* go tell Iris. It helps if you couch the 'Nate's leaving early' declaration as an invitation. She'll decline. She gets bored at lectures."

He grinned at me and scampered out of my office to go find Iris.

Dante liked lectures. About educational theory. Dante liked to watch TED events online for fun in his spare time. Dante was, in fact, even more nerdy than I was. Without being condescending about it. There was something incredibly refreshing about that.

We took my car as far as Kenmore and then got on the green line to avoid the hassle of trying to park near the school. The lecture was less difficult to find than I'd anticipated, because Dante had been entirely correct about its popularity; we just followed the crowd.

We were stopped at the entrance to the lecture hall by a kid in khakis and a black polo shirt with a half dozen cards on lanyards around his neck.

"Are you a student or faculty member?" he asked, looking down at the tablet he was holding and then back up at me with a slightly absent look. He glanced at Dante and frowned.

"No, I'm not," I answered.

"Okay. You're welcome to look for a seat in the 'guests' section, but due to demand we're going to ask that your cygenic either wait in the atrium or sit on the floor."

I froze, trying to formulate a response. There was a line forming behind me. I was holding things up. I didn't really give a fuck, because what kind of bullshit was it that Dante should have to sit on the floor like a goddamned animal, or worse, be forced out of the lecture hall entirely?

Dante tugged on my arm, and I looked at him. He had a look on his face that I had only ever seen before on Lisa—a sort of stern 'not here, not now' look.

"I'll stand," I finally said, letting Dante lead me away from the kid, who wasn't even really paying attention to me anymore. "I don't believe this," I muttered as we were walking down the aisle at the back of the hall, toward the staircase that led to the pit where there were already a gaggle of college kids standing because seating was full.

"It's not a big deal. I expected as much. Please

don't make a scene. I'd like to enjoy this. Please?" Dante said quietly. "I haven't actually gotten to attend a lecture since Professor Cunningham died."

I swallowed my anger down and let him lead me to the standing area.

The lecture itself was on the topic of lateral teaching and the importance of engaging students to get them to teach one another. Professor Ostrander pulled up slides of data showing studies that had been conducted all over the world, primarily in poverty-stricken areas, of "teacherless teaching" and its outcomes. Xe followed that with an outline of achievement-based skill-mastery teaching systems, addressed in a way that made it clear that xe presumed most of the audience were educators or those training to be. Xe was a powerful speaker, animated and passionate about the subject, and I found my throat tightening up during xyr big finish speech. The girl beside me was openly crying and nodding while her friend tried to console her. I looked at Dante.

Dante was looking up at the stage in total appreciative awe. There was something almost worshipful in his face, and I made note to ask later if it was the speaker or the subject that had made him look like that.

The room erupted into thunderous applause when xe concluded. After that died down, Professor Ostrander announced that xe'd be singing copies of xyr book in the atrium, and people began filing out.

There were refreshments in the atrium, some people forming little knots of discussion as others left. Dante expressed an interest in getting in line to purchase a copy of Professor Ostrander's book (if I was willing to purchase a copy—he'd love to be able to have it in hardcopy) and having it signed.

"Oh my gods," someone said from behind me, tapping me on the shoulder. I turned to find a heavy-set Asian girl in an almost painfully stylish outfit looking past me with open awe. Looking at Dante.

"Is he yours?" she asked, finally looking at me.

"For several intents and purposes. I'm the one he's out with tonight," I answered, looking to Dante. He was smiling, but it was a wholly perfunctory smile.

She looked from him and back to me uncertainly.

"Is it all right if I talk to him? I know some owners get very upset if anyone talks to their cygenics without their permission."

"Yes," I ground out. "You can talk to him."

"Are you Dante of The Dante Project?" she asked, all in a rush.

"I am," Dante said, his smile turning into something more genuine. "You're the first person I've met in quite some time who's known anything about it."

"I followed the shit out of that back in high school!" she said, practically squealing. "I thought you were the coolest thing! I wrote my college entrance essay about you and how you were what made me decide I wanted to be an education major! Oh my gods, I'm gushing and I haven't even introduced myself." She paused to fan herself with her hands. "I'm Kelly-Lynn Koh. I'm a writer for the blog 'Learn You Somethin.' I was here doing a live feed of the lecture for the blog, but this is just too much! Can I take a photo with you?"

Dante looked to me for confirmation, and it hurt that he should feel like he needed my permission. I nodded, swallowing. She huddled close to Dante and took a arm-length photo with her phone.

"What have you been doing for the last five years? The website just kind of stopped updating." She turned to me, a giddy smile on her face. "Can I ask who you are and how you're associated with the Dante project? Are you a professor here? Did you work with Professor Cunningham?"

"I actually work for the Turing Center for Cygenic Dignity," I faltered, looking at Dante. "I'm a case manager. Dante is one of my cases."

Dante smiled at me in a way that made my heart skip a beat, then turned to the girl and said, "I've been teaching literacy classes to cygenics at the Turing Center. I hope to eventually expand into educator education. Are you familiar with the agency and its mission at all?"

"No, I'm afraid I've never heard of it," she said with polite interest.

"Nate would be the one to best describe it, I think," Dante said, "as his association with the agency is longer than mine."

Kelly-Lynn Koh proceeded to conduct an impromptu interview of Dante and me, but mostly Dante, concerning the Turing Center and his work there and his methodology and the outcomes he hoped for, concluding with asking us for permission to be quoted on her blog. She excused herself shortly afterwards, saying she had an early class, leaving us with the address of her blog and telling us to look her up because we'd be appearing on it in a day or two.

"Well, she seemed nice," Dante said, watching her leave.

"I didn't know you had a fandom," I mused, putting an arm around his shoulder. "Should I be worried about being swarmed by groupies when we go out together in public?"

Dante laughed. I felt it.

"I don't think so, unless we exclusively attend educational conferences," he glanced toward the table, where Professor Ostrander was presumably still seated somewhere at the center of the throng of people who'd gathered.

"I think I'm more interested in food than I am in obtaining a signed hard copy. Shall we go to dinner?"

"Yeah, that sounds like a good idea. Got any ideas about what you want?"

"I don't know that I've ever been asked that question..." he said, looking slightly wistful as we exited the lecture hall and made our way back to the train. "Surprise me."

Dante

I should have known better than to let Nate take me to a restaurant, after his reaction to the relatively inoffensive usher at the lecture.

He'd decided on a little bistro he knew off Comm Ave. The waitress had asked him if he wanted a chair for me. He'd snapped at her that *of course* he wanted a chair for me.

He'd been visibly upset since, snapping again when the waitress asked him what he'd like for each of us, telling her to ask me what I wanted. She looked flustered and confused, and when she glanced at me I saw pity in her eyes. Sympathy that I had to deal with this man on a regular basis. I had no way of communicating to her that he was not, generally, like this.

Though I had no real basis upon which to make that observation... I'd only known him for a number of days, after all. This was the first time I'd seen him angry. I stayed quiet, watching him intently. How he behaved when angry was incredibly pertinent knowledge to me.

When the waitress had left with our orders, he leaned forward, elbows braced on the table, pushing the heels of his hands against his eyes. After a minute or so of stillness he looked up at me and asked, "How do you stand it? The asshole back at the lecture who wanted you to sit on the floor, the girl asking *me* if it was okay to talk to you, the fucking waitress asking *me* if you should be allowed to have a chair and not even asking me if you should get a menu... it's like you're invisible to them."

"It's like you're my master," I said, trying to keep my tone neutral.

"And that fucking kills me. I'm not your master, Dante. I don't fucking own you."

"They don't know that. You can't blame them for not knowing that."

"Hell I can't. No one acted this way with Lisa. She'd take me everywhere as a kid and people just treated her like..."

"Like a cygenic nanny with a human charge, presumably acting in loco parentis and executing the will of said charge's parents. A nanny is a figure of some authority and trust who must be dealt with as such. You were a child being escorted by his nanny. Now you're a man brazenly displaying your sex toy."

Nate hissed through his teeth and interrupted, "But you're not—"

"They think I am," I said, glaring at him, "and that's what matters regarding how they choose to react. Bristling at them for not having automatic knowledge that you'd prefer me to be treated as if I were human doesn't help anyone. Don't think you're doing me any favors by bullying the waitstaff."

"You don't deserve to be treated that way. Like you're not a person."

"I'm *not* a person, Nate. I'm a cygenic. I'm a thing. I'm a toy and a tool and a piece of wetware. I exist to be bought and sold and owned and used as my owner sees fit. That is what others see when they look at me. You and yours are an exception to the general rule. Your being angry at servicepeople for following the rules isn't helping."

Nate might have replied, but the waitress arrived with our food. I smiled and thanked her. She asked Nate if we needed anything else. He shook his head. She left.

"If it's any consolation to you, I appreciate very much that you feel so passionately about my right to personhood. Never since Professor Cunningham have I met a human who'd think it worthwhile to take me to a lecture. Or... speak to me, for that matter. Most of the humans I've known would think nothing of having me kneel at their feet. You do recall that you found me chained to the underside of a table, don't you?"

Nate shuddered a little, utterly ignoring his food. I wondered if that meant I should follow suit and ignore mine. He probably wouldn't punish me for having the audacity to eat before he started eating, but it seemed... callous.

"You don't deserve to be treated like this," Nate said, looking down. "Any of you. The way cygenics are treated... *This is slavery*."

"Only if we're people," I said, trying to keep the bitterness from my voice. "In any case, you can't change it by railing at waitstaff. I'd suggest you leave that poor girl an excellent tip. She probably expects you to be a pompous, demanding grandstander on the basis that you're the kind of man who'd bring his cygenic to a restaurant and then expect her to be psychic concerning your intentions about my treatment."

Nate nodded, sighing and picking at his food. I took that as a cue that it was acceptable for me to start eating. The silence quickly became awkward.

"When I was a child," I said as a means of breaking it, "Professor Cunningham had cards printed with a basic explanation of what I was and what his research entailed—and that I should be treated, as much as possible, as if I were a human child. So as not to invalidate the project. It was an incredibly effective social lubricant. We might look into something like that, if you intend to bring me out in public and wish to avoid this kind of awkwardness in the future."

"He had business cards that said 'He thinks he's people, isn't that cute? Please don't tell him otherwise.' printed on them?" Nate said, glaring at his food. I raised an eyebrow. He didn't see me do so.

"Yes, he did. And when he didn't have them readily on hand, he frankly explained me to any and all relevant people so that they would know how to respond to me. No one had to ask him if he wanted a chair for me, or inquired about my presence at the Museum of Science, or the Museum of Fine Arts, or any number of lectures and conferences over the course of my education. People need these things spelled out for them, because we live in a world of ambiguity and the default position of cygenics is not an elevated one."

Nate sighed again. Some time later, the waitress asked him if we'd like dessert. He answered in the negative. He paid with a card, and didn't discuss the prices with me, so I didn't know if he'd taken my advice to tip well.

On the train back to Kenmore, the car was

sufficiently crowded that we were both standing. In the closeness of the crowd, he wrapped his arm around me, pulling me against him. It was gesture that could have felt possessive, but from Nate it simply felt... close. Like he wanted to protect me. Like he thought I was worth holding onto. He put his head on my shoulder and said, into my ear, "Sorry I'm an ass. You deserve better."

I couldn't really answer him without turning around, so I just reached to his hand, still wrapped around me, and twined my fingers with his.

Nate

I was exhausted by the time we got home, pulling my jacket off and letting it fall to the floor somewhere halfway between the front door and the sofa, sitting down heavily and setting my head in my hands.

Dante picked up my coat and hung it up. I closed my eyes and leaned my head back against the sofa, unable to summon the energy to tell him that he didn't have to pick up after me. He did it everywhere he went, neatening and tidying things like it was his job.

Would I have thought anything about it if he'd been human, or just chalked it up to his being a fastidious person? It wasn't the kind of thing I was used to thinking about. It wasn't the kind of thing I wanted to think about.

I opened my eyes and found Dante kneeling on the floor at my feet, looking up at me.

"Dante," I began, leaning back from him, pressing myself into the sofa, "Dante get up. You shouldn't..."

"Don't tell me what I should and shouldn't do, Nate," he said, his voice clear and precise and inarguable. I swallowed. He looked up at me, his molten-silver eyes piercing. "I was thinking about this on the subway, playing out the events of the day.

Trying to figure out what set you off so badly. I think I've got it, so bear with me. I think I know what you *need*."

My mouth went dry and I sat there, paralyzed, watching him move with all the poise of a dancer to climb up and straddle my lap. He shifted his hips, grinding against me, and I could feel his cock pulsing, getting hard. I put my hands on his hips to still him, but found myself palming his hipbones, fingers splayed out, thumbs tucking neatly into the juncture of his thighs like they'd been made to do so.

"Dante, this..."

"Nate. You need to know how things stand between us. You're tense and you're angry and you're confused because everything's so horribly ambiguous. How you should treat me. How you should act around me. How others should act around me. What people should conclude about the two of us. You keep second-guessing yourself about what you should do and what's the best thing, the right thing. So... let me show you. Let me show you how I *want* it."

He leaned forward and took my mouth. Calling it a kiss wouldn't have done it justice. He was demanding and implacably all-consuming and perfect. I had no choice but to give myself up to it, to melt into it and surrender. He cradled the back of my head, holding me in place, rocking his hips to grind us together, and there was nothing else. My mind became utterly, gloriously, uncomplicatedly blank.

When he finally pulled away, I dragged air into my lungs like I'd been running.

"That's what I want, Nate," he said, his voice thick with desire. " You want that?"

"...Yes," I admitted, painfully, closing my eyes hard.

When I opened them again, he smiled wickedly at my assent. He moved downward, placing a gentle kiss at my throat, just above the notch in my collarbone.

"Can I touch you?" I asked, surprised at how small and needy my voice sounded.

"Please," he purred.

My hands found the hem of his T-shirt and slipped inside, running along his slightly-too-prominent ribs, up his back and the back of his neck. His skin was smoother than it had any right to be, fine and soft over lithe muscle. Inhumanly perfect. Because he wasn't human.

He flinched, breath drawn in a sharp gasp, when my fingertip brushed against the steel hardness of the jack on the back of his neck. He stopped still and breathed against my throat.

"I want to do right by you," I said with as much conviction as I could muster.

He lifted his head and met my eyes, and my mouth went dry. There was trepidation in those mercury-colored eyes, but more than that there was hunger.

"Then stop trying to figure me out and listen to what I *want*," Dante challenged. "I'm not really that mysterious, Nate. Stop trying to decide what you'd do if I was a human, or how best to pretend that I am one, and get over the fact that I'm a cygenic—and I very much want to have sex with you."

I couldn't argue against eyes like that. Against conviction like that.

I kissed him, and it was like he was drinking me

184

in. Hot, desperate, demanding. Like he was starving for it. Like he wanted to consume me.

And I knew that I'd let him.

I ran my hands along Dante's shoulders, around his sides and down the flat planes of his chest and the tight muscles of his abdomen. Ran my hands back up, peeling his shirt up in the process. I was met with a purr of satisfaction and Dante obligingly raised his arms, breaking the kiss for a few moments as the garment was lifted over his head and discarded. I ran my hands across all that exposed opalescent flesh, my eyes drawn to the way the light pulsed on the long, shimmering lines of electronics beneath his skin. The way the light caught on the shining steel rings that bisected each of his nipples. I ran a fingertip over one experimentally, and Dante arched.

"Oh *God*, glad I kept those..." he moaned, gazing at me with eyes gone glassy.

I smiled, looping one arm around the small of his back and cupping the back of his head, making him look at me.

"Can I take you to bed?" I asked, feeling my cheeks flush because I wasn't used to asking questions like that.

Dante murmured agreement, fumbling off my lap with more speed than grace, grabbing my wrists and pulling me up with him. Doing what he wanted with me. It was hard to think about why I shouldn't be letting him. When I got him on his back on my bed and kissed him again, he sucked and nibbled at my lip. I took hold of his shoulders, pressing him down into the softness of the sheets, breaking the kiss to nose my away along his throat. He arched under me, and I stroked his chest again, running my thumbs across his nipples and coaxing them into little points of hardness, playing with the jewelry. I caught one shining ring between my fingertips and tugged slightly, and he threw his head back and let out a stuttering moan. I took the opportunity to trail nibbling kisses down his throat and along his collarbone, and he laughed.

"You could... try that with your mouth... that thing you just did with your fingers," Dante panted. I was quite happy to oblige him, trailing my kisses further downward until I was lapping at one of those rigid points, catching one ring between my teeth, my hand toying with the other. Dante shuddered and moaned again, his hands grasping the sheets with white-knuckled urgency.

I ran my hand down his side, across the tautness of his belly and under the waistband of his pants to glide my hand teasingly over his cock. He bucked and took half a dozen gasping breaths before speaking, his voice sounding uncertain for the first time since he'd started this, "Please, Nate... Suck me?"

Hearing him say that had me as hard as I'd ever been. I let him feel it, grinding up against the length of his thigh as I crawled up to whisper into his ear.

"If I do anything that you don't like, I need you to let me know."

Dante nodded frantically, eyes still squeezed shut, hands balled into fists in the sheets.

"Please..." he murmured.

I couldn't deny him, not when he asked like that.

I hooked my thumbs under his waistband and slid his pants down, pulling him to the edge of the bed and kneeling on the floor.

He moaned when I took him into my mouth, his hands flying to my head, holding me there. He seemed to remember himself a second later, relaxing, fingertips barely caressing my scalp. He fit in my mouth like he belonged there. I'd expected him to be more demanding, given his desperation. To hold my head and fuck my mouth like Charles so often had. Dante didn't. He held himself still with a kind of discipline that had to come from effort, the muscles of his thighs bunching under my hands as I swallowed him right to the root and pulled back again to circle the head of his cock with my tongue. I brought my hand in to palm and cup his balls, and he practically *whimpered*. I looked up at him and pulled back a little, keeping my lips so close to his cock that he had to feel it when I said:

"It's okay if you come."

And then he did, like I'd said the magic words. The first spurt grazed my lip, and I flinched back in reflex to watch the remainder splatter onto his chest and belly. I licked my lips and grinned, watching his face as he basked in the afterglow. If Dante was beautiful most of the time, post-orgasmic Dante was... divine. Awe-inspiring. My mouth went dry, looking at him in bliss.

His eyes met mine, and he smiled, and I knew in that moment that I was completely and totally his. Just like that.

"That was *perfect*," he moaned, stretching like a contented cat. "So... you gonna fuck me?"

"You want me to?" I asked in answer, peeling my shirt and then my pants off, letting them fall to the floor.

"I think we both know the answer to that, Nate," he said with a grin. "You want me to turn over? Or up on my knees?"

187

"No," I replied, shaking my head. "I wanna see your face,"

He watched with silent interest, leaning up on his elbows with his legs still dangling off the edge of the bed, while I fished around in the drawer of the nightstand for a bottle of lube. When I looked back at him, he was fingering his left nipple, eyes closed. He looked almost studious about it, and something about that was way hotter than it should have been.

"You like those, huh?"

"I think it'll be a while before I get used to these... I mean, in a good way. I'll have to spend some time on... masturbatory exploration..."

He was already hard again.

I couldn't stand it. I practically lunged at him, wrapping my arm around him and pulling him in for a kiss that he absolutely melted into. I lubed up my hands and stroked him languidly as I slipped a finger into him. He squirmed and bit his lip and grinned.

"You're making me feel selfish. I should be doing something..."

"I thought this was about making you feel good, Dante. Wasn't that the premise we started on?"

He might have answered if I hadn't hooked my fingers inside him, wringing a long, low, incoherent moan from his throat.

I guided his knees over my shoulders and just stared down at him for a couple of seconds, working my fingers in and out of him. He was so unbelievably beautiful. He looked up at me with half-lidded eyes and offered a playful smile.

I slid into him in one long stroke, and the noise he made when I did was better than pornographic. I curled over him, hands planted on the bed, and tried not to come instantly. I could smell the come on his skin from earlier, mixed with sweat and the smell of the lube. Had to take a few long, deep breaths before I could start moving.

He slipped his legs off my shoulders and wrapped them around me when I did. Whimpered into my ear unintelligibly, quiet half-growled words that might have been pleas and might have just been filthy. I wasn't paying enough attention. The sheen of sweat on his brow was distracting, the way his hair fell across his face in silver-violet tendrils. The way he closed his eyes and drew his eyebrows together and bit his lip and panted. I collapsed onto one elbow to free my other hand and took hold of his cock, and he gasped and cried out and said my name as he came in my hand.

The sensation of him coming while I was buried to the hilt in the tight heat of him was too much, and I tumbled over the edge with him.

I pulled away and lay down beside him, legs dangling off the bed. His hand sought out mine and gripped it, fingers interlaced. Something felt right about that.

"You're not gonna make me sleep in the other room, right?" Dante asked playfully, an eternity later. "I don't think I can walk."

I rolled over and blanketed him with my body, nipping at the hollow of his throat, and he laughed.

I was probably a bad man for taking advantage of this gorgeous, brilliant creature who offered himself up to me. But with Dante curled against me, sweat slick and humming with pleasure, I couldn't think of a single reason why.

Dante

Every morning when I woke, I knew that my life had never, ever been this good.

Nate was a better sort of human than I'd ever encountered, the kind of altruist that I'd only read about in philosophical treatises. He was so incredibly indulgent of me and anything that I wanted to do; I was fairly certain that I could have convinced him to drop everything to fulfill any request of mine with nothing more than a pleading glance.

Because he needed to feel needed. Because he needed, desperately, to be told that he was good and worthwhile and wanted. There was a hollowness inside him that needed filling, and I hadn't entirely worked out how to fill it... but I'd decided that it was going to be my aim to do so.

The rewards in being what Nate needed were worth pursuing. The events of the last five years seemed like a terrible dream, a confused hitch in an otherwise perfectly civilized life. Professor Cunningham had been good to me, but he hadn't been... affectionate. Personable. I'd been a pupil, a project, something to be molded into the outcome expected of me, and eventually an indispensable and appreciated caregiver. Always his most prized possession.

Nate regarded me as something else entirely. I was hesitant to use the word "lover," but it would probably be the word he'd choose if asked. Or possibly the adorably sophomoric "boyfriend" or something as blandly congenial as "roommate" if he was trying to downplay our intimacy. He certainly wouldn't refer to me as "his cygenic." I was not one of his possessions. It was a novel state of affairs, not to be considered a possession.

My days were spent watching movies, reading, having real conversations. Teaching classes at the Turing Center five days a week, while Nate went to his office. Just existing, without the continual tension of knowing that someone might attack me at any moment for any number of reasons. That I could be killed or worse, and that there wouldn't be any recourse for that. Being registered meant that I could... relax. That I could pick up my life where I'd left it five years ago.

Upon being registered to the Turing Center, I was elevated to a level of social protection that I hadn't enjoyed since Professor Cunningham's death. That wasn't something I'd ever really expected to happen. Many, perhaps even most, cygenics who became dispossessed never got licensed again. It made us too traceable—the buyers of second-hand cygenics, in general, weren't the sorts of people who liked accountability or wanted to show up on their victims' registration histories.

Nate's skittishness on the subject notwithstanding, I was *owned* again. Anyone who pinged me now would find the Turing Center's information, would have someone to call who would answer. Would have someplace to return me to, if they felt motivated to do so, other than reclamation and recycling. It had been so horrifyingly simple; Nate had made a phone call and filled out a form, and suddenly my life had value. It meant, functionally, that I could walk the streets unescorted and not expect to be picked up by the police for it.

Slavery was freedom. How horrifically Orwellian.

But life was so much better than it had been in the past five years. Better than it had been before that, if I was being honest with myself.

There was a tenderness to Nate that no human had ever spared for me. He was more than happy to hold me and caress me, to let me lie in his lap as we watched TV and curl around him in bed to sleep. To kiss me and suck me and fuck me senseless. It was a powerful comfort, something that I keenly wanted to continue. I needed to become what he needed because... I wanted to be needed by him. I wanted him to *keep* me.

Which made me very conflicted about the idea of trying to pick up the pieces of my former life at all. It had occurred to me, after meeting that girl at Professor Ostrander's lecture, that I'd once had quite a lot of contacts via the Internet. They had probably been wondering what had become of me. Tutors and mentors and frequenters of message boards and social media sites that Professor Cunningham had let me participate in to hone my skills at rhetoric. People who'd read the papers he'd published on my educational progress, who took interest in the grand experiment of me. That girl at the lecture proved that there were people in the world who remembered what I had been and wanted to know what had become of me.

Nate would very certainly let me contact any and all of them if I expressed a desire to.

But I found that I rather preferred my current circumstances to those of my childhood. I was uninterested in becoming a curiosity again, the subject of papers and treatises, Vernon Cunningham's great longitudinal experiment in educational theory.

But if I spent a few years building a body of data on the results of teaching basic literacy and life skills to dispossessed cygenics before drawing attention to my actions... if I could offer evidence that I'd become something, that Professor Cunningham's experiment had turned out something of importance...

I was reading a site dedicated to educator education and pondering such things when I heard the back door open. Nate wouldn't be coming in through the back door, and I'd have heard his car. I felt the hairs on the back of my neck rise, as I very cautiously went to investigate.

'Taire

It was a couple of days before I saw the human leave the house without Dante with him.

My heart about stopped for a couple of seconds when I saw him, and I spent a solid minute just checking and rechecking and making sure this was actually the chance I'd been waiting so long for. He got in his car and drove away, and I looked at the GPS and it showed that Dante was still inside.

There would be only one shot at this.

It was go time.

I'd kind of expected to have to break a window to get the back door open, but I found that it wasn't even locked. I swallowed hard, because if this door wasn't locked that meant that there was something else keeping Dante in, like he was in another locked room inside or he was chained to something. That could be a problem. I'd have deal with it when I found out what was actually up. Maybe he was just pinned.

I hadn't really been in a house before. My first owner had kept me in one room of his apartment the entire time he had me, and the place Sir had kept us wasn't anything like this... was this how regular humans lived? It was all... open. I didn't even know what half the stuff in this room was for, everything was all shiny metal and tile, but it wasn't like a bathroom. A little ways on there was an archway into another room, and the floor started to have carpet. I'd be quieter on carpet, so I headed that way. That room had sofas and tables and shelves and a great big screen on the wall.

I didn't make it to a third room before Dante came and found me.

He came around a corner with some kind of tablet in his hand, looking spooked.

He looked okay. More than okay. He was dressed up in an outfit that probably cost enough to feed everyone in our old group for a week. I didn't know a lot about clothes, not really, but I knew enough to spot "expensive." He had that glowing *fullness* to him that meant he'd been eating food, too. Dante was high-end goods. Specialty goods. The kind that people actually bothered to take care of and keep nice. I laughed a little, without meaning to.

"Hey Dante," I said, swallowing hard.

Dante, for his part, looked at me with a "raccoon about to be flattened by a truck" glare that slowly turned into... something else. Like he was looking at something really important.

And then he grinned like one of the brain-dead.

Fuck. Wasn't any good reason for him to smile like that, meant he'd probably been reprogrammed. I'd had my suspicions about that from the first time I'd seen him walking around with the human, because he'd never looked tense. Never looked like he was scoping out paths of escape.

He rushed forward and hugged me. The tablet he'd been holding made a dull thud on the floor.

He just folded up around me, squeezing the air right out of me and it was all I could do to get another breath. Not because Dante was strong or anything; he was a lightweight. Could have shoved him off if I'd wanted to, no problem. But I couldn't breathe, because he was hugging me and he was real and he was here and this was actually happening. Because I could smell his hair and feel the warmth of his skin.

"'Taire! What're you doing here?" he asked, right up next to my ear. "God, never mind, you have no idea how happy I am that you're okay. I heard you got cut from KJ's group. I thought you were *dead*."

"Anybody with you? Like, right now I mean?" I said, panting, trying to keep it together.

"No," Dante said, loosening up a little and standing back and looking at me with eyes that really hurt because nobody had any business looking at me like that. I wasn't worth that kind of attention. "Nate went out to have someone look at his car because the check engine light came on. Don't take this the wrong way, I'm more happy to see you than you can possibly imagine, but what are you doing here?"

"I came to bail you out—come on, we have to get out of here before he comes back," I said, tossing my head toward the door and taking hold of Dante's upper arm. "We go back that way through the yard and there's this little stretch of woods that goes all the way down to the train tracks. We can hide out there until the trains stop running and walk tracks back downtown. It's how I got up here. Gotta dodge the humans but we should be okay..."

"Wait a second," Dante said, digging in his feet.

"Dante," I said, my voice tighter than normal. Not

keeping it together. Had to keep it together. I felt that little shudder in my muscles that I got sometimes when things were about to go to shit. My heart was going so fast and hard that I swore I could hear it in my ears.

"No, 'Taire, just listen," Dante said, taking a long, deep breath. Taking another. He was hoping I'd follow suit. I wasn't falling for that shit, not today. "You have no idea what's happened... I have so much that I need to tell you."

I didn't say anything. I just kept standing there, hands shoved in my pockets, shaking a little. This wasn't going the easy way. I'd brought something to use, in case Dante was reprogrammed... didn't want to have to use it, especially not when he was... acting like Dante.

"When was the last time you ate?" Dante asked, his voice all soft and floaty like it always got when he was trying to calm me down. "We've got food..."

"They reprogrammed you," I hissed without thinking about it. Breathed in. Breathed out. Pulled the blackbox out of my pocket and pointed it at him.

But he moved faster than I did.

He caught my hand and squeezed my wrist, digging his fingers in between the wrist bones so hard that I hissed through my teeth. I dropped the blackbox, he caught it. Saw him point it at me.

I fell down.

I could hear him breathing hard in the stillness that followed.

I couldn't move.

Because Dante had blackboxed me. Dante, who was supposed to be someone I could trust. Dante, who always had my back. Dante blackboxed me.

I heard him moving, soft footsteps on the carpet as he came at me.

"Sorry I had to do that. You can hate me later if you want, but I wasn't going to let you drag me out of here. I'm gonna put you in a more comfortable position, okay?"

He knew damned well that I couldn't answer, so it wasn't really a question. I felt myself swallow, without consciously trying to. My body just ticking over with automatic functions like breathing and blinking and swallowing without me having any conscious control over it. That's what a blackbox did. Locked me up inside my skull as bad as if I'd gone BSOD.

There'd been a guy back at Sir's place, one of my regulars, who liked to keep me blackboxed the whole time he was doing things with me. He'd knock me down and do whatever he wanted and I couldn't even wince or hiss or whimper about it. He broke my nose against the floor once, and licked the blood off my face. Never figured out why he didn't just go for the BSOD guys in the first place. BSOD's didn't care what happened to them.

Dante laid me on my side, legs curled up a little, halfway into a fetal ball. Because he knew I'd feel safer that way than laid out on my back like a corpse. This was the part where I'd probably have been screaming and crying if my body'd been hooked up to my brain... at least blackboxes gave you the dignity of not freaking out in any way anyone could see.

He was sitting down next to me now, and his hand came down to tousle my hair. To comb through it with his fingers, all calm and gentle and so fucking Dante.

I got twitchy sometimes about Dante hanging on me the way he did—always wanting to hug or hold or cuddle—but usually it was okay. Good, even. Because it didn't mean anything was coming when it was Dante. If he wanted it to go farther than cuddling, he'd fucking ask. He was safe. And it felt really nice to be able to just be that close to somebody, to know he was there and he was safe to be close to and it was okay.

I was blackboxed into stillness on the floor in a human's house. Dante had blackboxed me. It was most certainly not okay.

"I think I can fix this, 'Taire. If you just calm down and listen to me for a while. This guy I hooked up with? He's part of this emancipationist organization. They've got me *teaching*. I've been living here with Nate... he's been really good to me. I've been really happy, for the first time in longer than I can remember. And now that I know you're alive, now that I've got you here... God, 'Taire, I thought you were dead!"

He stopped talking, just petting my hair a little, and I could feel his hand trembling. He wanted to hug me. But he wasn't, because I couldn't tell him if it was okay or not. I wondered how long he'd boxed me for. Might have been five minutes, might have been an hour. No knowing when I'd come out of it unless he decided to tell me, and he didn't seem to feel like telling me.

But it was Dante. He was alive, and he was real, and he was there. He was petting my hair and talking to me about how happy he was to be holed up in the house of some human who was probably fucking him. Some human who was *keeping* him, who *owned* him.

"I was reading, when I heard you. Came to check

out the noise and there you were, back from the dead, walking around in Nate's living room." His hand shivered again, and I heard him swallow. "When you get back up, if you'll let me, I'd like to do a read on you and see if you're okay. We've got stuff here, nutrient syrup and everything. I could fill up your reservoir. I don't know if you remember how awesome that feels, when you've been empty for a while. We've got food, too, don't know the last time you ate. Even if you decide you're gonna..." he faltered, swallowing hard. "If you want to take off when you get up, I want to give you a good head start, you know? Get a solid meal in you and fill up your reservoirs and all. When was the last time you slept? I'd have your back if you wanted to sleep. It's safe to sleep here."

What was it like to have a place where it was safe to sleep? Dante wasn't stupid, and hearing him talk it was seeming less and less likely that he'd been reprogrammed. He was too Dante still. Talking about taking care of me. So if he didn't want to run while the running was good... had to be a reason for that. Dante always knew what he was doing.

I sobbed. It was the first indication that I had any kind of control over my body again, and Dante's reaction was immediate. He curled up around me, pressing his lips up against the back of my neck, not even really a kiss just... there. Right under the jack, where the skin was almost painfully sensitive.

"Is he fucking you?" I asked, and was suddenly sorry that those had been my first words because it sounded really shitty, even in my own ears.

"We've been intimate," Dante said, carefully, his words clean and precise. I sobbed again, closing my eyes, curling up the rest of the way into a tight little ball on the floor.

"And you still won't let me..." I didn't know how to finish what I was going to say. Everything sounded stupid. Let me rescue you, let me take you out of here... let me take care of you...

Like Dante always took care of me.

Like he was talking about taking care of me just now.

"No, I won't. I like this, okay? I like being able to look humans in the eye. Being able to have conversations. Being able to teach... I've never been able to do that, and it's what I spent my whole life training to do. Being able to just... be alive, without always worrying about what's going to happen next or who's going to fuck you over or how you're likely to get off-lined in the next day or two. You know what it's like to *relax*, 'Taire? What it's like to feel safe?" He sighed, his breath warm against the back of my neck, his arms twining around me. "Is it so hard to get why I enjoy it?"

"So you're fine with getting fucked for the perks?" I said through my teeth.

"Sleeping with Nate *is* one of the perks."

"The fuck is wrong with you?" I hissed. "Your brain would have to be fried for you to... like..." my voice choked out into ragged breaths.

"To like feeling good?" Dante asked, quietly. "To like having someone touch me and have it feel like it matters? You know how many people in this world have ever given a damn about how I feel?"

"And you think he does?" I spat between gasps. I laughed a little, wanting to say *I care how you feel, asshole!* but not saying it. Instead I choked out, "Let me tell you something, Dante. You are a fucking *appliance* to him. What do you figure will happen when he gets bored with you?"

"I expect I'll find somewhere else to live and hopefully continue teaching classes. I'm already building a network of associations at the Center. I'm meeting people. I'm actually getting to have conversations with people—with humans. That's what registration means, all right? It means that I've got options. That there are humans who think I'm useful and who'll want me around."

He pressed his lips to the back of my neck again.

"I want you to be around, 'Taire. I want you to stay and have a meal and meet Nate."

I laid there quietly, my eyes stinging. Had to keep it together. It was so hard to keep it together when Dante was holding me. He knew that, and this was dirty of him to make me agree to things while he was cuddled up against me. But I wasn't gonna ask him to stop, either.

"You remember the first smart-guy thing you ever said to me?" I asked, trying to keep my breath from hitching, "Like for real, the first time you and I were alone after... we met."

I could hear Dante swallow, feel his breath as it hitched a little.

"Remind me?"

"It was some poetry thing. You said it was from a play. You should know. If they didn't screw around with your head, you should fucking know, Dante."

He moved then, pulling up off of me and pulling at my shoulder so that I turned and for the first time

202

since he's blackboxed me he was looking at my face, looking at my eyes. It was almost too much, the way he fixed me with one of those "checking out the details" looks. He had eyes like human eyes that way—not like mine that just *looked* human; Dante's eyes could *act* human. He blinked a couple of times.

"As flies to wanton boys, are we to the gods; they kill us for their sport."

Something kind of pulled apart someplace in my chest, because that was right. That was the first thing he'd ever said to me that didn't have to do with what was going on right then. The first thing he'd said that let on how he was a smart guy. He remembered. Which meant that he was still Dante.

I was quiet for a really long time.

And then I heard the door open.

Nate

I came home to find Dante standing at the edge of the kitchen, helping a cygenic I'd never seen before to his feet. He was skinny, dirty, and beat up. Exactly the kind of cygenic that might turn up on the doorstep of the Center on any given day.

But this wasn't the Center. This was my house. Beat up strays were not supposed to show up at my house. They weren't supposed to know where my house was.

I had a moment of dull panic, wondering what the fuck was going on, but Dante turned to me and locked his eyes on me and there was something... authoritative about his gaze. Something I'd never seen in a cygenic's eyes, not even Lisa's. Something that said *I am taking care of this situation.*

"Nate, this is 'Taire," Dante said, his voice like cut glass. "He is my dearest friend and until several minutes ago I believed that he'd been put offline. We need to discuss the ramifications of his presence here."

I nodded numbly, putting the bag of groceries I was carrying down. I watched Dante sling his arm around the other cygenic's shoulders and start leading him to the living room. I followed and found myself sitting on the sofa opposite the two of them.

Dante's friend wouldn't look at me. Wouldn't look up at all. He was sitting hunched and tense, like he might bolt at any second. He was wiry, skinny as hell, but not slender—big in the bone structure. He'd be a built kind of guy, if he got regular meals. Square jaw, wide forehead, deep-set eyes. His nose was prominent, little crooked, crushed along the bridge in a way that indicated it had been broken. Probably more than once. The structure of his face was... not what cygenics usually looked like. Not sculpted and prettified and artistic. He looked so *average*. His hair was dark, almost black, reflecting a synthetic silver in the afternoon sun that came filtering through the curtains. Gunmetal. That was the name for that color. It looked like he'd been keeping it short with a pocket knife.

He glanced fleetingly at Dante before looking at his feet again. He had almost human eyes; watery gray with just a hint of metallic silver. It was mildly disconcerting.

Overall, it was like "human" was what someone had been aiming for in designing him. Not the idealized version that most cygenics represented, big-eyed and soft-mouthed and symmetrical, but something far more natural. A replica human instead of a doll.

"'Taire and I were mutual victims of the same sex-trafficking operation, the situation I found myself in immediately after my tour of duty at Mass General. He was instrumental in helping me to adapt to that situation and survive long enough to escape it," Dante said, running his hand up and down the other cygenic's back while he spoke. I was watching the tension bleed out of him slowly, like he was trying to resist. Like he didn't want to relax, but was relaxing anyway.

"We could go to the Center..." I started, only to have Dante interrupt me.

"No, he needs—" Dante began, catching my eyes again, looking at me with a kind of steely desperation. "He needs *me*. He needs a shower and a hot meal and a change of clothes and a good night's sleep. He needs to know he's *safe*. Whatever happens after that, if you can't let him stay, please just—before we get the agency involved—please just let me make sure he's all right. I need to know he's all right."

"You should be telling him what I'm good for, if you want him to keep me," the other cygenic, apparently 'Taire, said through his teeth. He was still looking at his feet, his hands balled into fists, every muscle tense.

"'Taire, this isn't about that," Dante said, stroking his hair. Something about the way he did it made me twitch a little.

"Like hell it isn't," 'Taire said, his voice tight, like he was trying not to cry. "You're trying to sell me to your master. Not doing a very good job at it, either."

He looked up at me, meeting my eyes, and I felt the breath go out of me like I'd been punched in the gut because he had those eyes that I knew so well from the Center. Those dull, hopeless, "You're gonna do whatever you want to me and there's nothing I can do about it, so why bother fighting?" eyes.

"I'd make myself useful to you, Master. Anything you wanted from me. Just... please. Please let me stay with Dante?"

"I'm not interested in owning you," I said, and immediately wished that I hadn't said it in those words because 'Taire's face a broke. A visible shattering behind his eyes, a tremor in his muscles that screamed bitterness and confusion and hopelessness. I realized that he was younger than I'd first thought, maybe even younger than Dante. Younger than dispossessed cygenics were supposed to be.

"Please..." he said, then closed his eyes hard and looked down, not elaborating on that.

Dante wrapped up around him, kissing the crown of his head. I felt the bottom drop out of my stomach, because I knew what I was seeing.

'Taire wasn't Dante's friend. He was his boyfriend. Someone with a long shared history of pain, someone who would actually understand him. Someone with whom relationships weren't transactional; an equal. Someone who didn't fucking *own* him.

Someone he loved.

Part of me had wondered, more and more often as I got older, if Lisa had loved me. I'd always loved her like a mother, but she hadn't gotten to choose about being my mom. In my more morose moments, I debated with myself whether she *could* love me, if any cygenic could really love, or could really love a human, or if love even counted if it was programmed in. I'd never talked about it with her; it would have hurt her to think that I doubted her love for me.

Nobody had programmed Dante to love 'Taire, or programmed 'Taire to love him back.

I didn't stand a chance against that.

"You're right about him needing a shower," I

said, lamely. "Why don't you two go deal with that and I'll throw together something for dinner?"

Dante looked up at me with that same painful gratitude on his face that he'd had that first night when I'd offered him some vanilla calcium supplement. Like he'd been expecting some monstrous response and was overjoyed that I was being reasonable.

'Taire, still wrapped in Dante's arms, looked at me like he was trying to find the catch.

I couldn't stand it, the both of them looking at me like that, so I got up and went to the kitchen, swallowing hard, wondering what the hell I was supposed to do now.

'Taire

"You want to shower alone, or..." Dante began, putting the clothes he'd got for me to wear down on the edge of the sink.

"Don't leave me," I yelped, sounding utterly pathetic.

Dante moved fast and was *there*, wrapped around me, his forehead pressed against mine. He kept on holding me until I could breathe again. I was in some human's house, and the human was wandering around out there somewhere, doing who knew what. Calling reclamation and recycling, maybe, or getting a blackbox ready, or just waiting.

But Dante was with me. It would be okay, as long as Dante was with me.

He started shucking off his clothes when he pulled away from me, and I took the hint.

Something shiny caught my eye and when he turned around I saw that he had his nipples pierced.

"When'd that happen?" I asked, finding that I couldn't look away. It looked painful, where metal met flesh. Skin around jacks was oversensitive, how did that have to be when it was already something as sensitive as a nipple...

"It's kind of a long story," he said, sighing.

"They hurt?"

"No. When I got them, yeah, but Nate ran a cellular regenerator over them for me. They don't hurt now. They're... fun."

I didn't know what to say to that. Dante shrugged and turned on the water.

I'd never have guessed that having the water be warm could make such a difference about how showers were. I knew it'd probably be nicer but... but this was bliss. There hadn't been hot water at Sir's place and my first master had only ever let me wash with a bucket and a cloth. I found myself purring under the spray, turning my face up to meet it, feeling the way the water ran down my neck and chest.

Dante washed my hair. He didn't have to; I wasn't so useless that I didn't know how to get myself clean—but I let him do it anyway just to feel his hands on me. Because he liked touching me, and I liked him touching me, and it had been so long for both of us. Because we had this, right now, and I didn't know if I was ever gonna get this again, if Dante's master would let us.

He turned me around and kissed me, right under the hot spray of the shower, and it didn't matter what was gonna happen even five minutes later because this was happening right now. Dante was in my arms, kissing me, pressing up against me. This was real.

He broke the kiss, pulling back just enough to look at me. To look me in the eyes like I was the most important thing in the world. I had to close my eyes, because when Dante looked at me like that I felt like my heart was trying to pull itself apart.

"I thought I'd lost you, 'Taire," he said, so soft I

could only just hear him over the rushing water. "Didn't even process it, not really, I've just been putting it out of my mind since I heard that you got cut from KJ's group."

"How'd you hear that?" I asked, opening my eyes but keeping them down. Looking at the water pooling in the little hollow just above his collarbone.

"There's a guy at the Center, Nines, used to be the leader of the group in the territory next to ours. He told me." Dante leaned in, his lips right next to mine. "But I don't want to talk about anything right now. I just want to enjoy this. You being alive and being with me, being here."

I hummed a little, agreement and appreciation as he ran his soap-slick hands up and down my back. Lower, sliding along my ass and thighs, making me feel light-headed. Should have expected this; Dante did always like to go straight for sex any time something big happened, good or bad.

Not that I minded at all.

He slid down to his knees, fluid as the water, and took me in his mouth. I bit my hand to keep from moaning, because I was pretty sure that Dante's master wasn't supposed to know that he was blowing me in the shower.

Dante's mouth was unreal. The things he did with his lips and tongue made me jealous, because I was pretty sure I'd never been that good. The fact that he wanted to do them to *me* made me want to cry. I didn't deserve to feel this good.

I didn't deserve to come as hard as I did. He pulled back, eyes closed, taking it on the face. Letting the shower wash it away. Smiling, looking up at me through wet eyelashes like he was some kind of perfect god of sex. My knees already felt weak, and it seemed natural to drop down next to him and hug him tight.

"I'm not gonna let anyone take you from me, 'Taire," he said into my ear. "Never again."

I wanted to believe him. I wanted so bad for that to be true.

But that kind of thing wasn't ever true for me.

I felt bad that he'd gotten me off and I didn't get him off, but he didn't seem interested in that right now, and I was actually really glad he didn't, because I didn't think I had it in me to be any good. I was just so damned tired. Having him suck me off had only made it worse. I didn't even want to move; I could have been really happy to just stay there on the floor of the shower with the hot water falling on us, with Dante holding me, forever.

We stayed kneeling there together for a little while before he got up and turned the water off.

The clothes he gave me to wear when we'd dried off smelled like laundry. Clean and soft and comfortable, sliding on like a second skin. Didn't chafe or itch or tug or anything. I hadn't ever had clothes this nice.

I expected him to bring me back to where his master was waiting, but he brought me to a different room instead, a bedroom. Like the client rooms back at Sir's place, only there weren't any cameras and it didn't reek. There was a cat laying in the middle of the bed. It took one look at me and jumped off, darting out of the room.

"That's Whiskers. He doesn't like strangers," Dante said, crossing the room to open up a cabinet and pulling out a jack injector. I froze. Jack injectors were scary shit, and Dante handling one seemed... wrong, somehow.

"When was the last time you had your reservoir filled up?" he said, catching my eyes.

"Not since I was little," I said, trying to swallow the lump in my throat.

"You're gonna like this," he said, smiling. A gentle, nice smile, the kind that brought my guard crashing down because it was Dante and Dante was a smart guy who knew that he was doing.

Dante wouldn't hurt me.

I still tensed up, watching him fill the jack injector up with something from a bottle. There was writing on it, probably said what it was. That didn't do me a damned bit of good, but Dante could read.

I couldn't help thinking about Tango and how he'd died as Dante lined the jack injector up to the back of my neck. As he pushed it until it slid in and clicked into place. As I felt the fluid going in.

It was like he'd flicked a switch. All the nagging alarms in the back of my head turned off at once, and the "good boy" chemicals started pumping out. Yes. Yes this was how it was supposed to be. This was how it was always supposed to have been. A warm sense of fullness all down my back. Muscles along my spine that were always tight going slack for the first time in longer than I could remember. I was moaning, low and loud, halfway sobbing with how good it was.

Dante was talking.

Not at me.

When the reeling stopped and the pure bliss faded back into something I could handle, Dante's master was standing in front of me looking scared. Dante had an arm curled around me. Protecting me. That felt... really good.

"He's been living with deficiency alarms for *years*, Nate," Dante was saying. "Far longer than I ever did. What did you expect? We should get some food in him, soon. Back the rush up with something real."

His master was looking at him and at me and at him again with the kind of confused uncertainty you didn't see much in humans. Like he was asking Dante what he should do. He smiled a little bit, scratching the back of his neck.

"I've got a soup on..."

"That's wonderful. That's perfect. Thank you," Dante said, and it didn't sound fake.

Dante's master looked like he was about to leave again, but Dante said, "Hey, Nate," and tossed his head for him to come closer. He did come closer, looking confused.

Dante leaned past me to kiss him. To put the hand that wasn't wrapped around me up to the side of his face, caressing it all gentle and sweet and nice. I watched Dante's master get into it, his neck muscles tensing and then relaxing again. Watched how Dante pulled him into it.

It didn't hurt as much as I'd thought it would, watching Dante kiss him. It wasn't like watching him kiss Sir, or Angelo, or one of the clients back at Sir's place. It wasn't all hollow and stiff. It looked... nice.

It looked the way it felt when Dante kissed *me*.

"We're going to make this work, okay?" Dante said to his master when the kiss broke. "You and 'Taire and I. We'll make it work."

214

Dante's master looked a little bit dazed, but he nodded before he walked out again.

"He's really nice with you, isn't he," I said quietly, once he was gone.

"Yeah," Dante said, petting my hair. "He is."

"He's not gonna want me. Not when he already has you."

"*I* want you. I think you're underestimating the importance of that."

I didn't really get what he meant by that, but I was too wiped out to argue about it.

I'd never figured on having a master again. On anyone wanting to own me, unless maybe another situation like Sir's place and even then... I wasn't young enough anymore to be a novelty, and I wasn't pretty like Dante, so who was gonna want me even for that? I'd figured that if humans got their hands on me it would just be to scrub out my head and throw me into manufacturing or something. Or just recycle me. I probably wasn't worth the trouble of reprogramming.

The idea rattled around in my head that I could... have someone telling me what to do again. I didn't want that. Except I kind of did. I wasn't any good at living on the street, not without Dante, and Dante always... told me what to do. KJ'd told me what to do. It felt better when someone was telling me what to do. Might have been hardwired into my head, wanting someone else calling the shots. That was the kind of thing humans would do.

And Maybe Dante's master would keep me, and I'd have Dante to tell me what to do and his Master too and... and they'd keep me safe.

It was like someone had loosened a knot someplace in my chest, just thinking about that.

Wasn't long after that that Dante made me get up and go back to the first room we'd been in, the one with the screen in it, and Dante's master brought out bowls of soup for all of us. He ate the same food he gave us. It was bizarre. Dante didn't act like it was.

I made an orgasmic noise when I tasted it, absolutely sure that I'd never been allowed to eat anything this good. I'd eaten human food before, even hot sometimes, but never anything like this. Never anything that a human would have thought it was okay to eat. I was kind of foggy on the details of where food came from, but I was pretty sure this hadn't come out of a can.

When my soup was gone, Dante's master turned to me and asked, "Are you feeling better, 'Taire?"

"Yes, sir," I said quietly, drawing my knees up, curling into the corner where back of the sofa met the arm, because curling up felt better. It was stupid. Wasn't going to make any difference. Never did.

"Good... that's good. Look, I'm kind of in over my head here, so... you can stay as long as you need to, all right? I'm not going to kick you out or anything. Do you know who you're registered to? We might need to get your registration fixed, it's a legal issue..."

"I'm not registered to anyone. My first owner didn't register me," I said, trying to curl up into myself even more. Dante was right there next to me. That kept me from losing it.

I couldn't ever remember talking to a human. Talked at by them, yeah. Repeating things I was told to say, for their entertainment. I'd done that. But not, like, having a conversation. This wasn't how humans acted. They didn't want your opinion. They didn't make offers. Humans gave orders. Humans did things to you. You took it, or you fought it if you were really royally stupid, but you didn't sit around talking about it.

I was tired. Really, really tired. A belly full of hot food wasn't helping that. All my internals were cooing at me, pumping out the happy chemical rewards because I'd got my reservoirs filled up and backed it with real food. Because I was clean and comfortable and safe. There had to have been a painkiller in the stuff he'd shot me up with, because what else could explain the perpetual headache just kind of rolling back into a soft dense fog? The thought made me twitch inwardly. Fucking head games. Just... handed food, like it was no big deal. Just given medicine, just made to feel calm and happy and anything but sharp. Helpless, here in a human's home.

Feeling good about it.

I'd have preferred being blackboxed, or pinned. That was at least clear, I knew where I stood with that. I didn't have to worry about what the human was playing at. Didn't have to worry about getting lost in it, getting stupid. It was better when it was scary, when it hurt, when I could just take myself out of it. This felt too good to take myself out of.

Dante's master smiled too much.

He didn't like me, he wasn't happy that I was here, but he kept smiling. He had the same kind of sad, tender little smile Dante had. It felt wrong to see a human smile like that, wrong in a way that made my throat tighten up.

Because what if it was real? What if this was actually going to be okay? What if Dante was right?

"Do you know what your original intended function was..." he started, and Dante's head shot up to glare at him like it wasn't an okay thing to ask. Kind of look that'd have gotten him twitchboxed or popped in the mouth by any other human, because you weren't supposed to look at humans like that. Dante's master didn't do that though. Didn't even look mad. He just looked sorry.

"I was a kid," I said, swallowing hard. "Dante says I got commissioned in Belarus. There's no laws there about cygenic kids. Guy who commissioned me... First thing I remember, ever, is him pulling me out of a cardboard box. Had me on my back like ten minutes later. He kept me in a closet. In a box. Brought me out when he wanted to play, had me pinned pretty much all the time he wasn't playing with me. Fed me on paste, and never anything else. He told me I was a good boy. His best boy. Taught me how to do... stuff. I'm good at it, now. He sold me when I got too old for him. There's videos you could probably find online of me... of me and Dante together, if you want."

The look on his face made it pretty clear that he didn't, so I kept talking.

"I was at that place he sold me to for years before the guy bought Dante. Didn't even think about trying to get out of it, think about life being anything else. Dante... kind of changed everything for me. He's the only one who's ever cared about it."

"You love him," Dante's master said. It wasn't a question. I sat there staring at him, trying to figure out what he wanted. I looked at Dante, wondering what there was to say to that and wondering what it meant and wondering if it was true. Because there was nothing I wouldn't do for Dante, down to getting wiped or getting off-lined, and maybe that's what love was?

Dante looked like he was hurt. He had this look on his face like he was trying not to lose it, and Dante never looked like that. I kind of wanted to lean in and kiss him, but I was pretty sure his master would be pissed if I did that.

"I don't know if that's a word I'm allowed to use," I said, looking down at my hands again. "Dante matters. Dante's all that matters. So if... I don't know what you want from me. Please. I just want to stay with Dante. I'll do anything you want me to do."

It felt wrong to be offering myself up to a human who didn't even want me. Made me feel hollow and broken and useless. He had Dante already. I felt my throat closing up and my eyes stinging, and crying in front of humans was the worst thing, because they either hated it and got pissed at you for crying or they liked it and that was worse, usually.

"I'm really tired," I said, trying to make it not sound like sobbing. "I came here from downtown and I've been tracking Dante everywhere since Angelo took him and I finally found him and he wouldn't come with me and he's not even reprogrammed and what am I even supposed to do now? I don't have... I don't... there's nothing. I'm not anything. You can fuck me or reprogram me or off-line me, whatever, I don't even care if I'm not gonna be with Dante. I just can't anymore, sneaking around and eating out of the trash and hoping I don't get caught... and then the shower, and the clothes, and Dante shoots me up with jack juice, and you give me food, and I feel like every thing's soft and foggy and... and I just want to lay the fuck down and I *can't*. So just do what you're gonna do, okay? Tell me what you want."

Dante wrapped himself up around me again, and it felt so good that I couldn't keep the sob in. I closed my eyes and held my breath and waited.

"You should take him to bed, Dante," Dante's master said, sounding far away. "We can talk about what happens next tomorrow."

And that was it. I was gonna get put in a bed, and I was gonna get to sleep, and maybe if I was really lucky Dante was gonna get to sleep with me.

Maybe he was gonna keep me.

Maybe it was gonna be okay.

Nate

I turned on the TV after Dante and his friend disappeared into Dante's room, but I didn't really watch it. I sat there on the sofa, staring in the general direction of the TV, feeling the same kind of numb I'd felt the first morning I'd woken up after Charles had gone. Walking around my house with all his stuff missing, still able to smell him in my clothes.

'Taire and Dante were so obviously, perfectly in love with each other. I didn't have any right to get in the way of that—to want Dante to care about me. It was stupid and selfish to even think of.

Whiskers hopped up on the sofa and made a little chirping noise, crawling up under my hand. I petted him absently.

"He's asleep," Dante said, padding quietly into the room. "In my bed."

"That... makes sense," I replied, not looking up at him because I was afraid of what I'd see there. Because I'd been stupid enough to think that Dante could love me. Because I'd been stupid enough to fall for him on the rebound and because I was the kind of idiot who could only fall for the wrong guy and I didn't want to see the look in his eyes as he tried to let me down easy.

"Where do you want me to sleep tonight?" he asked, his voice tight and brittle.

"You shouldn't be asking me that. I can't make that decision for you," I said. "I don't own you, Dante. I'm not your master."

The words came out harsher than I meant them to. Whiskers darted away, sensing the mood.

"I need to know if getting 'Taire back from the dead means losing you," he said, the brittleness in his voice turning icy. I did look up then, and found him standing there, looking at me with pain on his face. "I don't want to lose you, Nate. I don't want to choose between you. I want you. I want you so bad that it makes my heart hurt. But he *needs* me."

"And I don't," I said bitterly, looking down again. I heard him moving, but I didn't expect him to abruptly straddle my lap and grab my face. To make me look at him. I froze, mouth halfway open.

"You do need me, Nate. Do you think I don't know that? That what you and I have is complicated and thorny and socially problematic and entirely worth having despite that? I want you. I've wanted you from the beginning. I've fought for you to see that. You keep making me having this fight with you, and god damn it I *will* keep fighting. But I want him too. I don't want to have to choose between you."

I didn't resist when he leaned in to kiss me. I felt like I should have, but I couldn't. Dante straddling my lap, taking my mouth and making me his, like he had the first time.

Dante had a plan. Dante was all slick tongue and nibbling teeth and firm hands and *he had a plan* and I was in it.

And wasn't that enough? That Dante had me in his plans?

If I let him, he was probably going to put things in order. I'd seen that in his eyes right at that first moment when he was helping his friend up off the floor, that resolute confidence that shit would be handled and all I had to do was follow the plan.

It probably wasn't okay, on a lot of different levels, that thinking about those facts was making me hard. It probably indicated that I was fundamentally fucked up and should probably go see a therapist or something.

But Dante started grinding when he took notice, making a pleased noise against my mouth, and I knew that whatever Dante's plans were, I wanted to be in them.

He pulled away far enough to look me in the eyes, his hands still cupping the sides of my face, and asked,

"Can I take you to bed?"

"...Yeah," I said, closing my eyes. He backed off, letting me get up. He didn't pull me up like he had the first time; this was a less urgent affair. He led me to my bedroom with a hand in the middle of my back, smiling sensuously at me the whole time, and all I could think was that I had never done anything to deserve him. Brilliant, beautiful Dante. All lean muscle and smooth skin and casual, confident sureness in what he was doing. All the shit he'd obviously been through seemed to roll off him; here he was dealing with *my* stupid baggage. I was supposed to be the therapist, the one who helped cygenics work through their shit and try to get their lives to turn out okay.

"You want to take your clothes off, or should I help?" he asked playfully as he closed the bedroom door. I kicked out of my shoes and pulled my shirt up over my head without preamble, some part of me not quite convinced that this was happening. That Dante was here, with me, while another cygenic who clearly loved him was asleep in Baba's old room. That he'd picked *me*.

But then he was peeling out of his clothes and pushing me back onto the bed and climbing on top of me, and there wasn't time to really dwell on how surreal any of this was. All there was the slide of skin on skin, the taste of Dante's mouth on mine, the sound of my own labored breathing as he kissed his way down my throat. I turned my head, baring more of it for him, and he licked his way to the tender spot just under the edge of my jaw and sucked.

"Don't mark me up," I hissed, before I'd meant to. Kind of expected him to bite me and shush me and tell me not to worry. But he just paused, not sucking anymore, placing a painfully gentle kiss and then pulling back entirely to say,

"Okay. Won't. You want me to..."

"Kiss me," I said, swallowing hard, not wanting to have a conversation about my hangups because I didn't want to ruin this. He seemed to be okay with that, because he pulled me into another of those mind-searing kisses of his, hands on my shoulder pinning me down into the mattress. Dragging his fingers down my chest and belly, pinning my hips as he followed that path with his mouth, moving inexorably downward until I felt his breath on my straining cock the instant before he took me in his mouth. He was so

224

unbelievably *good* at this! I lost myself in it, in the velvet slide of his tongue and the tight heat of his throat and the absolutely evil things he could do with his lips. Watching him through half-lidded eyes as he pulled back and stuck his fingers in his mouth, licking them obscenely before moving to press them up against my ass. He paused, looking up at me, kissing the head of my cock as he did. Pressing his fingers in just a little bit. Watching me.

"Yeah," I whispered, when I realized that he was waiting for permission. He smiled, and it was a wicked, beautiful smile. He pushed his fingers inside me, swallowing me to the root. I closed my eyes and moaned, then bit my lip to keep from moaning because there was someone trying to sleep down the hall. Dante curled his fingers inside me and lightning shot up my spine and it took all my willpower not to come right then. I opened my eyes again to find him still looking at me, meeting my eyes and asking,

"Can I fuck you, Nate?"

I couldn't even form the word, I just nodded frantically, then he was getting up and standing at the edge of the bed, reaching past me to the lube on the night stand, lubing up his cock and looking down at me like... like I was what he wanted. Not something he was settling for, not just good enough, but actually what he wanted.

I closed my eyes as he slid his hands up the backs of my thighs to get my legs where he wanted them, urging me into position, because that was too much. Because I was pretty sure that watching him looking at me like that would make me come sooner than I wanted to. It occurred to me in the moment before he pressed forward that this was the first time I'd been fucked since Charles.

Dante was better than Charles.

He moved into me like water, filling up all the hollow places. Like he *belonged* in me. There wasn't any struggle, there wasn't any force. He didn't give me orders or make me beg. Everything was just... self-evident. Dante's cock slid into me in one long fluid motion, filling me up, making me his. He kept coming forward until he was leaning over my chest, his lips against my breastbone, sweat-damp hair brushing against my skin. I put my arms around him, holding him there, resisting the urge to drag my fingers down his spine because I didn't want to scratch him up.

"Nate, you are so... *good*..." he said, haltingly, as he started to move. Slow, shallow strokes at first, and I watched his throat as he swallowed hard, watched his mouth as he bit his lip in concentration, adjusting his angle in minute increments until he found the one that made me gasp and shudder and wrap my legs around him to pull him in. It made my cock, thus far neglected, press into his abs. He laughed, a choked, almost moaning sound, raising his head to smile at me.

"Good?" he said, his voice labored.

"So fucking good," I answered, closing my eyes again.

"Don't know how long I can last," he admitted. "It's a while since... ah... since I've done this and... and you're so *hot*..." he broke off into an incoherent moan, and there was something unbearable about hearing Dante lose coherence. His face in raw bliss and determination was the most perfect thing I'd ever seen. His cock buried inside me was the most perfect thing I'd ever felt.

I came, and it was like my soul was pouring out of me. It wasn't even the brilliant release that sex with Dante always brought; it was something deeper and purer and more consuming.

"I love you," I panted.

He crushed my mouth with his, a kiss that threatened to bruise my lips as he drove hard into me and shuddered and came. I felt every instant of it in absolute, mind-blowing clarity.

After a moment of perfect stillness, Dante moved to climb onto the bed beside me, pulling me up and wrapping around me to cuddle in the sticky, sweaty aftermath.

I'd told him I loved him.

Stupid, clingy, and inviting conflict since I was not the only one in the house making that claim. It wasn't that I didn't mean it... it was just... this wasn't the time to say that kind of thing. I'd known him for a *week*. If he hadn't fucked me senseless, I could have just kept sitting on that information until the time was right.

But he had. And here he was purring into my ear, curled against me, not arguing about it.

And I loved him.

Dante

I heard movement, and opened my eyes.

Hyper-alertness was the sort of skill one picked up living on the streets; the ability to snap awake and get on one's feet at any sign of danger whatsoever. It took me a moment to unravel the events of the evening and realize that it probably wasn't actually danger. But it was someone moving around the house.

Nate slept the sleep of the blameless, and nothing short of a scream could wake him. He remained blissfully oblivious as I slipped out of bed to investigate, pausing to locate my sleeping attire and dress.

I found 'Taire sitting on the sofa in the living room, looking lost. Whiskers was sitting on the coffee table, tail twitching angrily, looking at him with cold judgment.

"Did you kick the cat off the sofa?" I asked.

'Taire startled, looking up at me with terror in his eyes that immediately melted when he saw me. He was looking at me like I was the answer to all of his problems.

"I wasn't sure if I dreamed it," he said in a voice flooded with relief, "I had a dream and I woke up in that bed and these clothes and I was alone and..." he swallowed. "And I wasn't sure you were really here. Tried to find you but I don't know anything about this place."

"Can I turn on the light?" I asked, walking over to the light switch. He nodded, and I turned on the lights and came to sit beside him. Whiskers apparently found the light to be adding insult to injury, and flounced away in the manner uniquely perfected by affronted cats.

'Taire was hanging his head, looking at his hands.

"I didn't mean to wake anybody,...." he said.

"I had a screaming nightmare the first night I slept here," I confessed. "This is far less dramatic, in comparison."

"I don't think I can go back to sleep if I'm alone," he said, swallowing hard. "I mean the bed's comfy and all but... I did too much of that, last couple of months. Had some real bad scares, back when I was tracking you around Piss Street. Those guys who had you between Angelo and this guy... I swear I was so scared that you were gonna get wiped or off-lined, I just gave up on sleeping for a while."

I nodded, pushing back memories of those first few weeks at the brothel I'd burned down. I'd spent the first few days utterly unable to sleep, after the first attempt had been met with waking to a swift kick in the ribs. I'd eventually succumbed to exhaustion, and had been punished for that as well.

"It's safe to sleep here, 'Taire."

"How do you deal with it?" he asked, plaintively, "Feeling this fuzzy all the time? Does it stay like this? Like... the back of my head feels empty without something shouting at me about maintenance. And just... wearing clothes," he tugged at the front of his shirt, looking down at it like it was an alien thing, "and sleeping in beds and all? How do you keep sharp?"

"I don't. I don't have to. This is what relaxing feels like. You don't have to be on top of your game here; nothing's going to happen. Nate's a really excellent person. I know you haven't really had any positive experiences with humans at all, but I have. I spent twelve years living among and interacting with humans. Most of them aren't actively malicious. Some of them can even be very kind. Nate's one of the latter."

"My first master was real sweet with me too, you know that?" he said tightly. "I know it was fucked up because I was a kid... I mean I was a *little* kid right when he got me... but he was sweet, at first. He didn't want to hurt me. I didn't think it was fucked up then, because I didn't know any better. And then he sold me to Sir, and Sir was all about hurting, and the customers... and *that's* what humans are about, Dante. They want what they want out of you, and they get it. Sometimes they get it by being sweet, and sometimes they get it by being nasty, but they get what they want. Only way around that is not being around them, and... .and I don't think I can hack that. So what's he gonna want out of me that he doesn't already have from you, huh? I'm not like you, Dante. I'm not special."

I slid an arm around him and used my hand to guide his face back up so that I could kiss him. He allowed it. The same kind of mechanical, automatic non-resistance that he'd offered to clients at the brothel. Dissociated compliance, because it was better and safer to just let it happen. I didn't want that from

'Taire. I wanted to comfort him and... what comforted me wasn't always comforting to 'Taire. So I just pulled him close and held him for a while.

"You ought to pin me," he said eventually. "Keep me down, at least, so I'm good for whatever he wants to do with me in the morning. It's almost as good as sleeping anyhow."

"That's not happening, 'Taire," I said gently, untangling myself from him and standing and offering a hand. He looked a little wary, but he took it and got up.

"Where we goin'?"

"Bed. Come on. You shouldn't have to sleep alone."

He seemed more than a little confused when I took him by the wrist and hit the lights again, leading him down the hall in darkness. When we got back to Nate's room, 'Taire paused at the threshold like a spooked deer.

"He fucked you tonight," he whispered, swallowing. "I can smell..."

"If you want to be technical about it, I fucked him," I said softly. "Don't worry, 'Taire. He won't hurt you."

I turned to look at him, watching the bob of his Adam's apple as he swallowed, staring at Nate. In the moonlight, 'Taire was a chiaroscuro image of dark hair and pale skin and palpable anxiety.

"Is he gonna want to fuck me?" he asked, his voice small.

"Do you want him to?" I asked, putting a hand on his back, feeling the tension in his muscles. "I wasn't bullshitting you when I said that sleeping with him is one of the perks." I ran my hand up and down his back. Still tense. "You'd like it."

"If it's a thing I need to do to stay here, I'd rather know now," he hissed through his teeth, leaning back against my hand like he wanted to take a step back. I kept my hand steady, preventing retreat. 'Taire had spent enough time running.

"If you don't want it to happen, then it doesn't happen," I said, schooling my voice to soothing tones. "Hopping in bed with us doesn't obligate you to anything. Just... I know you can't sleep alone. I couldn't either. I'm pretty sure Nate's not great at it. I haven't asked or anything, but he's cuddly. I'd feel bad leaving him."

I could see him warring with himself, trying to fight my logic because he was scared. It felt extortionate, making him choose between sleeping alone or sleeping with both of us. But I'd already had this fight once with Nate. 'Taire was, not without good reason, terrified of humans. He wouldn't believe that he was safe until he was *shown*. Until I proved to him that Nate was trustworthy. Meanwhile, Nate wouldn't believe that I cared for him as much as I cared for 'Taire if he woke up alone and found me in 'Taire's bed. Co-sleeping was the only clear solution.

It would have been ideal to have Nate awake to negotiate this, to welcome 'Taire to sleep with us, and I briefly considered waking him... but if Nate said it, then 'Taire would take it as an order.

I was reasonably certain that I knew Nate well enough that he wouldn't be angry about waking to find both of us in his bed. It was a calculated risk, but those were my calculations: this wouldn't lead to catastrophic, irreparable consequences.

"I don't wanna make trouble," 'Taire whispered. "Humans get rid of you if you make trouble, and..."

"Shh. 'Taire, it's just sleeping. He's not going to hurt you. He's never hurt me—"

"You're special, Dante. I'm not," he interrupted, bitterly.

"You're special to me," I said, running my hand up and down his back until I felt the tension going out of it. "I just want to hold you, 'Taire. Let me?"

It was unfair of me to exploit the fact that 'Taire had a hard time saying no to any wish that I expressed so frankly, but when I climbed carefully back into bed, placing myself as a buffer between them, and felt 'Taire relax against me, I was entirely certain that it was for the greater good.

Nate

I woke up to the sound of breathing. Deep, even breaths in and out. Took me a moment to figure out what seemed out of place about it.

Too many breaths.

I opened my eyes and found myself looking at the back of Dante's head. He was cuddled up against me, one of my legs tangled between his, my arm around his waist. Past him, I saw 'Taire. He must have crawled into bed at some point during the night. He was on his back, one arm thrown up over his head, the other draped across his chest, holding one of Dante's hands. Even in sleep he looked worried; lines of anxiety permanently carved on his face.

I wanted to lean over and touch his face and ruffle his hair and tell him it wasn't his fault. That I wasn't gonna take out anything on him. That I wasn't gonna hurt him.

"I know you're awake," Dante whispered, snuggling a bit closer. "are you... okay with this? I didn't want to wake you, and I didn't want you to have to wake up alone, and 'Taire —"

"I'm not mad," I said, softly, kind of surprising myself with how much I meant it. I hugged him a little bit tighter, pressing a kiss to the back of his neck. He answered with a pleased murmur. I was coming to realize that, for Dante at least, the skin around the jack was acutely sensitive. The jacks on his wrists somewhat less so than the jack on the back of his neck, but any of them could produce a positive response when kissed.

I wondered if the same was true of 'Taire and immediately curtailed that line of thought as grossly inappropriate.

"You might want to put on some clothes before he wakes up," Dante said, something just the slightest bit smug creeping into his voice, grinding his ass against my crotch. My cock took immediate interest.

"You're incorrigible," I groaned, pulling away and sliding out of bed.

By the time I'd located my clothes and gotten dressed, Dante was wrapped around 'Taire and nuzzling his neck. It was a scene that made me pause because it managed, somehow, to be both sweet and innocent and disturbingly hot at the same time. 'Taire's casual admission from yesterday that there existed porn of the two of them sprang instantly and intrusively to mind. As did the fact that Dante was demonstrably exhibitionist, and 'Taire had expressly offered me sex as a placating tactic.

"Come back to bed," Dante murmured, "Not like you have anywhere to be this morning."

'Taire stirred a little at his words, blinking his eyes open and looking at Dante. I watched the anxiety on his face fade, replaced by a sleepy smile. It only lasted for a moment, and then the anxiety began to creep back in as he apparently gained more awareness of his present situation, but I'd seen it, just for a moment. I wanted to see it again.

Then those water-gray eyes were fixed on me and his face went blank, like he was waiting for orders. Like he was waiting to be told how he should look.

"Good morning," I said, feeling a bit at a loss and wondering if I shouldn't just excuse myself to take a shower or make breakfast or something.

"Nate," Dante said, making me look at him and instantly catching me in his gaze, direct and implacable, "come back to bed."

I couldn't argue with that.

I climbed back into bed behind Dante, not sure what to do with my hands, not quite daring to look at either of them. But Dante turned toward me, touching the side of my face. I let him guide me into a kiss, acutely aware that 'Taire was watching. Knowing that I was being judged made it especially important that this kiss be perfect; that I give Dante everything he wanted and more. That I could make Dante happy. It was stupid that I felt like I had to prove that, but I did. Had to show Dante's boyfriend that I was good enough for him. At least that was the plan—but Dante kissed me in a way that made me close my eyes, shorted out my brain and had me moaning into his mouth. My hands came up to cradle the back of his head, to play in his hair and run careful fingertips over the jack on the back of his neck. He purred. I opened my eyes to find 'Taire watching us with avid, almost studious interest. He caught me looking at him and the look on his face shifted back to blankness. I looked to Dante, and found that he was looking from 'Taire to me and back, something positively calculating in his eyes

Dante turned and kissed 'Taire on the mouth,

wrapping his arms around him and moving him, sliding himself underneath. I realized what he was doing and leaned back, as close as I could get to the edge of the bed without falling off. When Dante broke the kiss, he'd rolled 'Taire over so that he was between Dante and I. 'Taire froze when he realized that, looking at me and swallowing hard.

"Master," he said, meeting my eyes, his voice so perfect in its courteous capitulation that it hit me like a bucket of ice water, "what would you like me to do?"

And before I could answer, before I could tell him that I wasn't his master and to call me Nate, to tell him that I didn't want him to do anything, Dante started talking.

"Nate, you and I should show 'Taire just now good we can make him feel. You think you can make him feel as good as you make *me* feel?" He leaned close to me, murmuring into my ear, softly enough to be conspiratorial but loud enough that there was no doubt 'Taire could hear us, "Think we can make him come as hard as you made me come last night?"

"Would you like that?" I asked, closing my eyes, not sure if I was asking Dante or asking 'Taire or asking both of them at same time. It was all I could do to keep my voice steady.

It was 'Taire who answered, haltingly:

"Yes, sir."

'Taire

I said, "yes" because that was the thing you said to humans. Because doing what they wanted made it easier, made it safer. If saying yes to him meant that I got to stay with Dante, I could deal with it. Even though humans hurt. Even when the stuff they did didn't actually leave you bleeding and bruised, even when they were nice about it, humans *hurt*. Dante knew that, I knew he did. Couldn't really figure out what his angle was right now, pretty much shoving me at his master and smiling about it, like this was gonna end some other way.

There were times back at Sir's place when one of the customers would want both of us at once. Those were the worst, because having Dante watch made it so much harder for me to fake it with the customer. Watching Dante fake being into it... Dante was so good at faking. When it was just me and a human I could take myself out of it and not feel anything about it, say what the human told me to say and do what I was told to do, and make it not *matter*. When I had to watch it happening to Dante, when I had to know Dante was watching it happen to me, it was so much worse. Then after, back in our room, he'd hug me and kiss me and cry and mumble about getting out of that place and how we deserved better, and that hurt worse than anything.

But Dante was smiling down at me, one of those sweet sexy smiles he only got when he wanted to play. When he wanted me. The kind of smile I knew meant he was gonna make me feel good.

Was that something he could fake? Was that something he *would* fake, for this human?

Dante lay back down, wrapping himself around me from behind as I turned my head to look to his master. To see if it was okay, if he was allowed to hug me. If he was allowed to have his cock pressed up against my ass, reminding me that it was a damned long time since anyone had fucked me. Even before Dante'd gotten taken, when he and I had been living on the street together, we didn't actually fuck all that often because we didn't usually have anything to use as lube. Usually we just sucked each other, and stroked each other, and cuddled, and kissed, and it was more than enough. But Dante was grinding against me in a bed that smelled like sex, and I was pretty sure that I was gonna get fucked.

And it was probably just programming or past experience or whatever, but knowing that was getting me hard. No matter how I felt about how I was probably about to get fucked, my cock liked the idea.

Dante's master was looking at the two of us like he didn't know what to do, but his eyes were hungry. He wanted. What humans wanted, humans took. I froze, looking at him, licking my lips because they suddenly felt dry. Wished he'd just give me some orders to follow or start doing something so that I could figure out what he wanted from me, what I had to do to be good.

"You should kiss him, Nate," Dante said, leaning in to kiss the back of my neck, just under the jack. I closed my eyes and just let myself feel that. Tried to let myself relax into it because Dante knew what he was doing. Dante always knew what he was doing.

When Dante and his master had been kissing a couple of minutes ago... it had looked nice. Not like something I'd have minded happening to me.

I felt a hand on the side of my face and knew it wasn't Dante's hand. Tried not to tense up because tensing up just made everything hurt more than if you could relax and let it happen. Because I was pretty sure from all the petting and soft-talk that they wanted me relaxed.

"Can I kiss you, 'Taire?" Dante's master asked, right against my lips.

"Yeah?" I whispered, more like a question than an answer. But it was enough, because he came forward and pressed his lips against mine and he was so... gentle. Dante kissed the back of my neck again, and a little noise came out of me that wasn't quite a sob. I was caught there between the two of them, Dante's hand moving lazily up and down my chest and belly, Dante's master caressing the side of my face, Dante kissing and *tonguing* the skin just underneath the Jack, Dante's master kissing me on the lips... sweetly. Didn't bite me or stick his tongue down my throat or anything, just... just kind of brushed his lips against mine. Like he wanted me to feel it.

Like he wanted me to *like* it.

"You still like having your hair played with, 'Taire?" I heard Dante ask as he slid one of his legs between mine, pressing his thigh right up so that I could grind on it if I wanted to.

"Mmm-hmmm," I whined, not quite daring to actually speak because I didn't want his master to stop kissing me. The hand on the side of my face slid up and back, tangling in my hair, fingertips tracing lines on my scalp. I whimpered. Wasn't fair; Dante knew everything that got me off and he was letting the human in on it. His hands felt so nice, though. Dante's hands. Dante's master's hands. It was getting hard to keep track of whose were whose.

I never got into it like this, not with humans... humans never made it feel this good...

Dante's master put his forehead against mine, touching my face again, running his hands down the side of my neck, running his fingers down my chest. His nails dragged on the fabric of my T-shirt and it felt electric. I found myself leaning into it, making a desperate little noise. Arching like that, the tip of my cock pressed against his belly, and I wanted him to come closer so that I could get more contact.

"You having a good time, 'Taire?" Dante asked into my ear a second before sucking my earlobe into his mouth. I tilted my head and Dante's master moved to nuzzle at my neck and I actually *moaned.*

I opened my eyes and Dante's master was right there. He was looking at me and... and it didn't hurt. Because he had that same look in his dark, deep eyes that Dante had, like he was paying attention to me. Like this was actually about me, like it mattered how I felt—not just about my body or what he could get out of it.

I'd never thought humans could look like that.

I couldn't breathe until I closed my eyes.

The impulse came out of nowhere, and I felt my

cheeks flush because it was probably just training or programing or whatever, but Dante's master was right there and it was so easy to press my mouth against his, easy as breathing to be sucking on his tongue. He made a surprised noise that turned into a moan of approval, and I liked it.

I *liked* it.

"'Taire's really sensitive along the insides of his thighs," Dante said, his voice sounding thick, almost a purr. "You want Nate to touch you there, 'Taire?"

I broke the kiss and pulled back far enough to nod. Dante was being evil, and I might even have been mad about it if his master hadn't pushed my thighs apart and slid his hands along them, firm and warm and just a little demanding. He skirted just shy of my crotch and wound up with his hands on my hips, holding there. His hips came forward and I felt his cock, hot and hard and bigger than I'd expected, pressing against mine through the fabric of our clothes.

"Dante, I think your boyfriend wants me," Dante's master said, his voice deep and smooth and sounding pleased. It was always so good when humans were pleased with you.

"Nate, take your shirt off. Let him get a look at you," Dante said.

Dante's master sat up and peeled out of his shirt, dropping it over the side of the bed. He didn't even hesitate. Like Dante was the one in charge of all of this. Back when his master had been standing at the end of the bed, Dante'd basically ordered him to get back in it. And he'd listened.

Maybe he'd figured out, like I had a long time ago, that Dante knew what he was doing. That letting

Dante call the shots generally made things turn out okay.

Dante's master had nice skin; smooth and dark and clean. Nicer than I was used to seeing on humans. Humans like him didn't show up in places like Sir's place. He had the kind of skin that made me want to touch it, to see if it was as smooth as it looked.

"'Taire, you too," Dante purred.

I was slower to listen, and Dante kissed the back of my neck again, sliding his hands under the edge of my shirt, pulling me to sit up enough that he could get his hands underneath.

"Arms up," he whispered. I obeyed. He slid my shirt up and off me, my skin prickling with awareness as it was exposed. I had a nice body; it was something I'd been told a lot of times. I wasn't pretty like Dante, but my body was okay. I lay back down and looked at Dante's master looking at me. He looked pretty pleased with what he was seeing. He looked past me, looking at Dante, like he was checking with him. He smiled. He looked really nice when he smiled. Really... real. It wasn't a nasty smile, and it wasn't a hungry smile it was just...

It made me feel safe.

Dante ran his fingers down the length of my spine, and I arched, grinding against Dante's master, closing my eyes because it felt so incredibly good.

"If I wanted to suck you off, would that be okay?" Dante's master said into my ear.

"Yeah," I said, my voice sounding tight and desperate. "Yes. Please."

Dante shifted so that he was sitting up, pulling me up with him. Kneeling behind me. Dante's master pressed my thighs apart and crawled into the space he made, taking just enough time to look up at me and smile before moving in on me, sliding his hands under the waistband of my pants. I tried really hard not to think about other times humans had sucked me off, because most of the time it wasn't something that I wanted to happen. I tried to think of the times Dante's sucked me off instead, and how good he always made it.

Dante purring in my ear made that easier. Dante running his hands along my chest and fingering my nipples, kissing my neck and playing with my hair.

Dante's master slid my pants down and just... breathed on me for a couple of seconds. Kind of nuzzled up against my cock like he was getting friendly with it. The skin on his cheek wasn't quite smooth; it rasped a little. Because he hadn't shaved. Just that little bit of friction as the head of my cock glided across his cheek made me gasp.

Then he opened his mouth and sucked my cock inside, and I kind of stopped thinking at all for a while. Dante slid his hand up into my hair and made a fist, running his tongue in a circle all around the jack. I hissed, grabbing handfuls of bedsheets on either side of me, afraid to touch anything or anyone because I didn't want to interrupt. I didn't want any of this to stop. Teeth and tongue on the back of my neck. A hand tangled in my hair, tugging it. A hard cock grinding against my ass. Hands stroking up and down the insides of my thighs. The velvet slide of lips and tongue on my cock. A hand cupping and massaging my balls.

I closed my eyes and stopped trying to work out whose hands were whose because it didn't matter.

"I'm... I'm gonna come..." I whimpered, gritting my teeth, warning them because most of the time humans wanted to back off before I came. Wanted to get me desperate and keep me there, because I looked good desperate. But Dante's master responded by swallowing me down so that my cock was nestled up against the back of his throat. Dante sucked at my skin just under the jack hard enough that it had to be leaving a mark.

And I came, like I was breaking apart. Like nothing else mattered and I could just let go and feel it. I leaned back against Dante and let it roll through me, surprised that his master had let it happen. That I'd been allowed. That he was swallowing me down hard like it was exactly what he'd wanted to happen.

Dante's cock was pressing into the small of my back. He didn't seem to think it was too urgent a problem, because he was just cuddling me, purring into my ear. His master was sitting back, licking his lips and smiling at me like he'd won a prize.

"Isn't someone gonna fuck me?" I said, sounding more confused than sexy. You were supposed to sound sexy when you said stuff like that.

"Oh don't worry, 'Taire," Dante said into my ear, running his hand down my chest, digging his fingernails in just a little bit, "We're not done with you yet."

Dante

Things were going exceptionally well. I'd been very worried that 'Taire and Nate's assorted hangups would be an obstacle to this kind of intimacy—frankly hadn't expected the morning to hold more than cuddling and conversation and wearying negotiation while I pleaded the case that this was all right. But both of them were remarkable at following directions, and I had a talent for giving them.

I knew an opportunity when I saw one.

Awe-struck, post-orgasmic 'Taire laying in my arms was certainly an indication that I'd been a successful architect today. I tried not to look smug about it.

"Do you *want* someone to fuck you, 'Taire?" I asked playfully, nibbling on his ear. "Who do you want to fuck you? Me? Nate? Or would you rather watch while the two of us fuck? You getting fucked is by no means compulsory, if you'd rather not. There are so very many possibilities with three people..."

'Taire shuddered at my teasing words. Nate, still crouched between his legs, was looking up at me with a dawning comprehension in his lust-clouded eyes.

"I don't know... I just..." 'Taire stammered, still panting in the wake of orgasm.

"It's a lot to get used to. Why don't you just lie back and take it all in while Nate and I take care of each other?"

He nodded, and I directed him with caresses until he'd pulled himself up against the headboard, making space for Nate to come closer to me. Nate was looking painfully aroused, practically writhing.

And he was patiently waiting for my instructions.

I glanced at 'Taire, watching in fascination.

This was power. There were probably a thousand layers of analysis to be undertaken concerning the psychological ramifications of just how good it felt for both of them to be offering themselves up to my commands, considering the shifting power and agency I'd experienced in life. But I wasn't going to bother with them.

"Nate," I said, my voice thick with lust, "Lie on your back."

He obeyed without hesitation.

"'Taire, hand me that lube."

He did so.

I slicked Nate's cock down with teasing slowness, watching him gasp and squirm and bite his lip. I moved to straddle him, up on my knees, dragging my fingernails down his chest. Watching little lines of sensitivity raise up in their wake. Watching Nate close his eyes and moan.

I sank down on him, filling myself up with him, and it was perfect. I closed my eyes and stilled for a moment, exulting in this. Opened them again to find 'Taire looking at me in awe. I smiled at him, then looked to Nate, who still had his eyes closed. I braced my hands on his shoulders and *rode* him. This was a performance piece, and I did so enjoy performing. Knowing that 'Taire was watching, and that for once I was able to show him something beautiful. Knowing that I was driving Nate to slow, pleasurable insanity. Knowing that I could make this perfect... and that I could make this perfect in a thousand different ways, every day and night for the rest of our collective lives.

I came, moaning my pleasure in Nate's ear. I felt him come a moment after, answering with his own strangled cry, almost a sob, his arms going around me to hold me close. Listening to him breathe. Listening to 'Taire breathe. I shifted a little, rolling off of Nate to lay alongside him.

"'Taire, get over here," I purred. "Post-coital bliss is better shared."

'Taire came to my other side, curling against me so that I found myself pressed between the two of them, sweat-slick and almost uncomfortably hot and feeling incredibly pleased with myself.

This was going to work out beautifully.

Nate

Dante, with the infallibly logical excuse that the shower wasn't big enough for three people, had excused himself to the kitchen to make breakfast. Which left 'Taire and I to shower. Which he seemed to consider a joint activity. Which might have seemed more strange if I hadn't just participated in my first ménage-a-trois, and if it hadn't been brain-meltingly wonderful.

'Taire stood in the shower, his eyes closed and his face turned into the spray with what looked like worship. With the same kind of bliss that he'd had when I'd been sucking him off. He was actually pretty nice-looking, when his face wasn't lined with worry. Not achingly beautiful like Dante was, but open pleasure elevated his too-normal-for-a-cygenic features to something worth gazing at in appreciation.

"You like that, huh?" I asked, stepping in behind him. He seemed to catch himself, that look of bliss shifting to something warier as he looked over his shoulder at me. It wasn't the blank terror from before, at least.

"Is... is it all right, that I like it?" he asked.

"Yes. I like it when you like things. I like it when you're not worried."

He relaxed visibly, but it was about as tense as something could be and still be relaxation. There was a distinct sense of effort in it, like it was a performance. Small steps to trust, I supposed. It had seemed so effortless when Dante was giving me hints. I picked up the soap and started about the business of getting clean. 'Taire followed suit without a word when I handed it to him.

"Is... is it okay if I ask something?" he asked softly as I was rinsing off.

"Of course. I don't ever want you to hesitate to ask me things, 'Taire," I said, pulling him close, nuzzling his hair. He was a little taller than Dante, now that I had him standing. He was probably taller than me, actually—it was hard to tell because he constantly hunched over. Once he filled out from regular meals, he'd probably have no difficulty pushing me up against the wall.

If I could get Dante to tell him to do that.

"Why are you being so nice to me?" he asked, so softly that his voice was almost hidden by the sound of the water.

The question brought me up short, shattering the little fantasy I'd been constructing, and when I didn't answer immediately, he started stammering, "I mean, I'm not pretty like Dante is, and I'm not smart, and I'm not useful or anything... I'm just... I'm just a sex doll that got old. And you've been so... you touch me like... like it means something."

"Everyone deserves to feel good, 'Taire," I said gently. "I'm sorry life hasn't been good to you. But I love Dante, and Dante loves you, and he seems to be trying his damnedest to paste this love triangle closed

250

with more love. I say we go with it." I kissed his neck, and he gasped appreciatively. There was something intoxicating about how he reacted to every little kindness. It shouldn't have turned me on. "Gotta admit, you're already growing on me. And even if you weren't, having you around makes Dante happy... and that would probably be enough."

"So... you're gonna keep me?"

"Yeah," I said, sighing. "I am."

"You... you could... register me?" he asked, his voice wavering like he wasn't sure if he was allowed to ask that. "And people would ping me and know that I belong to somebody?"

"You want that?"

"No one ever wanted me enough to bother registering me. I mean... I've always had to look at those cygenics who get to wear collars and kneel at their masters' feet and get their hair played with," his voice hitched a little, and he swallowed, "and just wish someone wanted me that bad. I mean I know you don't want me, I'm not something you'd have picked out or anything but—"

"Shhhh," I hushed into his ear, holding him tight. "I'm gonna keep you. You get to stay here with Dante and me. I'll register you, if that's what you want. I'll keep you safe, 'Taire. You want to kneel at my feet and have me play with your hair, I can do that." I slid my hand up his back to card my fingers through his wet hair, and he whimpered. "But just so you know, Dante sits at the table with me, not on the floor. You might like that, too, if you give it a try."

"Anything you want, Master," 'Taire murmured, and I quelled the urge to correct him because if calling me "master" made him relax like this... well that was something we could work on later.

"Anything *you* want, 'Taire." I answered. "But we should get out of the shower or we're gonna use up all the hot water."

He hummed agreement, and we dried and dressed and headed out to find Dante. The hallway smelled like bacon. We found Dante was standing at the stove, dressed in a bathrobe, folding scrambled eggs.

"The phone rang while you were in the shower. I wasn't sure if I should answer it on your behalf, so I let it go to voicemail. You have a lot of other messages. It seems that someone—"

The phone rang again, and he turned his head to stare at it in exasperation. I walked over to pick it up.

"Do you ever check your goddamn voicemail?" Iris said, sounding like she was planning the details of my murder.

"What?"

"I have left you ten messages! And emails, and texts, and I've been entertaining the idea of just driving to your house and kicking your door down. If you're not gonna pick up your phone, you need to at least check your messages."

"I've had kind of a situation going on here, Iris, thanks for asking. What's the big emergency?"

"You and your boy toy have gone viral, apparently? Some blog ran an interview that the two of you gave at some lecture thing, and it got linked by a couple of big-name cygenic activism blogs and a couple of education blogs, and it kind of punted from there. I've had people from National on the phone wanting to know about it. There's a woman showing up to interview Dante. You and Dante need to be here. *Now.*"

"I don't know if I can. I've got company and I don't know if he's gonna be okay with coming to the Center yet."

"Nate. This is not optional. National is talking about invoking agency possession rights and throwing around words like 'chapter certification.' Dante is technically agency property, remember? If you don't show up *here*, people are going to show up *there*. You two need to get here and calm them the fuck down. I needed you here about an hour ago."

"Dante, go hop in the shower and put on a nice outfit when you get out," I said, putting my hand over the phone. "Iris wants us at the Center. It sounds pretty important. Apparently someone from National's going to interview you?"

'Taire had gone to stand next to Dante, and they were both looking at me now with mild alarm. I could hear Dante's eggs sizzling.

"It'll be okay," I said, hanging up the phone, not really giving a damn if Iris had anything else to say. It could wait until we were there.

Dante seemed to catch himself then, turning the eggs in the pan over one more time before turning off the heat and taking off in the direction of the bathroom. That left 'Taire standing next to the stove, looking at it like it confused him.

"We should eat while he's showering. Save time," I said lamely.

"This is eggs, right?" he asked, poking at them with the spatula, "I've only ever seen them come out of boxes frozen before. They look different."

"You've never had actual eggs?" I asked, trying not to sound horrified. He shook his head, looking over at the pan on the back burner, where Dante had cooked what looked like an entire pound of bacon.

"Never seen bacon that actually looked like the picture on the outside of the box, either. No one's ever felt like feeding me the kind of food humans eat."

"Which means you've never tasted real food. Today is your lucky day."

He looked up at me and smiled thinly, like he wasn't sure if he was supposed to be pleased by that. I went over and loaded up two plates, then led him to the table. He paused for just a moment when I put both plates on the table and pulled out a chair, so I said, "Sit."

And since it was an express order, he obeyed. Seemed relieved to be doing so.

"We're going to the Turing Center as soon as Dante's out of the shower and dressed and fed and all. It's where I work, and where Dante teaches. You don't have to come if you don't want to; you can stay here—"

"I'm going wherever Dante goes," he answered with more conviction than I'd ever heard in his voice. He flushed, and immediately amended, "If that's all right with you. Master."

"Of course it is. And please, don't call me 'Master.' Call me Nate."

"... Nate," he agreed uncertainly. "Thank you. I just... I spent a long time alone, you know? The whole time between when Dante got picked up and when I found him here, pretty much. KJ only kept me around because Dante wanted me around, soon as he was gone she wanted me gone too."

"KJ?"

"This chick who used to be in charge of the group we were in. She was old, like maybe 20. Smart. I mean, not smart like Dante's smart or anything, but..." he pushed his food around on the plate with his fork. He held the fork awkwardly, in a loose fist, like a toddler might. The same way he'd fumbled with the spoon last night and has just ended up drinking his soup from the bowl. "She was smart like she knew what was going on. She'd been on the street a long time. She didn't like me because I wasn't any kind of useful. I don't know how to do things."

"What would you be interested in learning to do, now that you've got the chance?"

"What would make me useful to you?" he answered instantly, looking up with a creepy earnestness in his too-human eyes.

"It's not about that. It's about what you want..."

"I want to be useful. I want you to have a reason to want me around besides Dante wanting me around. I've only ever been good for sex my whole life... nobody's ever wanted me to do anything else. I mean, I know I could be good for stuff, if I'd been programmed right. Like I know that other cygenics know how to cook and clean and keep a house. I want to be able to do that kind of stuff. I'm never gonna be smart like Dante is but..." his voice got small, and he looked down at his eggs again, "I wish I knew how to read."

I reached across the table and took his hand. He looked up at me, startled.

"Don't worry, 'Taire. We can teach you how to read. We can teach you anything you want. It doesn't even have to be useful. I just has to make you happy."

He smiled, weakly.

"I want to learn how to do this," he confessed, indicating the food on his plate. "Because this seems like fucking magic, you know? I don't even know where food comes from, or how you get it to taste like this." He finally speared a slice of bacon and brought it clumsily to his mouth, a little drip of grease rolling down his chin. I watched his eyes light up in the instant before he closed them and moaned, chewing with obvious and unfiltered pleasure.

I hoped that whatever bullshit Iris was panicking over wasn't going to take all day, because I'd much rather have spent the day hanging around with Dante and 'Taire.

Introducing the world to him was going to be *fun*.

'Taire

I was starting to wonder if I was ever gonna get over the dazed feeling, or if I was just gonna spend the rest of my life in a pleasant fog of orgasms and showers and food and undeserved praise. Having a master again, having one who kept talking about me being happy and not being scared and not being worried... having a human be nice to me... it was so weird. But I was pretty sure I could get used to it.

Riding in cars was something I'd only ever done a handful of times in my life, and Dante sat in the back seat with me and held my hand the whole way as Nate drove us through the city to a brick building that looked pretty much like the brick buildings all around it. I had no idea where we were; I'd never been on this end of the city. Everything looked clean and tidy. It was the kind of place you couldn't be stray. Which made the group of obvious strays hanging out in the first room we got to on the inside seem... kind of creepy, actually. Like I had to wonder how they'd got there and how they were gonna get away without running into anybody. There had to be a trick to it.

As soon as we got past that first room, a woman came rushing out from the hallway and started yelling at Nate. She was all snarling and big hand gestures, saying something about telephones and Nate having taken hours. She didn't seem to even notice me, but everything about her screamed "dangerous," and it was only Dante's hand clamping down on my shoulder that kept me from turning and running.

I looked at Dante, and he looked a little bit tense, but not scared. Nate didn't seem bothered at all. He sighed like he was just tired.

"Iris, I'm here. Dante's here. The freaking out can cease now. Also, this is 'Taire. Good morning, Iris. Shall we go to your office and you can tell me what all of this is about?"

"We can go to *your* office, and Dante can go to the classroom to talk to Madeline Patterson, from National, who has been waiting patiently for the last 20 minutes inquiring as to Dante's whereabouts and being very polite about the canned answers concerning the voluntary nature of his association with the Center and how we don't actually have a means of tracking clients who aren't housed in the group home system." Her eyes flicked to Dante and she said, "Do not. Fuck. This. Up."

"I wouldn't dream of it, ma'am," Dante answered in a tone that really ought to have gotten him slapped. "'Taire, you okay to stay with Nate while I go and get interviewed? You can come with me if you need to. You can both come with me, if you feel like it."

"She indicated it was *you* that she wanted to talk to," the woman said.

"And no one asked me if I was at all interested in being interviewed, so I think I'm entitled to bring guests if I so choose," Dante replied, staring at her hard. This wasn't how you were supposed to talk to humans. That wasn't allowed. But Dante was doing it anyway, and neither Nate or this woman seemed to think it was weird at all. No one was pulling a twitchbox to teach him a lesson about manners.

"Know what?," the woman said, gritting her teeth, "I don't even give a fuck at this point. Just know that I will fucking *gut* you if you cost me this chapter, so help me. I have worked my entire life to be where I am now and I'm not losing it over a viral video!"

Dante kept staring at her. "Think about the ramifications of working for an organization that would fire you over a viral video that doesn't even involve you, Miss Castillo."

"It's probably better if I just go to my office," Nate said, his voice taking on that same floaty quality that Dante got in his voice when he was trying to calm someone down. Was that a human thing? I'd always figured it was just a Dante thing. "You can come get me if you need me, right, Dante?"

The woman sighed hard, and grabbed the bridge of her nose. Then she looked at me.

"If he's gonna be a new intake, I want him in the waiting room," she said, pointing at me. "Not gonna deal with accusations of conflict of interest or playing favorites, not when there's a lady from National sniffing around."

"I'm not leaving him alone," Nate said, setting his jaw. "I can wait to process him until I've gotten through every other cygenic in this building, if you want, but 'Taire stays with me or with Dante until *he* decides otherwise."

"Then I suggest you do some intake interviews while you're waiting on Dante," the woman answered tightly, "who should already be in the classroom by now."

Dante kissed me on the temple and whispered, "You'll be fine. Stay with Nate," before he pulled away and walked past the woman, down the hallway and out of sight. I felt a cold tightening in my stomach, and I could swear I heard the blood rushing in my ears. It felt wrong to let Dante walk away like that, even if it was just into another room. This place didn't feel safe. My breath was getting quicker, and this was wrong, I needed to do something...

Nate pulled me into a hug. Warm and strong and *there*. He smelled like the soap from the shower. I felt my brain slowing down. The woman was talking again, but I couldn't pay attention to what she was saying. Nate was answering her, and he sounded pissed, and that should have scared me because when humans were pissed they *hurt*. Didn't matter if it was about you, just that you were there and you were hurtable so they hurt you, to feel better.

Except Nate was just... holding me. Like he was protecting me. Like no human ever had before, not in my whole life. It made my eyes sting.

It had got really quiet, and when the woman spoke again she wasn't yelling.

"Should I even ask what *this* is about?"

"Not in the mood you're obviously in, no," Nate answered, still sounding pissed. "I get it, okay? National is suddenly breathing down your neck and you've only been officially running this chapter for a month, and June still micromanages half the things you do from Washington because you let her. You're afraid someone's gonna snatch the rug out from under you. You keep asking yourself what June would do and what June would approve and thinking if you could just *be* June everything'd be okay. But then you made an off-the-books call on Dante's teaching plans, and you're scared it's gonna bite you in the ass because it's not what June would have done. *I get it.* But you don't get to freak out at me about it, and you especially don't get to freak out at Dante and 'Taire, because they do not deserve that."

"You dropped out of creation the second you picked that boy up. You dragged him here, and on *the same damned day* he started telling us how we were doing shit wrong and how he was gonna fix it. And you made puppy eyes at me, so I let him. Then you went and blabbed about it to some chick with a camera. And now I'm the one who's probably going to take the fall for it. And you've been dropped off creation the whole fucking time. And who the hell is *this* kid you're all cuddly with now? Say it with me, Nate: BOUNDARIES."

I felt Nate let go of me. I didn't want him too, but I knew better than to try and make it last, if he was indicating that it was over. It wasn't my place to want or need things from humans, especially from angry humans. I should have just been grateful that nobody had hit me yet. I resisted the urge to drop to the floor because I was pretty sure that that would upset him. I just kept still and kept my eyes down and waited for someone to tell me what to do.

"This is 'Taire. He's Dante's boyfriend. He's going to be living with Dante and me until further notice. And since he's not registered to the agency, he's not the agency's business."

"Then he can't be here."

"Since when is that a rule? Can you show me in the agency literature? Volunteers and interns bring their friends all the time. Linda brings her kids. Charles used to bring Baba. You want me to make him a guest badge? I have no problem doing that. But I'm not leaving him."

"This isn't a situation like an intern bringing a friend to volunteer or Linda bringing her kids because she can't find a babysitter. He's—"

"A cygenic. I know. And nobody owns him. I don't remember any explicit rules about that in the agency's literature, Iris. Do you?"

"No, but..."

"So I'm gonna go up to my office, and he's coming with me, and you know what? I won't even punch in. I'll take your advice and do some intake interviews off the clock. As a volunteer. And when Dante's done being interviewed by the lady from National, we can all go home and get out of your hair and if you want you can swing by my place after work and we can discuss this whole 'drastic change that's happened in Nate's life recently' thing over a bottle of wine. Okay?"

The woman stared at him, and sighed wearily, then threw up her hands. I flinched. She didn't seem to notice or care.

"Do whatever you're gonna do, Nate. It's not like I can stop you. I mean I guess I could fire your ass before they fire mine and then we'd both be in the same boat, but scorched earth's never been my style. So go ahead. Damage done. Take Boy-Toy-the-Second upstairs and make yourself useful. Stop and buy a bottle of decent Cabernet Sauvignon on the way home, since I know damned well you don't even drink wine and are hopeless with it. Ask someone at the liquor store to pick it out for you and tell them it's for an angry girlfriend. And pick up some fancy beer for yourself; I'm not watching you pour yourself a glass of wine you don't intend to drink. Shit's wasteful."

"Yes ma'am," Nate replied, not actually sounding pissed anymore. I felt relief wash through me, so strong that it was hard to keep standing. It would have been easier to deal with if I'd already been on my knees.

The woman walked away. Nate turned to me and put a hand on my shoulder and asked,

"You okay?"

I answered, "Yes, Master," before I remembered that I wasn't supposed to call him that.

"Uh-huh. Let's go upstairs and I can show you my office and if you're about to have a panic attack at least it won't be public, okay?"

"Yes... .please..." I said, swallowing.

"No one's gonna hurt you, 'Taire." he said gently. I resisted the urge to collapse against him and instead let him lead my upstairs with a hand on my shoulder.

I hoped Dante was okay. Dante was good at looking after himself. If Dante felt safe in this place... it was probably going to be okay.

Dante

Madeline Patterson turned out to be an impeccable blonde woman in her forties, wearing a powder blue cardigan and pressed khakis. She was the sort of woman one would find at the top of an image search for "nice white lady" and had a smile like a senator's wife. She was thumbing out a message on her phone when I found her.

"Miss Patterson, I presume?" I asked as I entered the room, "I apologize for the wait; I was delayed and, frankly, didn't know that I was going to be meeting anyone today."

"You must be Dante!" she said with saccharine cheerfulness, standing and offering her hand. I paused just a moment longer than was polite before accepting it. "I've heard so much about you!"

"Dare I ask from whom, ma'am?" I asked. She looked almost startled for a moment, a crack in her facade that she quickly smoothed over with another stretched-elastic smile.

"Well, as I'm sure you've been made aware of by now, you've become something of an overnight celebrity."

"Yes, I've been made aware of that. I haven't had a chance to look into it, yet. Something of a busy weekend, I'm afraid. But I suppose it was only to be expected; I had an academic following during childhood, and things never really die on the internet. I've considered rejoining the conversation, since there appears to be so much interest."

Without being invited to do so, I sat down. She followed suit, and opened her mouth as if to speak. I interrupted her.

"If I may ask, what was it in particular that's so important that I had to be called here on a Sunday morning to attend to it? Surely it could have waited until Monday? You seem to have Miss Castillo in a panic."

There was something sharp and brittle in the smile she gave me then, and I had the overwhelming impulse to summon Nate. If he brought 'Taire with him, all the better.

"As your work has become very public, it both has very exciting ramifications for the agency's future and could potentially have a great effect on public perception of the agency. So, it has been decided that you are, as of this moment, being invited to leave this branch and continue your work at the Turing Center's main offices in Berkeley, California, where experts in this sort of thing can help you decide how you will proceed. You'll be meeting with a team of coordinators to plan a curriculum and design the classroom you'll be working in, and your first class of students will be selected from among the most promising cygenics in each local chapter. How many students do you think you could manage in a proper lecture hall?"

I blinked at her, raising my eyebrows. "Miss Patterson," I began, only to be interrupted.

"Please, call me Madeline!"

"*Miss Patterson*," I said, sharpening my words ever so slightly, "it's very flattering that the Turing Center is taking such immediate interest in my work, but I'm afraid I'm not remotely interested in an undertaking of that magnitude at this time, much less in relocating to California."

"This is a decision that has already been made, Dante," she said, waving her hand as if swatting away flies. "I'm here to arrange and implement travel plans. Our flight departs at 6:00 this evening. You're coming to Berkeley."

"No, Miss Patterson, I most certainly am not. If the Turing Center feels a burning need to fund and document my work, they can do so by enriching the Boston chapter, because that is the chapter at which my work is and will be occurring if it occurs at all. I will continue teaching my current class, utilizing my current curriculum, in my current location or one that is reasonably nearby. I would be very appreciative of a technology grant, and perhaps some improved classroom space within a walkable distance of this chapter, if Turing National is asking what resources I'd like."

"I'm afraid you're misunderstanding the situation—"

"Miss Patterson, have you read your own Mission Statement and the Turing Center's Bill of Cygenic Rights?" I asked, steepling my hands. "Because I am communicating to you, in clear and absolute terms, my *lack of consent*. I am quite pleased with my current accommodations, Miss Patterson, and with my current employment. Forcing me to relocate and forcing upon

266

me tasks other than those of my choosing would be in direct violation of the core ethical premise of this organization."

"Dante, let me be entirely frank with you for a moment. Your work here was never cleared through National. Your changes to chapter programming can be construed as in violation with our standards. The fact that you made your little project a matter of public scrutiny is... unfortunate. I have the authority to remove this chapter's credentials and funding on those grounds. This is the sort of thing that could potentially damage the public's perception of the Turing Center and thus constitute a major blow to the cygenic rights agenda. I wouldn't expect you to understand the gravity of these actions, but your face and name are associated with a lot of media attention now. We have to clean that up. That means taking you to Berkeley and designing an approved program around this mess. You are registered to the organization. We have the right to relocate you if it's in the organization's best interests."

"If this meeting is going to continue, Miss Patterson, I request Mister Matheson's presence."

"He's the employee currently hosting you, isn't it? I assure you, his permission is not required for this."

I didn't dignify that with an answer. I simply looked at her coolly and stood up. She stood with me, looking a bit confused. I moved toward the door. She put her hand on my shoulder, just forcefully enough that it was clear that she expected me to stop.

"Do you want me to start screaming, Miss Patterson?" I said, turning slowly to glare at her.

"Because I could do that. I'm fairly certain that I could make myself heard in the next building, with a bit of effort, and certainly by *everyone* in this one."

Her jaw dropped, and I shrugged her hand off.

I found Nate in his office. 'Taire was sitting on the floor beside his desk, leaning on it, looking generally content as Nate conducted an interview with someone I didn't know.

"Dante," Nate began, his eyes lighting up when he saw me. 'Taire's head snapped in my direction, and he smiled weakly.

"Nate, tell this woman behind me that if she exercises her legal right to abduct me, you'll communicate the fact that she's done so to my entire internet readership."

"What's going on?" Nate asked, alarmed. The young man in the chair looked bewildered, gaze darting to each person in the room.

"Miss Patterson thinks that she's taking me to Berkeley to be a pawn in a public relations game. Apparently I've garnered too much attention to be anything other than a showpiece and poster child."

"Dante, these histrionics are entirely unnecessary," Miss Patterson began, sounding exasperated.

"They would be—if you'd assure me that your former insistence that decisions about my future had already been made in my absence, and that your intention to quietly bustle me onto a plane and take me to California in direct opposition to my wishes, was said hastily and in error. I'm just making sure that my local contacts are fully aware of the situation. It's important, I feel, for all of us to be on the same page. And for me to have a human representative, whose speech is protected by law and who will have the capacity to communicate the situation to others, if it comes to that. I am not going to Berkeley."

"The agency needs—"

"Fuck the agency's needs, Miss Patterson. If you decide to exercise your right as an *owner* to dictate the actions of your *slave*, I'm making sure the world knows you've done so. Just how do you think the public will react, Miss Patterson, when they come to learn that a purported cygenic rights organization utilized the fact that it is in ownership of me to undermine my consent? Do you think I'll willingly *teach* in Berkley? If you leave here with me today, it will be because you have taken me prisoner and I will be utterly and completely non-compliant. Did no one think to ask me about my opinion in all of this? Or was I simply considered as a resource?"

"The possibility that you would be intractable hadn't factored into the agency's plans," she said, sharply. "This is an enormous opportunity for you."

"Intractable?" I said with a bark of laughter, "*That's* an incredibly interesting choice of words, Miss Patterson. When I was 17 years old, a woman in a dingy beige room told me that if she marked me down as intractable that I would be wiped for reprogramming. She told me that I'm a computer with arms and legs, and that I don't get to want things. She told me that I wouldn't get another warning. And since that time, I have been enslaved in dull, dirty menial labor, and I have been raped and beaten and drugged, and I have been a homeless fugitive, living on the margins of human society—always in terror that the next human who took interest in me would erase my

269

mind. Because I have no legal rights. My body and my mind are owned things, to be used and abused and destroyed at the whim of my owners. I am fucking *done* with being tractable, Miss Patterson. Why don't you get on the phone with whatever powers that be sent you, and tell them that."

Madeline Patterson's face was the color of wet chalk, her eyes darting from me to Nate to 'Taire.

"Why is that cygenic sitting on the floor?" she asked, her voice faint.

"That's where he wanted to be," Nate answered.

"That's in breach of—"

"My priority was making him feel safe. He's not registered to the agency."

"The Boston chapter is clearly entirely out of control," she said, swallowing, appearing to regain a bit of her composure. "Authorities are going to have to be consulted concerning what's to be done about it."

"By all means, Miss Patterson," I said. "Consult all the authorities of your choosing. I'll be in my classroom, making a blog entry about the day's events. Don't worry, the laptop I use to conduct my lessons isn't agency property."

"That won't be necessary, Dante—" Miss Patterson stammered.

"Oh, I think it will. And further, I'd be very interested in knowing how you intend to stop me. *Mistress.*"

I walked out of the room, acutely aware that everyone was watching me go.

Nate

There was a minute or so of me staring dumbfounded and the blonde woman trying to talk at me before I came to my senses and scrambled out of my office in pursuit of Dante. 'Taire followed me. By the time I caught up with Dante, he was already in the classroom, sitting in front on his laptop, his hands shaking.

"What's going on?" I asked, sitting down next to him. I wanted to hug him, but I wasn't sure that would be welcome.

"They want to take me away, and they own me, so they can do it if they feel like it," Dante said, his voice slightly strangled. "I should have known better than to actually expect to be allowed to have a life and make choices—"

"Wait, back up. Where are they taking you and why? You said something about Berkeley? That's where the main offices are..."

"It's my childhood all over again. They're going to turn me into a project. A showpiece. They want to take me to Berkeley and away from you and 'Taire." He looked up suddenly, horror on his face. "You can't let them have 'Taire, Nate. Don't register him to these people. I need you to promise me that you'll keep him safe. If they get legal custody of him they'll very certainly use him to secure my cooperation to anything and everything they want me to do."

"Dante, I'm sure it's not... Look. This is probably actually an opportunity. If you go to Berkeley you'll get funding and media attention and collaboration—"

"I don't want any of that! I want you and I want 'Taire and I want my students and I want to make my own choices!"

"They'd probably let you bring 'Taire to Berkley, you know. If you—"

"Would you come to Berkeley for me? Do you honestly think they'd allow the three of us to continue to be intimate? Don't mock me, Nate. I've been down this road before. I wonder if they'll pin me at night and put me in a drawer, like the hospital did..."

"...You'd rather have me than Berkeley?"

"Fuck Berkeley, Nate. I *love* you. I love *'Taire*. I was starting to love the prospect of the future. I don't want to go anywhere. I don't want to give any of this up for some amorphous prospect of grander, more complicated things in service to this organization. I don't want a different life."

I did hug him then, and kissed the top of his head. He was shaking.

"What the hell is going on in here—" that blonde woman said from the doorway. I looked up at her, and she paled a little taking a step back. I could only guess at how angry I looked.

"Get out," I said, surprised at how menacing my voice sounded.

"Mister Matheson, I remind you that—"

"Get out, now. Or I'll come over there."

It was an utterly empty threat. It wasn't as if I'd

actually put my hands on her or anything. But the last of the color drained from her face and she backed out of the room quickly, half tripping over her own feet. I watched her go.

"Dante," I said quietly, "you'd better make that blog post. I think we're gonna need some cavalry."

The first protesters arrived within 15 minutes of Dante's blogging efforts. He put out a plea to the moderators of the "Learn You Somethin" blog to call out to their readership. They delivered admirably. Boston was a college town after all, and it was a weekend. By the time Madeline Patterson's reinforcements arrived, there were 30 young people outside, including a number of cygenics I'd never seen before. Some of them had already made signs, and one had shown up with a drum. I wasn't entirely certain how the drum was supposed to help, but it seemed to have facilitated chanting and singing. The kids who were filming the proceedings on their phones, and presumably live-feeding them to assorted media outlets, were probably helping more.

If this constituted "helping."

Dante was reveling in it like he'd planned it in great detail. He'd gone outside as soon as the first protesters had arrived to give a brief interview and dictate ways in which they could help. I'd been instructed to look after 'Taire. 'Taire, being hugely intimidated by a gaggle of angry young humans, even when they were angry on his behalf, had elected to stay inside with Iris and me. Madeline Patterson had stationed herself on the front steps and had been furiously texting, utterly refusing to talk to anyone, since Dante had stormed dramatically out of my office.

273

I was going to get fired. Iris was going to get fired. The entire Boston chapter was probably going to be shut down. National might burn down the building and salt the earth for good measure.

Dante was standing on a milk crate, leading a chorus of "Do You Hear The People Sing," when the man in the suit showed up.

"We're fucked," Iris said, looking out the window at the man coming up the sidewalk, flanked by shouting college kids. She drew another drag on her vapor cigarette. Her hands were shaking. "How the fuck did I let this happen? Last week everything was fine. What am I supposed to tell my family, Nate? You know how bad my abuelita's gonna get on my case? She always said going into 'charity work for the robots' was stupid and I should have gone to law school."

"This isn't your fault or my fault or Dante's fault. This is National being hypocritical about the agency's mission," I said tightly. "That bitch wanted to take Dante, and Dante didn't want to go. That's what this is about."

"They *own* Dante, Nate. If they call in cops, this isn't a fight that he's gonna win."

"Which is why we're not involving the police, Miss Castillo," Dante said from the door. 'Taire shot up from his post in the corner to go and hug him. Dante casually pulled him into an embrace, ruffling a hand in his hair. "Unless of course these people behind me feel like inviting them to come and witness our media spectacle. We all know how well it turns out when the police are called to disperse a group of peacefully protesting college students who are all armed with cameras and live feeds, after all. Did you know that the president of Harvard's PETCL chapter is out there? I heard him on his phone talking about obtaining damaged, disembodied cygenic limbs from recycling centers. I'm not sure what he's planning, but I doubt it's the kind of press the Turing Center is looking for."

The man in the suit was standing behind him in the doorway. Madeline Patterson was standing beside him, a slight mania in her eyes, her face pulled into a grimace that was desperately trying to be a smile.

He was a doughy-looking white man with salt and pepper hair, probably in his fifties or so. He was smiling with the kind of forced politeness I associated with college personnel and real estate agents.

Tagging at the back of the entourage was a girl who looked just familiar enough that I knew I'd met her before. Dante waited for her to catch up and with an outstretched arm invited her to come to the front of the group. Neither Madeline nor the man who'd yet to introduce himself looked pleased by that.

"Iris Castillo, may I introduce Kelly-Lynn Koh, one of the moderators of the blog 'Learn You Somethin.' She'd like to interview you, since you're the head of the Boston chapter of the Turing Center, and this situation seems to be shaping up as a 'National Agency vs. Local Chapter' altercation."

"There is no altercation going on here," the man said. "There has been a gross misunderstanding—"

"Miss Patterson said," Dante interrupted, his voice cutting and commanding in a way that produced wholly inappropriate feelings in my midsection, "and I quote, 'You are registered to the organization. We

275

have the right to relocate you if it's in the organization's best interests.' And she did not redact that. That is a significant threat to my personal wellbeing, and as I have no opportunity for *legal* recourse to defend myself, I've taken a social one. Now, if I had reason to believe that the Turing Center has utterly reversed its position on the 'problem' that I pose and has decided that I will be allowed to continue living where I see fit, doing the work I choose, with the people I care about, in the place of my choosing— in short, exercising rights that would seem both basic and sacrosanct were I a human—then I will happily go and announce that to the gathered crowd for them to promulgate on their internet venues of choice. You sent Miss Patterson here to 'clean up' the 'problem' that I created by having the temerity to teach literacy to cygenics who were doing nothing more useful with their time. As if that could damage your organization's reputation. I have demonstrated to you that your organization's reputation may be worthy of very harsh criticism indeed. So. Who are you, and what do you intend to do?"

"My name is Maddox Cooper. I'm the Turing Center's agency director for the Northeast district. And, as this situation has somehow blossomed in the last 48 hours from 'troubling' to 'fucked up beyond all repair'... I'm here to cut you a check. Is there somewhere for us all to sit down and discuss this like civilized adults? Miss Koh is welcome to take notes on the proceedings, if she's your chosen media outlet, but I request no video or pictures."

A matter of five minutes saw us in the dining room-cum-classroom, seated at one of the large cafeteria tables. Dante sat, flanked by 'Taire and I. Miss Koh sat on 'Taire's other side. Iris sat on my other side. Maddox Cooper and Madeline Patterson sat opposite us. Dante sat like a king holding court. I wondered what that made me, in relation.

"So, Miss Castillo. I would be incredibly interested in knowing what prompted you to decide to flagship an entirely new program, and allow it to come to public knowledge, without so much as a phone call or a memo to the regional offices in New York," Maddox Cooper said, managing to sound both casual and menacing.

Iris broke the pen she was holding.

"This was not an intended outcome, I assure you," she said quickly. "There was no formal agreement—"

"The fault is entirely mine, Mister Cooper," Dante said smoothly. "I suggested the educational program. I requested no resources that were being otherwise utilized. I simply plugged a borrowed laptop into an idle projector and invited cygenics from the waiting room to instead come and listen to me prattle on about the rudiments of phonics. The entire expenditure for this project has been $30 to purchase paper and pencils with—"

"And that was out of my pocket," I interjected. Dante smiled at me.

"And it's been going on for two weeks. It was only the happenstance of running into Miss Koh here while attending Nerve Ostrander's lecture at BU—"

"What were you doing at a lecture at BU?" Madeline Patterson asked sharply.

"What business of it is yours what I choose to do with my time, Miss Patterson? Why shouldn't I attend lectures? It was open to the public. I'm a member of the public. A member of the public who happens to have a great interest in radical education reform and lateral teaching praxis."

"In the New York chapter, cygenics registered to the agency are housed in agency group homes until they're placed in suitable work situation. They're not left to roam the streets unsupervised—"

"Do you think that I require supervision, Miss Patterson?" Dante asked. Simultaneously, Iris said, "We don't have the resources that New York has in terms of group home space or staffing!"

Maddox Cooper's gaze flicked from one of them to the other and landed squarely on Dante. It then swung, abruptly, to Miss Koh.

"Why was he worth interviewing?" he asked.

"Because he's Dante," she answered, a bit breathless. "Of The Dante Project. It was kind of a big deal in education theory circles when I was in high school. Professor Vernon Cunningham had Dante commissioned at five years' growth and raised him as a classical student. He was convinced that, given the history of civil rights and the work that cygenic rights organizations were doing at the time, by the time Dante was old enough for college he'd be allowed to enroll. It was a huge deal, the blog had thousands of followers all around the world, and Professor Cunningham was interviewed by magazines and websites and stuff. There's videos and transcripts of his talks and copies of his essays all over the place. But the economy tanked, and the Dante project fell off the radar—"

"And Professor Cunningham contracted cancer and died, leaving me to be possessed by the state of

Massachusetts and enslaved, be stolen from that enslavement and sold into prostitution—I may have failed to mention that in our first interview, Miss Koh, because I didn't think it seemly—escape from that and be a homeless fugitive, and finally find myself delivered into the loving care of the Turing Center. I was, briefly and refreshingly, treated as if I were a person capable of making my own decisions and undertaking my own initiative toward improving the lives of other cygenics! But I suppose that's a threat to the agency, as Miss Patterson here turned up to tell me in no uncertain terms that my actions were unacceptable and that she was to abscond with me to the other side of the country, where other people would tell me what to do and where and when and how. If I may employ the vernacular: Fuck that."

Madeline Patterson looked like she was boiling. Mister Cooper looked somewhat calmer and altogether colder.

"Dante, you're being invited to Berkeley because the main offices in Berkeley are much better equipped to handle the undertaking of a new program and its design and implementation than a marginal branch like Boston—"

"Then by all means, design and implement a program in Berkeley. But do so without me. I have no interest in being relocated, and I assure you I can get along quite well as I have been."

"I'm afraid you're too much in the public eye for that. We can't simply ignore you, Dante. There would be questions. We need to look at what this means for the agency. You don't seem to understand—"

"If I were a human, would you be arguing from

the stance that relocating me against my will was a viable option, Mister Cooper?"

"I obviously would not, but—"

"Mister Cooper, are you familiar with the Turing Test?"

"I'm sure you'll be happy to remind me."

"The Turing Test, devised by the same Alan Turing for whom your organization is named, is a test of a machine's ability to exhibit intelligent behavior equivalent to, or indistinguishable from, that of a human. Can you, Mister Cooper, distinguish my response at the specter of being taken against my will from my home and the people whom I love, from that of a human?"

Mister Cooper narrowed his eyes, and made a note on his tablet, but said nothing. There was tense silence for a long moment before Dante said, in a voice that cut like a razor, "Am I a person or not, Mister Cooper? And if I am not, doesn't the world deserve to know what a sham this operation is? If you're not committed to treating cygenics as people, what differentiates your organization from any other point of resale?"

"This means, of course, that we're going to have to fund the Boston chapter more fully and see to it that it's properly staffed," Mister Cooper said with a labored sigh. "I am going to cut a check to Miss Castillo here, and within 72 hours I want an itemized list of what the money will be spent on. You and I will go outside and tell your army of angrily passionate social media creators that there has been a misunderstanding and that you are *not* being relocated to Berkeley. You will assure them that the Turing

Center is going to be extensively funding programming of your design and implementation here in Boston and I will tell them that we have been very gracious and are very excited to be able to provide you with this opportunity, and many photos and videos of us shaking hands and smiling will be taken and disseminated. Is that agreeable to you, Dante?"

"Mister Cooper—" Miss Patterson began, only to be interrupted.

"You lost your talking privileges hours ago, Miss Patterson, when you so spectacularly failed to assess and address this situation. I haven't decided yet whether you still have a position in this organization. It is not in your best interest make that decision easier for me."

He turned to Dante, and gazed the length of the table. He paused for a moment at 'Taire, a flicker of confusion in his eyes, but he didn't ask.

"There are going to be photo-shoots and interviews. Some of them will be scripted, and when they are, you will keep to the script. You can expect to feature widely in assorted media and literature, and you will have to talk about your work extensively. You may henceforth consider yourself *employed* by this agency, Dante. As much as Miss Castillo or Mister Matheson are."

"Oh?" he said with a small smile, "Am I going to be paid?"

"That's for you and Miss Castillo to discuss. Wages are an acceptable allotment of funds."

Dante smiled broadly, and looked from me to 'Taire and back to me with an air of absolute victory. He leaned across the table and offered a hand to Mister

Cooper, who looked started for a moment before taking it.

"Mister Cooper, you have restored my faith in humanity!" He looked coolly at Miss Patterson. "Which she had tested quite severely. Let's go and tell the cause-heads to call off their attack."

"They probably already have," Miss Koh confessed. "I've been live-blogging this meeting. It's been feeding to the PETCL site and everything with about 55 seconds of lag."

"I hate living in the future," Mister Cooper said with a sigh. "Let's go out for photo-ops."

Dante

The next weeks were frenetic.

Re-canning a can of angry college students turned out to be less easy than opening it had been, and the Center enjoyed a brief but exceptionally energetic round of volunteerism, which was exceptionally handy for building the new classroom, complete with a touch screen board and five digital work stations which I could reasonably spread to as many as 30 students at a time.

Nines had become sufficiently literate in all the ways that mattered that we'd put him to work doing entrance interviews, which meant that for the first time Nate was actually able to dispense the counseling services he'd initially been hired to dispense.

'Taire, when not joining my classes, had taken an incredible interest in food and turned this interest into hanging around the kitchen. Zee was talking about starting a community garden in the lot behind the building so that the Center would have access to fresh vegetables.

I had given an utterly grating number of redundant interviews. Everything from school papers to educational journals to student media to mainstream news organizations were suddenly terribly interested

in where The Dante Project and been and where it was
going and how the Turing Center was helping it get
there and what it all meant for cygenic rights. The fact
that some of them were scripted was quite frankly a
relief.

I was thus probably somewhat more brusque than
necessary when Iris barged into my classroom during
my planning period with a strange woman in tow, fully
expecting her to be a representative of some outlet or
another.

"Zara, Dante, Dante, Professor Zara Ahmadi—
formerly of MIT," Iris said quickly, "Zara's gonna be
our new programmer, she wanted to talk to you about
what you do here. I need to get back on the phone with
Bankroll Cooper. Talk to you later!"

Professor Zara Ahmadi was a tall, thin, brown
woman in a scarlet hijab. She had a pair of mid-
century horn rim glasses. She might have been any age
between 20 and 50; she had that kind of face.

"I'm so glad that I saw your interview on 'Learn
you Somethin,'" she said congenially, clasping her
hands in front of her. "I'd never have even heard of the
Turing Center otherwise, and it seems like such an
awesome agency! I'm so excited to actually be able to
work with you—I was reading The Dante Project back
when I was a freshman in college. It's what made me
decide to go into programming."

"That's very flattering, Miss Ahmadi, thank you.
What is it that you think I can tell you that you haven't
already been able to read in my vastly extensive body
of recent work?"

"The BSOD's—that's who I intend to work with
before I even think about offering skillset overlays—

where do you need them to be at to join your class? I don't want to bring them any farther than that, not unless they ask for it. I know the agency's policy is to program them with a baseline ISTJ personality and overlay a desired skillset like domestic tasks and childcare on it, but..."

"But that's incredibly limiting," I finished for her, brightening considerably, "And you're interested in achieving..."

"Something more focused on the consent of the parties involved and their personal goals and desires. I read the transcript of your interview with Maddox Cooper, and I'm fairly confident that I am roughly as radical about the nature of personhood and consent as you'd demand someone be before being allowed to go fiddling around in someone else's head. So, for BSOD's, starting as close to the ground as possible and proceeding with education—"

"Dante?" Nate called from the door. I smiled and rose to meet him, disregarding the action's unconscionable rudeness to Professor Ahmadi.

"I came to see if you wanted to go catch lunch off campus. Who's your friend?"

"Professor Zara Ahmadi, our new programmer. Iris only just introduced us. Professor, would you care to continue this conversation over lunch? Oh, and this is Nate Matheson. If you've been reading my blog—"

Professor Ahmadi lit up with a grin, rushing over.

"I've read so much about your work here and what you've been doing through the agency's consent crisis!" she gushed, fanning herself. "It's not often you actually see someone who's willing to back up discussions of cygenic personhood with personal action—"

"Please, ma'am," Nate said, scratching the back of his neck, "I just do what Dante tells me. He's the brains of the operation." I leaned in to kiss him on the cheek. Professor Ahmadi looked very slightly scandalized.

"Hey Dante have you seen... oh," 'Taire said walking into the room and looking at the three of us. "I was looking for Nate. Are you done with lesson stuff for the day? Taisha, the intern, was telling me about the farmers market off Copley, and how there's a cart that makes crepes and you can pick out the fruit you want on them, and how berries are in season right now, and I was wondering... because I mean we could all... unless you've still got teacher stuff..."

"That sounds wonderful! I've got a minivan and can seat six, if transit's an issue."

"'Taire, Zara, Zara, 'Taire," Nate said, "Zara's our new programmer, 'Taire is..."

"Much loved," I finished, smiling at him fondly before looking back to Nate.

"Also, Dante," Nate said, "Kelly-Lynn Koh left a message for you in the general messages folder. She wants to schedule another interview."

"Oh god, are we sure that's a good idea?" I groaned, "Look what happened last time. It might spark a revolution."

"You say that like it's a bad thing," Professor Ahmadi said. I smiled at her, and took Nate's hand, looping an arm around 'Taire shoulders and kissing his temple.

"Let's go get lunch," I said, "You can drive, Miss Ahmadi, and we can talk about the radical potential of the future."

About the Author

Monique Poirier is a time-traveler from the year 1983; an author, costumer, convention-goer, and activist currently living in Pawtucket, Rhode Island. She began writing science fiction and fantasy when she was twelve, and discovered erotica at 16; she hasn't stopped writing since. She is a councilwoman of the Seaconke Wampanoag Tribe, and a lineal descendant of Ousamequin Massasoit. Her erotica has been featured in many Circlet anthologies, including *Fantastic Erotica: The Best of Circlet Press 2008-2012.* Her short stories are collected in one volume in *This World Between: Erotic Stories.* Her steampunk work has also been extensively published in anthologies and publications. She can be reached at Poirier.Monique@gmail.com or on Tumblr at Poiriermonique.tumblr.com

If you enjoyed this book you might also enjoy:

This World Between: Erotic stories
by Monique Poirier

Eight entrancing erotic tales from the rich imagination of Monique Poirier, an author who first began sending stories to Circlet Press in 2009 and we have loved every one. Spanning eras and universes, these stories span the gamut of sexuality and genre. A woman with a broken time machine haunts a big box store looking for a mechanic who can get her out of therewhen. An angel trolls the depths of a dark netherworld where only a demon can ease his affliction. Steampunk pasts, space operatic futures, and mysterious magical nows co-exist in *This World Between.* And in every story, the passionate meetings that occur are expressed in gloriously carnal detail, leaving the characters forever changed.

Robotica,
by Kal Cobalt

Five erotic stories of robot-human relations, exploring the future of humanity, sex, and desire. In Cobalt's futures, artificial intelligences can have very real emotions, and humans can be just as confused, turned on by, and obsessed with their robot lovers as they are by any others. The stories have a delicious homoerotic edge even as they question what gender means to a robot mind. Or heart.

Simulacrum
by Rian Darcy

In the virtual world of Simulnet, no one knows who you really are, making it the perfect playground for the imagination... and for a serial killer. The police ask Shaun to partner with an enigmatic programmer to hunt a murderer in the sex clubs and ramen shops of cyberspace. But as they investigate, Shaun finds himself wanting to know more about his mysterious partner... but ultimately the questions Shaun needs to answer are the ones deep in his own heart.

If You Liked This Title, You Might Also Like:

The Circlet Treasury of Erotic Wonderland
Edited by J. Blackmore

The Circlet Treasury of Erotic Steampunk
Edited by J. Blackmore & Cecilia Tan

The Circlet Treasury of Lesbian Erotic Science Fiction and Fantasy
Edited By Cecilia Tan

The Siren and the Sword:
Book One of the Magic University Series
By Cecilia Tan

The Tower and the Tears:
Book Two of the Magic University Series
By Cecilia Tan

The Incubus and the Angel:
Book Three of the Magic University Series
By Cecilia Tan

Spellbinding: Tales from Magic University
Edited by Cecilia Tan

The Poet and The Prophecy
Book Four of the Magic University Series
By Cecilia Tan

No Safewords2
Edited by Laura Antoniou

The Eidolon Initiative
by Vinnie Tesla

Made in the USA
Middletown, DE
29 January 2021